THE TRAGEDY OF HAMLET, PRINCE OF DENMARK
哈姆雷特

[英]威廉·莎士比亚/著　朱生豪/译

时代出版传媒股份有限公司
安徽文艺出版社

图书在版编目（CIP）数据

哈姆雷特/（英）威廉·莎士比亚（William Shakespeare）著；朱生豪译.—合肥：安徽文艺出版社，2019.2（2025.6重印）

（莎士比亚戏剧典藏）

ISBN 978-7-5396-6142-1

Ⅰ．①哈… Ⅱ．①威… ②朱… Ⅲ．①悲剧—剧本—英国—中世纪 Ⅳ．①I561.33

中国版本图书馆CIP数据核字(2017)第173833号

出版人：姚 巍
选题策划：姜婧婧　原典纪　　统筹策划：刘 畅
责任编辑：姜婧婧　刘 畅　　装帧设计：张诚鑫

....

出版发行：安徽文艺出版社　www.awpub.com
地　　址：合肥市翡翠路1118号　邮政编码：230071
营 销 部：(0551)63533889
印　　制：安徽新华印刷股份有限公司　(0551)65859551

....

开本：787×1092　1/32　印张：13.25　字数：310千字
版次：2019年2月第1版
印次：2025年6月第10次印刷
定价：52.00元(精装)

....

(如发现印装质量问题，影响阅读，请与出版社联系调换)

版权所有，侵权必究

剧中人物

克劳狄斯　丹麦国王
哈姆雷特　前王之子,今王之侄
福丁布拉斯　挪威王子
霍拉旭　哈姆雷特之友
波洛涅斯　御前大臣
雷欧提斯　波洛涅斯之子
伏提曼德　朝臣
考尼律斯　朝臣
罗森格兰兹　朝臣
吉尔登斯吞　朝臣
奥斯里克　朝臣
马西勒斯　军官
勃那多　军官
弗兰西斯科　兵士
雷奈尔多　波洛涅斯之仆
英国使臣
众伶人
二小丑　掘坟墓者
乔特鲁德　丹麦王后,哈姆雷特之母
奥菲利娅　波洛涅斯之女

贵族,贵妇,军官,兵士,教士,水手,使者及侍从等,哈姆雷特父亲的鬼魂

地点

艾尔西诺

第一幕

第一场
艾尔西诺；城堡前的露台

【弗兰西斯科立台上守望。勃那多自对面上。

勃那多 那边是谁？

弗兰西斯科 不，你先回答我；站住，告诉我你是什么人。

勃那多 国王万岁！

弗兰西斯科 勃那多吗?

勃那多 正是。

弗兰西斯科 你来得很准时。

勃那多 现在已经过了十二点钟。你去睡吧,弗兰西斯科。

弗兰西斯科 谢谢你来替换了我。天冷得厉害,我心里也老大不舒服。

勃那多 你守在这儿,一切都很安静吗?

弗兰西斯科 一只小老鼠也不见走动。

勃那多 好,晚安!要是你碰见霍拉旭和马西勒斯,我的守夜的伙伴们,就叫他们赶紧一点来。

弗兰西斯科 我想我听见他们的声音了。喂,站定!那边是谁?

【霍拉旭及马西勒斯上。

霍拉旭 都是自己人。

马西勒斯 丹麦王的臣民。

弗兰西斯科 祝你们晚安!

马西勒斯 啊!再会,正直的军人!谁替换了你?

弗兰西斯科 勃那多代替我值班。祝你们晚安!(下)

马西勒斯 喂!勃那多!

勃那多 喂——啊!霍拉旭也来了吗?

霍拉旭 这儿有一个他。

勃那多 欢迎,霍拉旭!欢迎,马西勒斯!

马西勒斯 什么!这东西今晚又出现过了吗?

勃那多　我还没有瞧见什么。

马西勒斯　霍拉旭说那不过是我们的幻想。我告诉他,我们已经两次看见这一个可怕的怪象,他总是不肯相信;所以今晚我请他也来陪我们守一夜,要是这鬼再出来,就可以证明我们并没有看错,还可以叫他对它说几句话。

霍拉旭　嘿,嘿,它不会出现的。

勃那多　你先请坐下,虽然你一定不肯相信我们的故事,我们还是要把我们这两夜来所看见的情形再向你絮叨一遍。

霍拉旭　好,我们坐下来,听听勃那多怎么说。

勃那多　昨天晚上,当那照耀在旗杆西端的天空的明星正在向它现在吐射光辉的地方运行的时候,马西勒斯跟我两个人,那时候钟刚敲了一点——

马西勒斯　住声!不要说下去了。瞧,它又来了!

【鬼上。

勃那多　正像已故的国王的模样。

马西勒斯　你是有学问的人,对它说话,霍拉旭。

勃那多　它的样子不像已故的国王吗?看好,霍拉旭。

霍拉旭　像得很,它使我心里充满了恐怖和惊奇。

勃那多　它希望我们对它说话。

马西勒斯　你去问它,霍拉旭。

霍拉旭　你是什么鬼物?胆敢僭窃丹麦先王神武的雄姿,在这样深夜的时分出现。凭着上天的名义,我命令你说话!

马西勒斯　它生气了。

勃那多　瞧,它悄悄地去了!

霍拉旭　不要去!说呀!说呀!我命令你,快说!(鬼下)

马西勒　它去了,不愿回答我们。

勃那多　怎么,霍拉旭!你在发抖,你的脸色这样惨白。这不是幻想吧?你有什么高见?

霍拉旭　当着上帝的面前,倘不是我自己的眼睛向我证明,我也不会相信这样的怪事。

马西勒斯　它不像我们的国王吗?

霍拉旭　正像你就是你自己一样。它身上的那副战铠,就是他讨伐野心的挪威的时候所穿的;它脸上的那副怒容,活像他有一次在一场激烈的争辩中,把那些波兰人打倒在冰上那时候的神气。怪事怪事!

马西勒斯　前两次他也是这样不先不后地在这个静寂的时辰,用军人的步态走过我们的眼前。

霍拉旭　我不知道究竟应该怎样想;可是大概推测起来,这恐怕预兆着我们国内将要有一番非常的变故。

马西勒斯　好吧,坐下来。谁要是知道的,请告诉我,为什么我们要有这样森严的戒备,使全国的军民每夜不得安息?为什么每天都在制造铜炮,还要向国外购买战具?为什么赶造这许多船只,连星期日也不停止工作?这样夜以继日地辛苦忙碌,究竟将要有什么事情发生呢?谁能够告诉我?

霍拉旭　我可以告诉你,至少一般人都是这样传说。刚才他的形象还像我们出现的那位已故的王上,你们知道,曾经接受骄矜好胜的挪威的福丁布拉斯的挑战。在那一次决斗中间,我们的勇武的哈姆雷特——他的英名是举世称颂的——把福丁布拉斯杀死了。按照双方根据法律和武士精神所订立的协定,福丁布拉斯要是战败了,除了他自己的生命以外,必须把他所有的一切土地拨归给胜利的一方。同时我们的王上也提出以相当的土地作为赌注,要是福丁布拉斯得胜了,也就归他没收占有,正像在同一协定上所规定的,他失败了,哈姆雷特可以把他的土地没收占有一样。现在要说起那位福丁布拉斯的儿子,他生得一副烈火似的性格,已经在挪威的四境召集了一群无赖之徒,供给他们衣食,驱策他们去干冒险的勾当。他唯一的目的我们的当局看得很清楚，无非是要用武力和强迫性的条件，夺回他父亲所丧失的土地。照我所知，这就是我们种种准备的主要动机，我们这样戒备的唯一原因，也是全国所以这样慌忙骚乱的缘故。

勃那多 我想正是为了这一个缘故。我们那位王上在过去和目前的战乱中间，都是一个主要的角色，所以无怪他的武装的形象要向我们出现示警了。

霍拉旭 那是扰乱我们心灵之眼的一点微尘。从前在富强繁盛的罗马，当那雄才大略的裘力斯·恺撒驾崩之前不久的时候，披着殓衾的死人都从坟墓里出来，在街道上啾啾鬼语，拖着火尾、喷着血露的星辰在白昼陨落，支配潮汐的月亮被吞蚀像一个没有起色的病人。这一类预报重大变故的征兆，在我们国内也已经屡次见到了。可是不要想！瞧！瞧！它又来了！

【鬼重上。

霍拉旭 我要挡住它的去路，即使它会害我。不要走，幻象！要是你会开口，对我说话吧。要是我有可以为你效劳之处，使你的灵魂得到安息，那么对我说话吧。要是你预知祖国的命运，靠着你的指示，也许可以及时避免未来的灾祸，那么对我说话吧。或者你在生前曾经把你搜刮得来的财宝埋藏在地下，我听见人家说，鬼魂往往在他们藏金的地方徘徊不散。（鸡啼）要是有这样的事,你也对我说吧。不要走,说呀!拦住它,马西勒斯。

马西勒斯 要不要用我的戟子打它?

霍拉旭 好的,要是它不肯站定。

勃那多 它在这儿!

霍拉旭 它在这儿!(鬼下)

马西勒斯 它去了!我们不该用暴力对待这样一个有尊严的亡魂。因为它是像空气一样不可侵害的,我们无益的打击不过是恶意的徒劳。

勃那多 它正要说话的时候,鸡就啼了。

霍拉旭 于是它就像一个罪犯听到了可怕的召唤似的惊跳起来。我听人家说,报晓的雄鸡用它尖锐的啼声,唤醒了白昼之神,一听到它的警告,那些在海里、火里、地下、空中到处浪游的有罪的灵魂,就一个个钻回各自的巢穴里去,这句话现在已经证实了。

马西勒斯 它在鸡鸣的时候隐去了。有人说,我们的救主将要诞生以前,这报晓的鸟儿彻夜长鸣。那时候,他们说,没有一个鬼魂可以出外行走,夜间的空气非常清净,没有一颗星用毒光射人,没有一个神仙用法术迷人,妖巫的符咒也失去了力量,一切都是圣洁而美好的。

霍拉旭 我也听人家这样说过,倒有几分相信。可是,瞧,清晨披着赤褐色的外衣,已经踏着那边东方高山上的露水走过来了，我们也可以下班了。照我的意思，我们应该把我们今夜看见的事情告诉年轻的哈姆雷特。因为凭着我的生命起誓，这一个鬼魂虽然对我们一言不发，见了他一定有话要说。你们以为按着我们的忠心和责任说起来，是不是应当让他知道这件事情？

马西勒斯　很好，我们去告诉他吧。我知道今天在什么地方最容易找到他。（同下）

第二场
城堡中的大厅

【国王、王后、哈姆雷特、波洛涅斯、雷欧提斯、伏提曼德、考尼律斯、群臣、侍从等上。

国王 虽然我们亲爱的王兄哈姆雷特新丧未久,我们的心里应当充满了悲痛,我们全国都应当表示一致的哀悼,可是我们凛于后死者责任的重大,不能不违情逆性,一方面固然要用适度的悲哀纪念他,一方面也要为自身的利害着想;所以,在一种悲喜交集的情绪之下,让幸福和忧郁分据了我的两眼,殡葬的挽歌和结婚的笙乐同时并奏,用盛大的喜乐抵消沉重的不幸,我已经和我旧日的长嫂——当今的王后,这一个多事之国的共同的统治者,结为夫妇。这一次婚姻事先曾经征求各位的意见,多承你们诚意的赞助,这是我必须向大家致谢的。现在我要让你们知道,年轻的福丁布拉斯看轻了我们的实力,也许他以为自从我们亲爱的王兄崩逝以后,我们的国势已经瓦解,所以挟着他的从中取利的梦想,不断向我们书面要求把他的父亲依法割让给我们英勇的王兄的土地归还。这是他一面之词。现在要讲到我们的态度和今天召集各位来此的目的。我们的对策是这样的:我这儿已经写好了一封给挪威国王的信,年轻的福丁布拉斯的叔父,他因为卧病在床,不曾与闻他侄子的企图,在信里我请他注意他的侄子擅自在国内征募壮丁,训练士卒,积极进行各种准备的事实,要求他从速制止他的进一步的行动;现在我就派遣你,考尼律斯,还有你,伏提曼德,替我把这封信送去给挪威老王,除了训令上所规定的条件以外,你们不得僭用你们的权利,和挪威成立逾越范围的妥协。你们赶紧就去吧,再会!

考尼律斯　　我们不敢不尽力执行陛下的旨意。
伏提曼德

国王　我相信你们的忠心,再会!(伏提曼德、考尼律斯同下)现在,雷欧提斯,你有什么话说?你对我说你有一个请求,是什么请求,雷欧提斯?只要是合理的事情,你向丹麦王说了,他总不会不答应你。你还有什么要求,雷欧提斯,是我不会在你没有开口以前就自动给了你的?丹麦王室和你父亲的关系,正像头脑之于心灵一样密切。丹麦国王乐意为你父亲效劳,正像嘴里所说的话,可以由双手去执行一样。你要些什么,雷欧提斯?

雷欧提斯　陛下,我要请求您允许我回到法国去。这一次我回国参加陛下加冕的盛典,略尽臣子的微忱,实在是莫大的荣幸,可是现在我的任务已尽,我的心愿又向法国飞驰,但求陛下开恩允许。

国王　你父亲已经答应了你吗?波洛涅斯,你怎么说?

波洛涅斯　陛下,我却不过他几次三番的恳求,已经勉强答应他了,请陛下放他去了吧。

国王　好好利用你的时间,雷欧提斯,尽情发挥你的才能吧!可是来,我的侄儿哈姆雷特,我的孩子——

哈姆雷特　(旁白)超乎寻常的亲族,漠不相干的路人。

国王　为什么愁云依旧笼罩在你的身上?

哈姆雷特　不,陛下,我已经在太阳里晒得太久了。

王后　哈姆雷特,脱下你的黑衣,对你的父王应该和颜悦色一点,不要老是垂下了眼皮,在泥土之中找寻你的高贵的父亲。你知道这是一件很普通的事情,活着的人谁都要死去,从生存的空间踏进了永久的宁静。

哈姆雷特　嗯,母亲,这是一件很普通的事情。

王后　既然是很普通的,那么你为什么瞧上去好像老是这样郁郁于心呢?

哈姆雷特　好像,母亲!不,是这样就是这样,我不知道什么"好像"不"好像"。好妈妈,我的墨黑的外套、礼俗上规定的丧服、勉强吐出来的叹气、像滚滚江流一样的眼泪、悲苦沮丧的脸色,以及一切仪式,外表和忧伤的流露,都不能表达出我的真实的情绪。这些才真是给人瞧的,因为谁也可以做作成这种样子。它们不过是悲哀的装饰和衣服,可是我的郁结的心事却是无法表现出来的。

国王　哈姆雷特,你这样孝思不匮,原是你天性中纯笃过人之处。可是你要知道，你的父亲也曾失去过一个父亲，那失去的父亲自己也失去过父亲。那后死的儿子为了尽他的孝道起见，必须有一个时期服丧守制，然而固执不变的哀伤，却是一种逆天悖理的愚行，不是堂堂男子所应有的举止。它表现出一个不肯安于天命的意志，一个经不起艰难痛苦的心，一个缺少忍耐的头脑和一个简单愚昧的理性。既然我们知道那是无可避免的事，无论谁都要遭遇到同样的事，那么我们为什么要这样固执地把它耿耿于怀呢？嘿！那是对上天的罪戾，对死者的罪戾，也是违反人情的罪戾。在理智上它是完全荒谬的，因为从第一个死了的父亲起，直到今天死去的最后一个父亲为止，理智永远在呼喊："这是无可避免的。"我请你抛弃了这种无益的悲伤，把我当作你的父亲；因为我要让全世界知道，你是王位的直接继承者，我要给你尊荣和恩宠，不亚于一个最慈爱的父亲之于他的儿子。至于你要回到威登堡去继续求学的意思，那是完全违反我们的愿望的。请你听从我的劝告，不要离开这里，在朝廷上领袖群臣，做我们最密近的国亲和王儿，使我们因为每天能够看见你而心生快慰。

王后　不要让你母亲的祈求全归无用，哈姆雷特。请你不要离开我们，不要到威登堡去。

哈姆雷特　我将要勉力服从您的意志，母亲。

国王　啊，那才是一句有孝心的答复。你将在丹麦享有和我同等的尊荣。御妻,来。哈姆雷特这一种自动的顺从使我非常高兴。为了表示庆祝起见,今天丹麦王每一次举杯祝饮的时候,都要放一响高入云中的祝炮,让上天应和着地上的雷鸣,发出欢乐的回声。来。(除哈姆雷特外,均下)

哈姆雷特 啊,但愿这一个太坚实的肉体会融解、消散,化成一堆露水或者那永生的真神不曾制定禁止自杀的律法!上帝啊!上帝啊!人世间的一切在我看来是多么可厌、陈腐、乏味而无聊。哼!哼!那是一个荒芜不治的花园,长满了恶毒的莠草。想不到居然会有这种事情!刚死了两个月!不,两个月还不满!这样好的一个国王,比起这个来,简直是天神和丑怪。这样爱我的母亲,甚至不愿让天风吹痛了她的脸庞。天上和地下!我必须记着吗?嘿,她会偎依在他的身旁,好像吃了美味的食物,格外促进了食欲一般。可是,只有一个月的时间,我不能再想下去了!脆弱啊,你的名字就是女人!短短的一个月以前,她哭得像个泪人儿似的,送我那可怜的父亲下葬。她在送葬的时候所穿的那双鞋子现在还没有破旧,她就,她就——上帝啊!一头没有理性的畜生也要悲伤得长久一<u>些</u>——她就嫁给我的叔父,我的父亲的弟弟,可是他一点不像我的父亲,正像我一点不像赫拉克勒斯一样。只有一个月的时间,她那流着虚伪之泪的眼睛还没有消去它们的红肿,她就嫁了人了。啊,罪恶的匆促,这样迫不及待地钻进了乱伦的衾被!那不是好事,也不会有好结果。可是碎了吧,我的心,因为我必须噤住我的嘴!

【霍拉旭、马西勒斯、勃那多同上。

霍拉旭 祝福,殿下!

哈姆雷特 我很高兴看见你身体健康,霍拉旭。

霍拉旭 我也是这样,殿下。我永远是您的卑微的仆人。

哈姆雷特 不,你是我的好朋友。我愿意和你朋友相称。你怎么不在威登堡,霍拉旭?马西勒斯!

马西勒斯 殿下——

哈姆雷特 我很高兴看见你。(向勃那多)你好,朋友。——可是你究竟为什么离开威登堡?

霍拉旭 无非是偷闲躲懒罢了,殿下。

哈姆雷特 我不愿听见你的仇敌说这样的话,你也不能用这样的话刺痛我的耳朵,使它相信你对你自己所做的诽谤;我知道你不是一个偷闲躲懒的人。可是你到艾尔西诺有什么事?趁着你未去之前,我们要陪你痛饮几杯哩。

霍拉旭 殿下,我是来参加您的父王的葬礼的。

哈姆雷特 请你不要取笑,我的同学,我想你是来参加我的母后的婚礼的。

霍拉旭 真的,殿下,这两件事情相去得太近了。

哈姆雷特 这是一举两得的办法,霍拉旭!葬礼中剩下来的残杯冷炙,正好宴请婚宴上的宾客。霍拉旭,我宁愿在天上遇见我的最痛恨的仇人,也不愿看到那样的一天!我的父亲,我仿佛看见我的父亲。

霍拉旭　啊,在什么地方,殿下?

哈姆雷特　在我的心灵的眼睛里,霍拉旭。

霍拉旭　我曾经见过他一次,他是一位很好的君王。

哈姆雷特　他是一个堂堂男子,整个儿地说起来,我再也见不到像他那样的人了。

霍拉旭　殿下,我想我昨天晚上看见他。

哈姆雷特　看见谁?

霍拉旭　殿下,我看见您的父王。

哈姆雷特　我的父王!

霍拉旭　不要吃惊,请您静静地听我把这件奇事告诉您,这两位可以替我做见证。

哈姆雷特　看在上帝的分上,讲给我听。

霍拉旭　这两位朋友,马西勒斯和勃那多,在万籁俱寂的午夜守望的时候,曾经连续两夜看见一个自顶至踵全身甲胄,像您父亲一样的人形,在他们的面前出现,用庄严而缓慢的步伐走过他们的身边。当着他们惊奇骇愕的面,他三次步行过去,他手里所握的鞭杖可以碰到他们的身上,他们吓得几乎浑身都瘫痪了,只是呆立着不动,一句话也没有对他说。怀着惴惧的心情,他们把这件事悄悄地告诉了我,我就在第三夜陪着他们一起守望;正像他们所说的一样,那鬼魂又出现了,出现的时间和他的形状,证实了他们的每一个字都是正确的。我认识您的父亲,那鬼魂是那样酷肖他的生前,我这两手也不及他们彼此的相似。

哈姆雷特　可是这是在什么地方?

马西勒斯　殿下,就在我们守望的露台上。

哈姆雷特　你有没有对它说话?

霍拉旭　殿下,我说了,可是它没有回答我。不过有一次我觉得它好像抬起头来,像要开口说话似的,可是就在那时候,晨鸡高声啼了起来,它一听见鸡声,就很快地隐去不见了。

哈姆雷特　这很奇怪。

霍拉旭　凭着我的生命起誓,殿下,这是真的。我们认为按着我们的责任,应该让您知道这件事。

哈姆雷特　不错,不错,朋友们,可是这件事情很使我迷惑,你们今晚仍旧要去守望吗?

马西勒斯
勃　那　多　是,殿下。

哈姆雷特　你们说他穿着甲胄吗?

马西勒斯
勃　那　多　是,殿下。

哈姆雷特　从头到脚?

马西勒斯
勃　那　多　从头到脚,殿下。

哈姆雷特　那么你们没有看见他的脸吗?

霍拉旭　啊,看见的,殿下。他的脸甲是掀起的。

哈姆雷特　怎么,瞧上去像在发怒吗?

霍拉旭　他的脸上悲哀多于愤怒。

哈姆雷特　他的脸色是惨白的还是红红的?

霍拉旭　非常惨白。

哈姆雷特　他把眼睛注视着你吗?

霍拉旭　他直盯着我瞧。

哈姆雷特　我希望我也在那边。

霍拉旭　那一定会使您骇愕万分。

哈姆雷特　多分会的,多分会的。他停留得长久吗?

霍拉旭　大概有一个人用不快不慢的速度从一数到一百的那段时间。

马西勒斯

勃 那 多   还要长久一些,还要长久一些。

霍拉旭   我看见他的时候,不过是这么久。

哈姆雷特   他的胡须是斑白的吗?

霍拉旭   是的,正像我在他生前看见的那样,乌黑的胡须里略有几根变成白色。

哈姆雷特   我今晚也要守夜去,也许它还会出来。

霍拉旭   我可以担保它一定会出来。

哈姆雷特   要是它借着我的父王的形貌出现,即使地狱张开嘴来,叫我不要作声,我也一定要对它说话。要是你们到现在还没有把你们所看见的告诉别人,那么我要请求你们大家继续保持沉默。无论今夜发生什么事情,都请放在心里,不要在口舌之间泄漏出来。我一定会报答你们的忠诚。好,再会。今晚十一点钟到十二点钟之间,我要到露台上来看你们。

众人   我们愿意为殿下尽忠。

哈姆雷特   让我们彼此保持着不渝的交情,再会!(霍拉旭、马西勒斯、勃那多同下)我父亲的灵魂披着甲胄!事情有些不妙,我恐怕这里面有奸人的恶计。但愿黑夜早点到来!静静地等着吧,我的灵魂。罪恶的行为总有一天会发现,虽然地上所有的泥土会把它们遮掩。(下)

第三场
波洛涅斯家中一室

【雷欧提斯及奥菲利娅上。

雷欧提斯　我需要的物件已经装在船上,再会了,妹妹,在好风给人方便,路上没有阻碍的时候,不要贪睡,让我听见你的消息。

奥菲利娅　你还不相信我吗?

雷欧提斯　对于哈姆雷特和他的调情献媚,你必须把它认作一时的感情冲动,一朵初春的紫罗兰早熟而易凋,馥郁而不能持久,一分钟的芬芳和喜悦,如此而已。

奥菲利娅　不过是如此吗?

雷欧提斯　不过如此,因为像新月一样逐渐饱满的人生,不仅是肌肉和体格的成长,而且随着身体的发展,精神和心灵也同时扩大。也许他现在爱你,他的真诚的意志是纯洁而不带欺诈的。可是你必须留心,他有这样高的地位,他的意志并不属于他自己,因为他自己也要被他的血统所支配。他不能像一般庶民一样自己选择,因为他的决定足以影响到整个国本的安危,他是全身的首脑,他的选择必须得到各部分肢体的同意。所以要是他说,他爱你,你可以相信他在他的地位之上,也许会把他的说话见之行事,可是那必须以丹麦的公意给他赞许为限。你再想一想要是你用过于轻信的耳朵倾听他的歌曲,让他攫走了你的心,在他的狂妄的渎求之下,打开了你的宝贵的童贞,那时候你的名誉将要蒙受多大的损失?留心,奥菲利娅,留心,我的亲爱的妹妹,不要放纵你的爱情,不要让欲望的利箭把你射中。一个自爱的女郎,不应该向月亮显露她的美貌,圣贤也不能逃避谗口的中伤。春天的草木往往还没有吐放它们的蓓蕾,就被蛀虫蠹蚀;朝露一样晶莹的青春,常常会受到罡风的吹打。所以留心着吧,戒惧是最安全的方策,即使没有旁人的诱惑,少年的血气也要向他自己叛变。

奥菲利娅　我将要记住你这段很好的教训,让它看守着我的心。可是,我的好哥哥,你不要像有些坏牧师一样,指点我上天去的险峻的荆棘之途,自己却在花街柳巷流连忘返,忘记了自己的箴言。

雷欧提斯　啊!不要为我担心。我耽搁得太久了,可是我的父亲来了。

【波洛涅斯上。

雷欧提斯　两重的祝福是双倍的恩荣,第二次的告别是格外可喜的。

波洛涅斯　还在这儿,雷欧提斯!上船去,上船去,真好意思!风息在帆顶上,人家都在等着你哩。好,我为你祝福!还有几句教训,希望你铭刻在记忆之中:不要想到什么就说什么,凡事必须三思而行。对人要和气,可是不要过分狎昵。相知有素的朋友,应该用钢圈箍住在你的灵魂上,可是不要对每一个泛泛的新知滥施你的交情。留心避免和人家争吵,可是万一争端已起,就应该让对方知道你不是可以轻侮的。倾听每一个人的意见,可是只对极少数人发表你自己的意见;接纳每一个人的批评,可是保留你自己的判断。尽你的财力购置贵重的衣服,可是不要炫新立异,必须富丽而不浮艳,因为服装往往可以表现人格。法国的名流要人,在这一点上是特别注重的。不要向人告贷,也不要借钱给人,因为债款放了出去,往往不但丢了本钱,而且还失去了朋友。向人告贷的结果,容易养成因循懒惰的习惯。尤其要紧的,你必须对你自己忠实,正像有了白昼才有黑夜一样,对自己忠实,才不会对别人欺诈。再会,让我的祝福使你记住这一番话!

雷欧提斯 父亲,我告别了。

波洛涅斯 时候不早了,去吧,你的仆人都在等着。

雷欧提斯 再会,奥菲利娅,记住我对你说的话。

奥菲利娅 你的话已经锁在我的记忆里,那钥匙你替我保管着吧。

雷欧提斯 再会!(下)

波洛涅斯 奥菲利娅,他对你说些什么话?

奥菲利娅 回父亲的话,我们刚才谈起哈姆雷特殿下的事情。

波洛涅斯 嗯,这是应该考虑一下的。听说他近来常常跟你在一起,你也从来不拒绝他的求见;要是果然有这种事,——人家这样告诉我,也无非是叫我注意的意思,——那么我必须对你说,你还没有懂得你做了我的女儿,按照你的身份,应该怎样留心你自己的行动。究竟在你们两人之间有些什么关系?老实告诉我。

奥菲利娅 父亲,他最近曾经屡次向我表示他的爱意。

波洛涅斯 爱情!呸!你讲的话完全像是一个不曾经历过这种危险的不懂事的女孩子。你相信他的那种你所说的表示吗?

奥菲利娅 父亲,我不知道我应该怎样想才好。

波洛涅斯 好,让我来教你。你应该这样想,你是一个小孩子,把这些假意的表示当作了真心的奉献。你应该把你自己的价值抬高一些。

奥菲利娅 父亲,他向我求爱的态度是很光明正大的。

波洛涅斯 嗯,他的态度。很好,很好。

奥菲利娅 而且,父亲,他差不多用尽了一切指天誓日的神圣的盟约,证实他的言语。

波洛涅斯 嗯,这些都是捕捉愚蠢的山鹬的圈套。我知道在热情燃烧的时候,一个人无论什么盟誓都会说出口来。这些火焰,女儿,是光多于热的,一下子就会光消焰灭,因为它们本来是虚幻的,你不能把它们当作真火看待。从现在起,你还是少露一些你的女儿家的脸。你应该自抬身价,不要让人家以为你是可以随意呼召的。对于哈姆雷特殿下,你应该这样想,他是个年轻的王子,他比你在行动上有更大的自由。总而言之,奥菲利娅,不要相信他的盟誓,因为它们都是诱人堕落的鸩媒,用庄严神圣的辞令,掩饰淫邪险恶的居心。我言尽于此,简单一句话,从现在起,我不许你跟哈姆雷特殿下谈一句话。你留点儿神吧,进去。

奥菲利娅 我一定听从您的话,父亲。(同下)

第四场
露台

【哈姆雷特、霍拉旭及马西勒斯上。

哈姆雷特 风吹得人怪痛的,这天气真冷。

霍拉旭 是很凛冽的寒风。

哈姆雷特 现在是什么时候了?

霍拉旭 我想还不到十二点。

马西勒斯 不,已经打过了。

霍拉旭 真的?我没有听见。那么鬼魂出现的时候快要到了。(内喇叭奏花腔及鸣炮声)这是什么意思,殿下?

哈姆雷特　王上今晚大宴群臣，通宵醉舞，每次他喝下了一杯葡萄美酒，铜鼓和喇叭便吹打起来，欢祝万寿。

霍拉旭　这是向来的风俗吗？

哈姆雷特　嗯，是的。可是我虽然从小就熟习这种风俗，却也不是常常举行的。这一种酗酒纵乐的风俗，使我们在东西各国受到许多诽毁。他们称我们为酒徒醉汉，将下流的污名加在我们头上，使我们各项伟大的成就都因此而大为失色。在个人方面也常常是这样，有些人因为身体长了丑陋的黑痣，——这本来是天生的缺陷，不是他们自己的过失，——或者生就一种令人侧目的怪癖，虽然他们此外还有许多纯洁优美的品性，可是为了这一个缺点，往往会受到世人的歧视。

【鬼上。

霍拉旭　瞧，殿下，它来了！

哈姆雷特　天使保佑我们！不管你是一个善良的灵魂或是万恶的妖魔，不管你带来了天上的和风或是地狱中的罡风，不管你的来意好或坏，因为你的形状是这样和蔼可亲，我要对你说话。我要叫你哈姆雷特，君王，父亲！尊严的丹麦先王，啊，回答我！不要让我在无知的蒙昧里抱恨终天。告诉我为什么你的长眠的骸骨不安窀穸，为什么安葬着你的遗体的坟墓张开它的沉重的大理石的两颚，把你重新吐放出来。你这已死的尸体从这样全身甲胄，出现在月光之下，使黑夜变得这样阴森,使我们这些为造化所玩弄的愚人充满了不可思议的恐怖,究竟是什么意思呢?说,这是为了什么?你要我们怎样?(鬼向哈姆雷特招手)

霍拉旭 它招手叫您跟着它去,好像它有什么话要对您一个人说似的。

马西勒斯 瞧,它用很有礼貌的举动,招呼您到一个僻远的所在去,可是别跟它去。

霍拉旭 千万不要跟它去。

哈姆雷特 它不肯说话,我还是跟它去。

霍拉旭 不要去,殿下。

哈姆雷特 嗨,怕什么呢?我把我的生命看得不值一枚针,至于我的灵魂,那是跟它自己同样永生不灭的,它能够把它加害吗?它又在招手叫我前去了,我要跟它去。

霍拉旭 殿下,要是它把您诱到潮水里去,或者把您领到下临大海的峻峭的悬崖之巅,在那边它现出了狰狞的化形,使您丧失理智,变得疯狂,那可怎么好呢?您想,无论什么人一到了那样的地方,望着下面千仞的峭壁,听见海水奔腾的怒吼,即使没别的原因,也会吓得心惊胆战的。

哈姆雷特 它还是在向我招手。去吧,我跟着你。

马西勒斯 您不能去,殿下。

哈姆雷特 放下你们的手!

霍拉旭 听我们的劝告,不要去。

哈姆雷特　我的命运在高声呼喊,使我全身每一根微细的血管都变得像怒狮的筋骨一样坚硬。(鬼招手)它仍旧在招我去。放开我,朋友们。(挣脱二人之手)凭着上天起誓,谁要是拉住了我,我要叫他变成一个鬼!走开!去吧,我跟着你。(鬼魂及哈姆雷特同下)

霍拉旭　幻想占据了他的头脑,使他不顾一切。

马西勒斯　让我们跟上去,我们不应该服从他的话。

霍拉旭　那么去吧。这种事情会引出些什么结果来呢?

马西勒斯　丹麦国里恐怕有些不可告人的坏事。

霍拉旭　上天的意旨支配一切。

马西勒斯　不,我们还是跟上去。(同下)

第五场
露台的另一部分

【鬼魂及哈姆雷特上。

哈姆雷特　你要领我到什么地方去?说,我不愿再前进了。

鬼魂　听我说。

哈姆雷特　我在听着。

鬼魂　我的时间快要到了,我必须再回到硫黄的烈火里去受煎熬的痛苦。

哈姆雷特　唉,可怜的亡魂!

鬼魂 不要可怜我,你只要留心听着我将要告诉你的话。

哈姆雷特 说吧,我在这儿听着。

鬼魂 你听了以后,必须替我报仇。

哈姆雷特 什么?

鬼魂 我是你父亲的灵魂,因为生前孽障未尽,被判在晚间游行地上,白昼忍受火焰的烧灼,必须经过相当的时期,等生前的过失被火焰净化以后,方才可以脱罪。可是我不能违犯禁令,泄漏我的狱室中的秘密,我可以告诉你一个故事,它的最轻微的一句话,都可以使你魂飞魄散,你年轻的血液凝冻成冰,使你的双眼像脱了轨道的星球一样向前突出,你的纠结的鬈发根根分开,像愤怒的豪猪身上的刺毛一样森然耸立。可是这一种永恒的神秘,是不能向血肉的凡耳宣示的。听着,听着,啊,听着!要是你曾经爱过你的亲爱的父亲——

哈姆雷特 上帝啊!

鬼魂 你必须替他报复那逆伦惨恶的杀身仇恨。

哈姆雷特 杀身的仇恨!

鬼魂 杀人是重大的罪恶,可是这一件谋杀的惨案,是最骇人听闻而逆天害理的罪行。

哈姆雷特 赶快告诉我,让我驾着像思想和爱情一样迅速的翅膀,飞去把仇人杀死。

鬼魂 我的话果然令你激动。要是你听见了这种事情而漠然,无动于衷,那你除非比舒散在忘河之滨的蔓草还要冥顽不灵。现在,哈姆雷特,听我说,一般人都以为我在花园里睡觉的时候,一条蛇来把我螫死,这一个虚构的死状,把丹麦全国的人都骗过了。可是你要知道,好孩子,那毒害你父亲的蛇,头上戴着王冠呢。

哈姆雷特 啊,果然给我猜到了!我的叔父!

鬼魂 嗯,那头乱伦的奸淫的畜生,他有的是过人的诡诈、天赋的奸恶,凭着他的阴险的手段,诱惑了我的外表上似乎非常贞淑的王后,满足他的无耻的兽欲。啊,哈姆雷特,那是一个多么悬殊的差异!我的爱情是那样纯洁真诚,始终信守着我在结婚的时候对她所发的盟誓,她却会对一个天赋的才德远不如我的恶人降心相从!可是正像一个贞洁的女子,虽然淫欲罩上神圣的外表,也不能把她煽动一样,一个淫妇虽然和光明的天使为偶,也会有一天厌倦于天上的唱随之乐,而宁愿搂抱人间的朽骨。可是且慢!我仿佛嗅到了清晨的空气,让我把话说得简短一些。当我按照每天午后的惯例,在花园里睡觉的时候,你的叔父趁我不备,悄悄溜了进来,拿着一个盛着毒草汁的小瓶,把一种使人麻痹的药水注入我的耳腔之内,那药性发作起来,会像水银一样很快地流过了全身的大小血管,像酸液滴进牛乳里般地把淡薄而健全的血液凝结起来。它一进入我的身体里,我全身光滑的皮肤上便立刻发生无数疱疹,像害着癞病似的满布着可憎的鳞片。这样我在睡梦之中,被一个兄弟同时夺去了我的生命、我的王冠和我的王后。甚至于不给我一个忏罪的机会,使我在没有领到圣餐也没有受过临终涂膏礼以前,就一无准备地负着我的全部罪恶去对簿阴曹。可怕啊可怕!要是你有天性之情,不要默尔而息,不要让丹麦的御寝变成了藏奸养逆的卧榻,可是无论你怎样进行复仇,你的行事必须光明磊落,更不可对你的母亲有什么不利的图谋,让她去受上天的裁判,和她自己内心中的荆棘的刺戳吧。现在我必须去了!萤火的微光已经开始暗淡下去,清晨快要到来了。再会,再会!哈姆雷特,记着我。(下)

哈姆雷特 天上的神明啊!地啊!再有什么呢?我还要向地狱呼喊吗?啊,呸!忍着吧,忍着吧,我的心!我的全身的筋骨,不要一下子就变成衰老,支持着我的身体呀!记着你!是的,你可怜的亡魂,当记忆不曾从我这混乱的头脑里消失的时候,我会记着你的。记着你!是的,我要从我的记忆的碑板上,拭去一切琐碎愚蠢的记录,一切书本上的格言,一切陈言套语,一切过去的印象,我的少年的阅历所留下的痕迹,只让你的命令留在我的脑筋的书卷里,不搀杂一些下贱的废料。是的,上天为我做证!啊,最恶毒的妇人!啊,奸贼,奸贼,脸上堆着笑的万恶的奸贼!我的写字板呢?我必须把它记下来:一个人尽管满面都是笑,骨子里却是杀人的奸贼,至少我相信在丹麦是这样的。(写字)好,叔父,我把你写下来了。现在我要记下我的话,那是,"再会,再会!记着我"。我已经发过誓了。

霍拉旭 （在内）殿下!殿下!

马西勒斯 （在内）哈姆雷特殿下!

霍拉旭 （在内）上天保佑他!

马西勒斯 （在内）但愿如此!

霍拉旭 （在内）嘿啰,呵,呵,殿下!

哈姆雷特 嘿啰,呵,呵,孩儿!来,鸟儿,来。

【霍拉旭及马西勒斯上。

马西勒斯 怎样,殿下!

霍拉旭 有什么事,殿下?

哈姆雷特 啊!奇怪!

霍拉旭 好殿下,告诉我们。

哈姆雷特 不,你们会泄漏出去的。

霍拉旭 不,殿下,凭着上天起誓,我一定不泄漏。

马西勒斯 我也一定不泄漏,殿下。

哈姆雷特 那么你们说,哪一个人会想得到有这种事?可是你们能够保守秘密吗?

霍 拉 旭
马斯勒斯 是,上天为我们做证,殿下。

哈姆雷特 在全丹麦从来不曾有那一个奸贼——不,是一个十足的坏人。

霍拉旭 殿下,这样一句话是用不着什么鬼魂从坟墓里出

31

来告诉我们的。

哈姆雷特　啊,对了,你说得有理,所以,我们还是不必多说废话,大家握握手分开了吧。你们可以去照你们自己的意思干你们自己的事,——因为各人都有各人的意思和各人的事,——至于我自己,那么我对你们说,我是要去祈祷的。

霍拉旭　殿下,您这些话好像有些疯疯癫癫似的。

哈姆雷特　我的话冒犯了你,真是非常抱歉。是的,我从心底里抱歉。

霍拉旭　哪儿的话,殿下。

哈姆雷特　不,凭着圣伯特力克的名义,霍拉旭,我真是非常冒犯了你。讲到这一个幽灵,那么让我告诉你们,它是一个老实的亡魂。你们要是想知道它对我说了些什么话,我只好请你们暂时不必问。现在,好朋友们,你们都是我的朋友,都是学者和军人,请你们允许我一个卑微的要求。

霍拉旭　是什么要求,殿下?我们一定应允您。

哈姆雷特　永远不要把你们今晚所见的事情告诉别人。

霍拉旭
马西拉勒　殿下,我们一定不告诉别人。

哈姆雷特　不,你们必须宣誓。

霍拉旭　凭着良心起誓,殿下,我决不告诉别人。

马西勒斯　凭着良心起誓,殿下,我也决不告诉别人。

哈姆雷特　把手按在我的剑上宣誓。

马西勒斯　殿下，我们已经宣誓过了。

哈姆雷特　那不算，把手按在我的剑上。

鬼魂　（在下）宣誓！

哈姆雷特　啊哈！孩儿！你也这样说吗？你在那儿吗，好家伙？来，你们没听见这个地下的人怎么说的吗？宣誓吧。

霍拉旭　请您教我们怎样宣誓，殿下。

哈姆雷特　永不向人提起你们所看见的这一切。把手按在我的剑上宣誓。

鬼魂　（在下）宣誓！

哈姆雷特　又在那边了吗？那么我们换一个地方。过来，朋友们。把你们的手按在我的剑上，宣誓永不向人提起你们所听见的这一切。

鬼魂　（在下）宣誓！

哈姆雷特　说得好，老鼹鼠！你能够在地底钻得这么快吗？好一个开路的先锋！好朋友们，我们再来换一个地方。

霍拉旭　哎哟，真是不可思议的怪事！

哈姆雷特　那么你还是用见怪不怪的态度对待它吧。霍拉旭，天地之间有许多事情，是你们的哲学里所没有想到的呢。可是，来，上帝的慈悲保佑你们，你们必须再做一次宣誓。我今后也许有时候要故意装出一副疯疯癫癫的样子，你们要是在那时候看见了我的古怪的举动，切不可像这样交叉着手臂,或者这样摇头摆脑的,或者嘴里说一些吞吞吐吐的词句,例如"呃,呃,我们知道",或者"只要我们高兴,我们就可以",或是"要是我们愿意说出来的话",或是"有人要是怎么怎么",诸如此类的含糊其词的话语,表示你们知道我有些什么秘密。你们必须答应我避免这一类言行,上帝的恩惠和慈悲保佑着你们,宣誓吧。

鬼魂 (在下)宣誓!(二人宣誓)

哈姆雷特 安息吧,安息吧,受难的灵魂!好,朋友们,我用全心的真情,信赖着你们两位。要是在哈姆雷特的微弱的能力以内,能够有可以向你们表示他的友情之处,上帝在上,我一定不会有负你们。让我们一同进去。请你们记着在无论什么时候都要守口如瓶。这是一个颠倒混乱的时代。唉,倒霉的我却要负起重整乾坤的责任!来,我们一块儿去吧。(同下)

第二幕

第一场
波洛涅斯家中一室

【波洛涅斯及雷奈尔多上。

波洛涅斯　把这些钱和这封信交给他,雷奈尔多。

雷奈尔多　是,老爷。

波洛涅斯　好雷奈尔多,你在没有去看他以前,最好先探听探听他的行为。

雷奈尔多 老爷,我本来就有这个意思。

波洛涅斯 很好,很好,好得很。你先给我调查调查有些什么丹麦人在巴黎,他们是干什么事情的,叫什么名字,有没有钱,住在什么地方,跟哪些人做伴,用度大不大。用这种转弯抹角的方法,要是你打听到他们也认识我的儿子,你就可以更进一步,表示你对他也有相当的认识。你可以这样说:"我知道他的父亲和他的朋友,对他也略为有点认识。"你听着没有,雷奈尔多?

雷奈尔多 是,我在留心听着,老爷。

波洛涅斯 "对他也略为有点认识,可是,"你可以说,"不怎么熟悉,不过假如果然是他的话,那么他是个很放浪的人,有些怎样怎样的坏习惯。"说到这里,你就可以随便捏造一些关于他的坏话。当然啰,你不能把他说得太不成样子,那是会损害他的名誉的,这一点你必须注意。可是你不妨举出一些纨绔子弟们所犯的最普通的浪荡的行为。

雷奈尔多 譬如赌钱,老爷。

波洛涅斯 对了,或是喝酒、斗剑、赌咒、吵嘴、嫖妓之类,你都可以说。

雷奈尔多 老爷,那是会损害他的名誉的。

波洛涅斯 不,不,你可以在言语之间说得轻淡一些。你不能说他公然纵欲,那可不是我的意思,可是你要把他的过失讲得那么巧妙,让人家听着好像那不过是行为上的小小的不检,一个血气方刚的少年的一时胡闹,算不了什么事的。

雷奈尔多　可是老爷——

波洛涅斯　为什么叫你做这种事?

雷奈尔多　是的,老爷,请您告诉我。

波洛涅斯　呃,我的用意是这样的,我相信我可以有这种权利:你这样轻描淡写地说我儿子的一些坏话,就像你提起一件略有污损的东西似的,听着,要是跟你谈话的那个人,也就是你向他探询的那个人,果然看见过你所说起的那个少年犯着你刚才所列举的那些罪恶,他一定会用这样的话对你表示同意:"好先生——"也许他称你"朋友""仁兄",按照着各人的身份和各国的习惯。

雷奈尔多　很好,老爷。

波洛涅斯　然后他就——他就——我刚才要说一句什么话？哎哟,我正要说一句什么话;我说到什么地方啦?

雷奈尔多　您刚才说到"用这样的话表示同意"。

波洛涅斯　说到"用这样的话表示同意",嗯,对了,他会用这样的话对你表示同意:"我认识这位绅士,昨天我还看见他,或许是前天,或许是什么什么时候,跟什么什么人在一起,正像您所说的,他在什么地方赌钱,在什么地方喝得醺醺大醉,在什么地方因为打网球而跟人家打起架来,"也许他还会说,"我看见他走进什么什么一家生意人家去",那就是说窑子或是诸如此类的所在。你瞧,你用说谎的钓饵,就可以把事实的真相诱上你的钓钩。我们有智慧、有见识的人,往往用这种旁敲侧击的方法,间接达到我们的目的。你也可以照着我上面所说的那一番话,探听出我的儿子的行为。你懂得我的意思没有?

雷奈尔多 老爷,我懂得。

波洛涅斯 上帝和你同在。再会!

雷奈尔多 那么我去了,老爷。

波洛涅斯 你自己也得留心观察他的举止。

雷奈尔多 是,老爷。

波洛涅斯 叫他用心学习音乐。

雷奈尔多 是,老爷。

波洛涅斯 你去吧!(雷奈尔多下)

【奥菲利娅上。

波洛涅斯 啊,奥菲利娅!什么事?

奥菲利娅 哎哟,父亲,我吓死了!

波洛涅斯 凭着上帝的名义,吓什么?

奥菲利娅 父亲,我正在房间里缝纫的时候,哈姆雷特殿下跑了进来,走到我的面前。他的上身的衣服完全没有扣上纽子,头上也不戴帽子,他的袜子上沾着污泥,没有袜带,一直垂到脚踝上。他的脸色像他的衬衫一样白,他的膝盖互相碰撞,他的神气是那样凄惨,好像他刚从地狱里逃出来,要向人讲述它的恐怖一样。

波洛涅斯　他因为不能得到你的爱而发疯了吗?

奥菲利娅　父亲,我不知道,可是我想也许是的。

波洛涅斯　他怎么说?

奥菲利娅　他握住我的手腕紧紧不放,拉直了手臂向后退立,用他的另一只手这样遮在他的额角上,一眼不眨地瞧着我的脸,好像要把它临摹下来似的。这样经过了好久的时间,然后他轻轻地摇动一下我的手臂,他的头上上下下地颠了三颠,于是他发出一声非常惨痛而深长的叹息,好像他的整个的胸部都要爆裂,他的生命就在这一声叹息中间完毕似的。然后他放松了我,转过他的身体,他的头还是向后回顾,好像他不用眼睛的帮助也能够找到他的路,因为直到他走出了门外,他的两眼还是注视在我的身上。

波洛涅斯　跟我来,我要见王上去。这正是恋爱不遂的疯狂。一个人受到这种剧烈的刺激,什么不顾一切的事情都干得出来,我真后悔。怎么,你最近对他说过什么使他难堪的话没有?

奥菲利娅　没有,父亲,可是我已经遵从您的命令,拒绝他的来信,并且不允许他来见我。

波洛涅斯　这就是使他疯狂的原因。我很后悔看错了人。我以为他不过玩弄玩弄你,恐怕贻误你的终身。可是我不该这样多疑!正像年轻人干起事来,往往不知道瞻前顾后一样,我们这种上了年纪的人,总是免不了鳃

鳃过虑。来,我们见王上去。这种事情是不能蒙蔽起来的,要是隐讳不报,也许会闹出乱子来。来。(同下)

第二场
城堡中一室

【国王、王后、罗森格兰兹、吉尔登斯吞及侍从等上。

国王　欢迎,亲爱的罗森格兰兹和吉尔登斯吞!这次匆匆召请你们两位前来,一方面是因为我非常思念你们,一方面也是因为我有需要你们帮忙的地方。你们大概已经听到哈姆雷特的变化,我把它称为变化,因为无论在外表上或是精神上,他已经和从前大不相同。除了他父亲的死以外,究竟还有些什么原因,把他激成了这种疯疯癫癫的样子,我实在无从猜测。你们从小便跟他在一起长大,素来知道他的脾气,所以我特地请你们到我们宫廷里来盘桓几天,陪陪他,替他解解愁闷,同时乘机窥探他究竟有些什么秘密的心事,为我们所不知道的,也许一旦公开之后,我们就可以替他下对症的药饵。

王后　他常常讲起你们两位,我相信世上没有哪两个人比你们更为他所亲信了。你们要是不嫌怠慢,答应在我们这儿小做勾留,帮助我们实现我们的希望,那么你们的盛情雅意,一定会受到丹麦王室隆重的礼谢的。

罗森格兰兹 我们是两位陛下的臣子,两位陛下有什么旨意,尽管命令我们。像这样言重的话,倒使我们置身无地了。

吉尔登斯吞 我们愿意投身在两位陛下的足下,两位陛下无论有什么命令,我们都愿意尽力奉行。

国王 谢谢你们,罗森格兰兹和善良的吉尔登斯吞。

王后 谢谢你们,吉尔登斯吞和善良的罗森格兰兹。现在我就要请你们立刻去看看我的大大变了样子的儿子。来人,领这两位绅士到哈姆雷特的地方去。

吉尔登斯吞 但愿上天加佑,使我们能够得到他的欢心,帮助他恢复常态!

王后 阿门!(罗森格兰兹,吉尔登斯吞及若干侍从下)

【波洛涅斯上。

波洛涅斯 启禀陛下,我们派往挪威去的两位钦使已经喜气洋洋地回来了。

国王 你总是带着好消息来报告我们。

波洛涅斯 真的吗,陛下?不瞒陛下说,我把我对于我的上帝和我的宽仁厚德的王上的责任,看得跟我的灵魂一样重呢。要是我的脑筋还没有出毛病,想到了岔路上去,那么我想我已经发现了哈姆雷特发疯的原因。

国王 啊!你说吧,我急着要听呢。

波洛涅斯 请陛下先接见了钦使,我的消息留着做盛筵以

国王　　后的佳果美点吧。

国王　　那么有劳你去迎接他们进来。（波洛涅斯下）我的亲爱的王后,他对我说他已经发现了你的儿子心神不定的原因。

王后　　我想主要的原因还是他父亲的死和我们过于迅速的结婚。

国王　　好,我们可以试探试探他。

【波洛涅斯率伏提曼德及考尼律斯重上。

国王　　欢迎,我的好朋友们！伏提曼德,我们的挪威王兄怎么说？

伏提曼德　他叫我们向陛下转达他的友好的问候。他听到了我们的要求,就立刻传谕他的侄儿停止征兵。本来他以为这种举动是准备对付波兰人的,可是一经调查,才知道它的对象原来是陛下。他知道此事以后,痛心自己因为年老多病、受人欺罔,震怒之下,传令把福丁布拉斯逮捕,福丁布拉斯并未反抗,受到了挪威王一番申斥,最后就在他的叔父面前立誓决不兴兵侵犯陛下。老王看见他诚心悔过,非常欢喜,当下就给他三千克朗的年俸,并且委任他统率他所征募的那些军士,去向波兰人征伐,同时他叫我把这封信呈上陛下,(将书信呈上)请求陛下允许他的军队借道通过陛下的领土。他已经在信里提出若干条件,作为保证。

国王　这样很好,等我们有空的时候,还要仔细考虑一下,然后答复。你们远道跋涉,不辱使命,很是劳苦了,先去休息休息,今天晚上我们还要在一起欢宴。欢迎你们回来!(伏提曼德、考尼律斯同下)

波洛涅斯　这件事情总算圆满结束了。王上,娘娘,要是我向你们长篇大论地解释君上的尊严,臣下的名分,白昼何以为白昼,黑夜何以为黑夜,时间何以为时间,那不过徒然浪费了昼夜的时间。所以,既然简洁是智慧的灵魂,冗长是肤浅的藻饰,我还是把话说得简单一些吧。你们的那位殿下是疯了,我说他疯了,因为假如要说明什么才是真疯,那就除了说他发疯了以外,还有什么话好说呢？可是那也不用说了。

王后 多谈些实际，少弄些玄虚。

波洛涅斯 娘娘，我发誓我一点不弄玄虚。他疯了，这是真的。唯其是真的，所以才可叹，它的可叹也是真的。——蠢话少说，因为我不愿弄玄虚。好，让我们同意他已经疯了。现在我们就应该求出这一个结果的原因，或者不如说，这一种病态的原因，因为这个病态的结果不是无因而至的，这就是我们现在要做的一步工作。我们来想一想吧。我有一个女儿——当她还不过是我的女儿的时候，她是属于我的——难得她一片孝心，把这封信给了我。现在，请猜一猜这里面说些什么话。"给那天仙化人的，我的灵魂的偶像，最美丽的奥菲利娅——"这是一句恶劣的句子，可是你们听下去吧；"让这几行诗句留下在她的皎洁的胸中——"

王后 这是哈姆雷特写给她的吗？

波洛涅斯 好娘娘，等一等，听我念下去：

"你可以疑心星星是火把，

　　你可以疑心太阳会移转，

你可以疑心真理是谎话，

　　可是我的爱永没有改变。

亲爱的奥菲利娅啊！

　　我的诗写得太坏。

我不会用诗句来抒写我的愁怀，

> 可是相信我,最好的人儿啊!
>
> 我最爱的是你。
>
> 再会!
>
> 　　　　　　　　永远属于你的,哈姆雷特。"
>
> 这一封信是我的女儿出于孝顺之心拿来给我看的。此外,她又把他一次次求爱的情形,在什么时候,用什么方法,在什么所在,全都讲给我听了。

国王　可是她对于他的爱情抱着怎样的态度呢?

波洛涅斯　陛下以为我是怎么样的一个人?

国王　一个忠心正直的人。

波洛涅斯　但愿我能够证明自己是这样一个人。可是假如我看见这场热烈的恋爱正在进行——不瞒陛下说,我在我的女儿没有告诉我以前,就早已看出来了——假如我知道有了这么一回事,却在暗中玉成他们的好事,或者故意视若无睹,假作痴聋,一切不闻不问,那时候陛下的心里觉得怎样?我的好娘娘,您这位王后陛下的心里又觉得怎样?不,我一点儿也不敢懈怠我的责任,立刻我就对我那位小姐说:"哈姆雷特殿下是一位王子,不是你可以仰望的;这种事情不能让它继续下去。"于是我把她教训一番,叫她深居简出,不要和他见面,不要接纳他的来使,也不要收受他的礼物。她听了这番话,就照着我的意思实行起来。说来话短,他遭到拒绝以后,心里就郁郁不快,于是饭也吃不下了,觉也睡不着了，他的身体一天憔悴一天，他的精神一天恍惚一天，这样一步步发展下去，就变成现在他这一种为我们大家所悲痛的疯狂。

国王 你想是这个原因吗？

王后 这是很可能的。

波洛涅斯 我倒很想知道知道，哪一次我肯定地说过了"这件事情是这样的"，而结果却并不这样？

国王 照我所知道的，那倒是没有。

波洛涅斯 要是我说错了话，把这个东西从这个上面拿了下来吧。（指自己的头及肩）只要有线索可寻，我总会找出事实的真相，即使那真相一直藏在地球的中心。

国王 我们怎么可以进一步试验试验？

波洛涅斯 您知道，有时候他会接连几个钟头在这儿走廊里踱来踱去。

王后 他真的常常这样踱来踱去。

波洛涅斯 趁他踱来踱去的时候，我就让我的女儿去见他，你我可以躲在帷幕后面注视他们相会的情形。要是他不爱她，他的理智不是因为恋爱而丧失，那么不要叫我襄理国家的政务，让我去做个耕田的农夫吧。

国王 我们要试一试。

王后 可是瞧，这可怜的孩子忧忧愁愁地念着一本书来了。

波洛涅斯 请两位陛下避一避开。让我走上去招呼他。

（国王、王后及侍从等下）

【哈姆雷特读书上。

波洛涅斯　啊,恕我冒昧。您好,哈姆雷特殿下?

哈姆雷特　呃,上帝怜悯世人!

波洛涅斯　您认识我吗,殿下?

哈姆雷特　认识认识,你是一个卖鱼的贩子。

波洛涅斯　我不是,殿下。

哈姆雷特　那么我但愿你是一个老实人。

波洛涅斯　老实,殿下!

哈姆雷特　嗯,先生;在这世上,一万个人中间只不过有一个老实人。

波洛涅斯　这句话说得很对,殿下。

哈姆雷特　要是太阳能在一头和天神亲吻的死狗尸体上孵育蛆虫——你有一个女儿吗?

波洛涅斯　我有,殿下。

哈姆雷特　不要让她在太阳光底下行走。怀孕是一种幸福,可是你的女儿要是怀了孕,那可糟了。朋友,留心哪。

波洛涅斯　(旁白)你们瞧,他念念不忘地提着我的女儿。可是最初他不认识我,他说我是一个卖鱼的贩子。他的疯病已经很深很深了。说句老实话,我在年轻的时候,为了恋爱也曾大发其疯,那样子也跟他差不多哩。让我再去对他说话。——您在读些什么,殿下?

哈姆雷特　都是些空话,空话,空话。

波洛涅斯　有些什么内容,殿下?

哈姆雷特　一派诽谤,先生。这个专爱把人讥笑的坏蛋在这儿说着,老年人长着灰白的胡须,他们的脸上满是皱纹,他们的眼睛里沾满了眼屎,他们的头脑是空空洞洞的,他们的两腿是摇摇摆摆的。这些话,先生,虽然我十分相信,可是照这样写在书上,总有些有伤厚道。因为就是拿您先生自己来说,要是您能够像一只蟹一样向后倒退,那么您也应该跟我差不多老了。

波洛涅斯　(旁白)这些虽然是疯话,却有深意在内。——您要走进里边去吗,殿下?

哈姆雷特　走进我的坟墓里去?

波洛涅斯　(旁白)他的回答有时候是多么深刻!疯狂的人往往能够说出理智清明的人所说不出来的话。我要离开他,立刻就去想法让他跟我的女儿见面。——殿下,我要向您告别了。

哈姆雷特　先生,那是再好没有的事。但愿我也能够向我的生命告别,但愿我也能够向我的生命告别,但愿我也能够向我的生命告别。

波洛涅斯　再会,殿下。(欲去)

哈姆雷特　这些讨厌的老傻瓜!

【罗森格兰兹及吉尔登斯吞重上。

波洛涅斯　你们要去找哈姆雷特殿下,那边就是。

罗森格兰兹　上帝保佑您,大人!(波洛涅斯下)

吉尔登斯吞 我的尊贵的殿下！

罗森格兰兹 我的最亲爱的殿下！

哈姆雷特 我的好朋友们！你好,吉尔登斯吞？啊,罗森格兰兹！好孩子们,你们两人都好？

罗森格兰兹 不过像一般庸庸碌碌之辈,在这世上虚度时光而已。

吉尔登斯吞 无荣无辱便是我们的幸福。我们不是命运女神帽子上的纽扣。

哈姆雷特 也不是她鞋子的底吗？

罗森格兰兹 也不是,殿下。

哈姆雷特 那么你们是在她的腰上,或是在她的怀抱之中吗？

吉尔登斯吞 说老实话,我们是在她的私处。

哈姆雷特 在命运身上秘密的那部分吗？啊,对了,她本来是一个娼妓。你们听到什么消息没有？

罗森格兰兹 没有,殿下,我们只知道这世界变得老实起来了。

哈姆雷特 那么世界末日快要到了。可是你们的消息是假的。让我再问你们一些私人的问题：我的好朋友们,你们在命运手里犯了什么案子,她把你们送到这儿牢狱里来了？

吉尔登斯吞 牢狱,殿下！

哈姆雷特 丹麦是一所牢狱。

罗森格兰兹　那么世界也是一所牢狱？

哈姆雷特　一所很大的牢狱，里面有许多监房囚室，丹麦是一间最坏的囚室。

罗森格兰兹　我们倒不这样想，殿下。

哈姆雷特　啊，那么对于你们它并不是牢狱，因为世上的事情本来没有善恶，都是各人的思想把它们分别出来的。对于我，它是一所牢狱。

罗森格兰兹　啊，那是因为您的梦想太大，丹麦是个狭小的地方，不够给您发展，所以您把它看成一所牢狱啦。

哈姆雷特　上帝啊！倘不是因为我有了噩梦，那么即使把我关在一个果壳里，我也会把自己当作一个拥有着无限空间的君王的。

吉尔登斯吞　那种噩梦便是您的野心。因为野心者本身的存在，也不过是一个梦的影子。

哈姆雷特　一个梦的本身便是一个影子。

罗森格兰兹　不错，因为野心是那么空虚轻浮的东西，所以我认为它不过是影子的影子。

哈姆雷特　那么我们的乞丐是实体，我们的帝王和大言不惭的英雄，却是乞丐的影子了。我们进宫去好不好？因为我实在不能陪着你们谈玄说理。

罗森格兰兹
吉尔登斯吞　我们愿意侍候殿下。

哈姆雷特　没有的事，我不愿把你们当作我的仆人一样看待。老实对你们说吧,在我旁边侍候我的人太多啦。可是,凭着我们多年的交情,老实告诉我,你们到艾尔西诺来有什么贵干?

罗森格兰兹　我们是来拜访您来的,殿下,没有别的原因。

哈姆雷特　像我这样一个叫花子,我的感谢也是不值钱的,可是我谢谢你们。我想,亲爱的朋友们,你们专程而来,只换到我的一声不值半文钱的谢谢,未免太不值得了。不是有人叫你们来的吗?果然是你们自己的意思吗?真的是自动的访问吗?来,不要骗我。来,来,快说。

吉尔登斯吞　叫我们说些什么话呢,殿下?

哈姆雷特　无论什么话都行,只要不是废话。你们是奉命而来的,瞧你们掩饰不了你们良心上的惭愧,已经从你们的脸色上招认出来了。我知道是我们这位好国王和好王后叫你们来的。

罗森格兰兹　为了什么目的呢,殿下?

哈姆雷特　那可要请你们指教我了。可是凭着我们朋友间的道义,凭着我们少年时候亲密的情谊,凭着我们始终不渝的友好的精神,凭着其他一切更有力量的理由,让我要求你们开诚布公,告诉我究竟你们是不是奉命而来的?

罗森格兰兹　(向吉尔登斯吞旁白)你怎么说?

哈姆雷特　(旁白)好,那么我看透你们的行动了。——要是你们爱我,别再抵赖了吧。

吉尔登斯吞 殿下,我们是奉命而来的。

哈姆雷特 让我代你们说明来意,免得你们泄漏了自己的秘密,有负国王、王后的托付。我近来不知为了什么缘故,一点兴致都提不起来,什么游乐的事都懒得过问。在这一种抑郁的心境之下,仿佛支载万物的大地,这一座美好的框架,只是一个不毛的荒岬。覆盖群动的苍穹,这一顶壮丽的帐幕,这一个点缀着金黄色的火球的庄严的屋宇,只是一大堆污浊的瘴气的集合。人类是一件多么了不得的杰作!多么高贵的理性!多么广大的能力!多么优美的仪表!多么文雅的举动!在行为上多么像一个天使!在智慧上多么像一个天神!宇宙的精华!万物的灵长!可是在我看来,这一个泥土塑成的生命算得什么?人类不能使我发生兴趣;不,女人也不能使我发生兴趣。虽然从你的微笑之中,我可以看到你的意思。

罗森格兰兹 殿下,我心里并没有这样的思想。

哈姆雷特 那么当我说"人类不能使我发生兴趣"的时候,你为什么笑起来?

罗森格兰兹 我想,殿下,要是人类不能使您发生兴趣,那么那班戏子们恐怕要来自讨一场没趣了,我们在路上追上他们,他们是要到这儿来向您献技的。

哈姆雷特 扮演国王的那个人将要得到我的欢迎,我要在他的御座之前致献我的敬礼。冒险的武士可以挥舞他的剑盾,情人的叹息不会没有酬报,躁急易怒的角色可以平安下场,小丑将要使那班善笑的观众捧腹,我们的女主角必须坦白诉说她的心事,否则那无韵诗的句子将要脱去板眼。他们是一班什么戏子?

罗森格兰兹 就是您向来所欢喜的那一个班子,在城里专演悲剧的。

哈姆雷特 他们怎么走起江湖来呢?固定在一个地方演戏,在名誉和进益上都要好得多哩。

罗森格兰兹 我想他们不能在一个地方立足,是为了时势的变化。

哈姆雷特 他们的名誉还是跟我在城里那时候一样吗?他们的观众还是那么多吗?

罗森格兰兹 不,他们现在已经今非昔比了。

哈姆雷特 怎么会这样的?他们的演技退落了吗?

罗森格兰兹 不,他们还是跟从前一样努力。可是,殿下,他们的地位已经被一群羽毛未丰的黄口小儿占夺了去。这些娃娃的嘶叫博得了台下疯狂的喝彩,他们是目前流行的宠儿,他们的声势压倒了所谓普通的戏班,以至于许多腰佩长剑的悲剧伶人,都因为惧怕批评家鹅毛管的威力,而不敢到那边去。

哈姆雷特 什么!是一些童伶吗?谁维持他们的生活?他们的薪工是怎么计算的?他们一到不能唱歌的年龄,

就不再继续他们的本行了吗？要是他们攒不了多少钱，长大起来多分还是要做普通戏子的，那时候他们不是要抱怨他们的批评家们不该在从前把他们捧得那么高，结果反而妨碍了他们自己的前途吗？

罗森格兰兹 真的，两方闹过不少的纠纷，全国的人都站在旁边恬不为意地呐喊、助威，怂恿他们互相争斗。曾经有一个时期，一本脚本非到编剧家和演员争吵得动起武来，是没有人愿意出钱购买的。

哈姆雷特 有这等事？

吉尔登斯吞 啊，多少人的头都打破了。

哈姆雷特 那也没有什么稀奇。我的叔父是丹麦的国王，当我父亲在世的时候对他扮鬼脸的那些人，现在都愿意拿出二十、四十、五十、一百块金洋来买他的一幅小照。哼，这里面有些不是常理可解的地方，要是哲学能够把它推究出来的话。（内喇叭奏花腔）

吉尔登斯吞 这班戏子来了。

哈姆雷特 两位先生，欢迎你们到艾尔西诺来。把你们的手给我，按照通俗的礼节，我应该向你们表示欢迎。让我不要对你们失礼，因为这些戏子来了以后，我不能不敷衍他们一番，也许你们见了会发生误会，以为我招待你们还不及招待他们的殷勤。我欢迎你们，可是我的叔父父亲和婶母母亲可弄错啦。

吉尔登斯吞 弄错了什么，我的好殿下？

哈姆雷特 天上刮着西北风,我才发疯的。风从南方吹来的时候,我不会把一头鹰当作了一头鹭鸶。

【波洛涅斯重上。

波洛涅斯 祝福你们,两位先生!

哈姆雷特 听着,吉尔登斯吞,你也听着,两人站在我的两边,听我说,你们看见的那个大孩子,还在襁褓之中,没有学会走路哩。

罗森格兰兹 也许他是第二次裹在襁褓里,因为人家说,一个老年人是第二次做婴孩。

哈姆雷特 我可以预言他是来报告我戏子们来了的消息。听好。——你说得不错,在星期一早上,正是正是。

波洛涅斯 殿下,我有消息要来向您报告。

哈姆雷特 大人,我也有消息要向您报告。当罗歇斯在罗马演戏的时候①——

波洛涅斯 那班戏子们已经到这儿来了,殿下。

哈姆雷特 嗤!嗤!

波洛涅斯 凭着我的名誉起誓——

哈姆雷特 那时每一个伶人都骑着驴子而来——

波洛涅斯 他们是全世界最好的伶人,无论悲剧、喜剧、历史剧、田园剧、田园喜剧、田园史剧、历史悲剧、历史田园悲喜剧,不分场的古典剧或是近代的自由诗剧,他们

---

① 罗歇斯(Roscius)为古罗马著名伶人。

无不擅长；塞内加的悲剧不嫌其太沉重，普鲁图斯的喜剧不嫌其太轻浮①。无论在规律的或是即兴的演出方面，他们都是唯一的演员。

哈姆雷特　以色列的士师耶弗他②啊，你有一件怎样的宝贝！

波洛涅斯　他有什么宝贝，殿下？

哈姆雷特　嗨，

　　他有一个独生娇女，

　　爱她胜过掌上明珠。

波洛涅斯　（旁白）还是在提着我的女儿。

哈姆雷特　我念得对不对，耶弗他老头儿？

波洛涅斯　要是您叫我耶弗他，殿下，那么我有一个爱如掌珠的娇女。

哈姆雷特　不，下面不是这样的。

波洛涅斯　那么是应当怎样的呢，殿下？

哈姆雷特　你去查那原歌的第一节吧。瞧，有人来打断我的谈话了。

【优伶四五人上。

哈姆雷特　欢迎，各位朋友，欢迎欢迎！我很高兴看见你们

---

①　塞内加（Seneca）、普鲁图斯（Plautns）均为罗马剧作家，前者善写悲剧，后者善写喜剧。

②　耶弗他（Jephthah）得上帝之助，击败敌人，乃以其女献祭。事见《旧约·士师记》。

都是这样健好。啊,我的老朋友!你的脸上比我上次看见你的时候,多长了几根胡子,格外显得威武啦。你是要到丹麦来向我挑战吗?啊,我的年轻的姑娘!凭着圣母起誓,您穿上了一双高底木靴,比我上次看见您的时候更苗条得多啦。求求上帝,但愿您的喉咙不要沙哑得像一面破碎的铜锣才好!各位朋友,欢迎欢迎!我们要像法国的猎鹰一样,看见什么就飞扑上去。让我们立刻就来念一段剧词。来,试一试你们的本领,来一段激昂慷慨的剧词。

伶甲 殿下要听的是哪一段?

哈姆雷特 我曾经听见你向我背诵过一段台词,可是它从来没有上演过。即使上演,也不会有一次以上,因为我记得这本戏并不受大众的欢迎。它是不合一般人口味的鱼子酱。可是照我的意思看来,还有其他在这方面比我更有权威的人也抱着同样的见解,它是一本绝妙的戏剧,场面支配得很是适当,文字质朴而富于技巧。我记得有人这样批评它,说是没有耐人寻味的名言隽句,可是一点不见矫揉造作的痕迹。他把它称为一种老老实实的写法,兼有刚健与柔和之美,壮丽而不流于纤巧。其中有一段话是我最喜爱的,那就是埃涅阿斯对狄多讲述的故事,尤其是讲到普里阿摩斯被杀的那一节①。要是你们还没有把它忘记,请从这一行念起。让我看,让我看:——

  野蛮的皮洛斯像猛虎一样②,

不,不是这样;它是从皮洛斯开始的:——

  野蛮的皮洛斯蹲伏在木马之中,
  黝黑的手臂和他的决心一样,
  像黑夜一般阴森而恐怖。
  在这黑暗狰狞的肌肤之上,
  现在更染上令人惊怖的纹章,
  从头到脚,他全身一片殷红,
  溅满了父母子女们无辜的血。
  那些燃烧着熊熊烈火的街道,
  发出残忍而惨恶的凶光,
  照亮敌人去肆行他们的杀戮,
  也焙干了到处横流的血泊。
  冒着火焰的熏炙,像恶魔一般,
  全身胶黏着凝结的血块,
  圆睁着两颗血红的眼睛,
  他来往寻找普里阿摩斯老王的踪迹。

---

  ① 以下所引剧词,叙述特洛亚亡国惨状,大约系莎翁模拟古典剧风之作。普里阿摩斯(Priam),为特洛亚之王。
  ② 皮洛斯(Pyrrhus),希腊英雄亚契尔斯(Achilles)之子,以骁勇残忍著称。

　　　　你接下去吧。
波洛涅斯　上帝在上,殿下,您念得好极了,真是抑扬顿挫,曲尽其妙。
伶甲
　　　　那老王正在气喘吁吁,
　　　　在希腊人的重围中苦战。
　　　　一点不听他手臂的指挥,
　　　　他的古老的剑锵然落地。
　　　　皮洛斯瞧他孤弱可欺,
　　　　疯狂似的向他猛力攻击,
　　　　凶恶的剑锋上下四方挥舞,
　　　　却把心胆俱丧的老王击倒。
　　　　这一下打击有如天崩地裂,
　　　　惊动了没有感觉的伊利恩①,
　　　　冒着火焰的屋顶霎时坍下,
　　　　那轰然的巨响像一个霹雳,
　　　　震聋了皮洛斯的耳朵。瞧!
　　　　他的剑还没砍下普里阿摩斯的
　　　　白发的头颅,却已在空中停住。
　　　　像一个涂朱抹彩的暴君,
　　　　对自己的行为漠不关心,

---

　　① 伊利恩(Ilium),特洛亚之别名。

他兀立不动。
　　　在一场暴风雨未来以前,
　　　天上往往有片刻的宁寂,
　　　一块块乌云静悬在空中,
　　　狂风悄悄地收起它的声息,
　　　死样的沉默笼罩整个大地。
　　　可是就在这片刻之内,
　　　可怕的雷鸣震裂了天空。
　　　经过暂时的休止,杀人的暴念
　　　重新激起了皮洛斯的精神。
　　　库克罗普斯①为战神铸造甲胄,
　　　那巨力的锤击,还不及皮洛斯的
　　　流血的剑向普里阿摩斯身上劈下
　　　那样凶狠无情。
　　　去,去,你娼妇一样的命运!
　　　天上的诸神啊!剥去她的权力,
　　　不要让她僭窃神明的宝座。
　　　拆毁她的车轮,把它滚下神山,
　　　直到地狱的深渊。

波洛涅斯　这一段太长啦。

哈姆雷特　它应当跟你的胡子一起到理发匠那儿去剃一

---

①　库克罗普斯(The Cyclops),传说中之一族独眼巨人。

剃。念下去吧。他只爱听俚俗的歌曲和淫秽的故事，否则他就要瞌睡的。念下去。下面要讲到赫卡柏了①。

伶甲

可是啊！谁看见那蒙脸的王后——

哈姆雷特 "那蒙脸的王后"？

波洛涅斯 很好，"蒙脸的王后"是很好的句子。

伶甲

满面流泪，在火焰中赤脚奔走，

一块布覆在失去宝冕的头上，

也没有一件蔽体的衣服，

只有在惊惶中抓到的一幅毡巾，

裹住她瘦削而多产的腰身。

谁见了这样伤心惨目的景象，

不要向残酷的命运申申毒詈？

她看见皮洛斯以杀人为戏，

正在把她丈夫的肢体脔割，

忍不住大放哀声，那凄凉的号叫——

除非人间的哀乐不能感动天庭——

即使光明的日月也会陪她流泪，

诸神的心中都要充满悲愤。

波洛涅斯 瞧，他的脸色都变了，他的眼睛里已经含着眼

---

① 赫卡柏(Hecuba)，特洛亚王普里阿摩斯之后。

泪！不要念下去了吧。

哈姆雷特　很好，其余的部分等会儿再念给我听吧。大人，请您去找一处好的地方安顿这一班伶人。听着，他们是不可怠慢的，因为他们是这一个时代的缩影。宁可在死后得到一首恶劣的墓铭，不要在生前受他们一场刻毒的讥讽。

波洛涅斯　殿下，我按着他们应得的名分对待他们就是了。

哈姆雷特　哎哟，朋友，还要客气得多哩！要是照每一个人应得的名分对待他，那么谁逃得了一顿鞭子？照你自己的名誉地位对待他们。他们越是不配受这样的待遇，越可以显出你的谦虚有礼。领他们进去。

波洛涅斯　来，各位朋友。

哈姆雷特　跟他去，朋友们。明天我们要听你们唱一本戏。（波洛涅斯偕众伶下，伶甲独留）听着，老朋友，你会演《贡扎古之死》吗？

伶甲　会演的，殿下。

哈姆雷特　那么我们明天晚上就把它上演。也许我因为必要的理由，要另外写下有十几行句子的一段剧词插进去，你能够把它预先背熟吗？

伶甲　可以，殿下。

哈姆雷特　很好。跟着那位老爷去。留心不要取笑他。（伶甲下）（向罗森格兰兹、吉尔登斯呑）我的两位好朋友，我们今天晚上再见。欢迎你们到艾尔西诺来！

吉尔登斯吞 再会,殿下!(罗森格兰兹、吉尔登斯吞同下)
哈姆雷特 好,上帝和你们同在!现在我只剩一个人了。啊,我是一个多么不中用的蠢材!这一个伶人不过在一本虚构的故事、一场激昂的幻梦之中,却能够使他的灵魂融化在他的意象里,在它的影响之下,他的整个的脸色变成惨白,他的眼中洋溢着热泪,他的神情流露着仓皇,他的声音是这么呜咽凄凉,他的全部动作都表现得和他的意象一致,这不是很不可思议的吗?而且一点也不为了什么!为了赫卡柏!赫卡柏和他有什么相干,他对赫卡柏又有什么相干,他却要为她流泪?要是他也有了像我所有的那样使人痛心的理由,他将要怎样呢?他一定会让眼泪淹没舞台,用可怖的字句震裂听众的耳朵,使有罪的人发狂,使无罪的人惊骇,使愚昧无知的人惊慌失措,使所有的耳目迷乱了它们的功能。可是我,一个糊涂颠顶的家伙,垂头丧气,一天到晚像在做梦似的,忘记了杀父的大仇;虽然一个国王给人家用万恶的手段掠夺了他的权位,杀害了他的最宝贵的生命,我却始终哼不出一句话来。我是一个懦夫吗?谁骂我恶人?谁敲破我的脑壳?谁拔去我的胡子,把它吹在我的脸上?谁捏我的鼻子?谁当面指斥我胡说?谁对我做这种事?嘿!我应该忍受这样的侮辱,因为我是一个没有心肝、逆来顺受的怯汉,否则我早已用这奴才的尸肉,喂肥了四境之内的乌鸢了。嗜血的、荒淫的恶贼！狠心的、奸诈的、淫邪的、悖逆的恶贼！啊！复仇！——嗨，我真是个蠢材！我的亲爱的父亲被人谋杀了，鬼神都在鞭策我复仇，我这做儿子的却像一个下流女人似的，只会用空言发发牢骚，学起泼妇骂街的样子来，真是了不得的勇敢！呸！呸！活动起来吧，我的脑筋！我听人家说，犯罪的人在看戏的时候，因为台上表演的巧妙，有时会激动天良，当场供认他们的罪恶。因为暗杀的事情无论干得怎样秘密，总会借着神奇的喉舌泄露出来。我要叫这班伶人在我的叔父面前表演一本跟我的父亲的惨死情节相仿的戏剧，我就在一旁窥察他的神色。我要探视到他的灵魂的深处，要是他稍露惊骇不安之态，我就知道我应该怎么办。我所看见的幽灵也许是魔鬼的化身，借着一个美好的形状出现，魔鬼是有这一种本领的。对于柔弱忧郁的灵魂，他最容易发挥他的力量。也许他看准了我的柔弱和忧郁，才来向我作祟，要把我引诱到沉沦的路上。我要先得到一些比这更切实的证据。凭着这一本戏，我可以发掘国王内心的隐秘。（下）

第三幕

第一场
城堡中一室

【国王、王后、波洛涅斯、奥菲利娅、罗森格兰兹及吉尔登斯吞上。
国王 你们难道不能用迂回婉转的方法，探出他为什么这样神魂颠倒，让紊乱而危险的疯狂困扰他的安静的生活吗？

罗森格兰兹　他承认他自己有些神经迷惘,可是绝口不肯说因了什么缘故。

吉尔登斯吞　他也不肯虚心接受我们的探问。当我们想要从他嘴里知道他自己的一些真相的时候,他总是用假作痴呆的神气回避不答。

王后　他对待你们还客气吗?

罗森格兰兹　很有礼貌。

吉尔登斯吞　可是不大出于自然。

罗森格兰兹　对于我们的问题保持缄默,可是对我们倒盘问得很是详细。

王后　你们有没有劝诱他找些什么消遣?

罗森格兰兹　娘娘,我们来的时候,刚巧有一班戏子也要到这儿来,给我们追上了。我们把这消息告诉了他,他听了好像很高兴。现在他们已经到了宫里,我想他今晚就要看他们的表演的。

波洛涅斯　一点不错,他还叫我来请两位陛下同去看看他们演得怎样哩。

国王　那好极了,我非常高兴听见他在这方面感兴趣。请你们两位还要更进一步鼓起他的兴味,把他的心思移转到这种娱乐上面。

罗森格兰兹　是,陛下。(罗森格兰兹、吉尔登斯吞同下)

国王　亲爱的乔特鲁德,你也暂时离开我们,因为我们已经暗中差人去唤哈姆雷特到这儿来,让他和奥菲利娅见见面，就像是他们偶然相遇的一般。她的父亲跟我两人将要权充一下密探，躲在可以看见他们，却不能被他们看见的地方，注意他们会面的情形，从他的行为上判断他的疯病究竟是不是因为恋爱上的苦闷。

王后　我愿意服从您的意旨。奥菲利娅，但愿你的美貌是哈姆雷特疯狂的原因，更愿你的美德能够帮助他恢复原状，使你们两人都能安享尊荣。

奥菲利娅　娘娘，但愿如此。（王后下）

波洛涅斯　奥菲利娅，你在这儿走走。陛下，我们就去躲起来吧。（向奥菲利娅）你拿这本书去读，他看见你这样用功,就不会疑心你为什么一个人在这儿了。人们往往用至诚的外表和虔敬的行动,掩饰一颗魔鬼般的内心,这样的例子是太多了。

国王 （旁白）啊,这句话是太真实了！它在我的良心上抽了多么重的一鞭！涂脂抹粉的娼妇的脸颊,还不及掩藏在虚伪的言辞后面的我的行为更丑恶。难堪的重负啊！

波洛涅斯 我听见他来了。我们退下去吧,陛下。（国王及波洛涅斯下）

【哈姆雷特上。

哈姆雷特 生存还是毁灭,这是一个值得考虑的问题。默然忍受命运的暴虐的毒箭，或是挺身反抗人世的无涯的苦难，在斗争中结束这一切，这两种行为，哪一种是更勇敢的？死了，睡去了，什么都完了。要是在这一种睡眠之中，我们心头的创痛，以及其他无数血肉之躯所不能避免的打击，都可以从此消失，那正是我们求之不得的结局。死了，睡去了，睡去了也许还会做梦。嗯，阻碍就在这儿：因为当我们摆脱了这一具朽腐的皮囊以后，在那死的睡眠里，究竟将要做些什么梦，那不能不使我们踌躇顾虑。人们甘心久困于患难之中，也就是为了这一个缘故。谁愿意忍受人世的鞭挞和讥嘲、压迫者的凌辱、傲慢者的冷眼、被轻蔑的爱情的惨痛、法律的迁延、官吏的横暴和微贱者费尽辛勤所换来的鄙视？要是他只要用一柄小小的刀子，就可以清算他自己的一生？谁愿意负着这样的重担，在烦劳的生命的压迫下呻吟流汗，倘不是因为惧怕不可知的死，那从来不曾有一个旅人回来过的神秘之国，是它迷惑了我们的意志，使我们宁愿忍受目前的折磨，不敢向我们所不知道的痛苦飞去？这样，理智使我们全变成了懦夫，决心的赤热的光彩，被审慎的思维盖上了一层灰色，伟大的事业在这一种考虑之下，也会逆流而退，失去了行动的意义。且慢！美丽的奥菲利娅！——女神，在你的祈祷之中，不要忘记替我忏悔我的罪孽。

奥菲利娅 我的好殿下，您这许多天来贵体安好吗？

哈姆雷特 谢谢你,很好,很好,很好。

奥菲利娅 殿下,我有几件您送给我的纪念品,我早就想把它们还给您。请您现在收回去吧。

哈姆雷特 不,我不要。我从来没有给你什么东西。

奥菲利娅 殿下,我记得很清楚您把它们送给了我,那时候您还向我说了许多甜蜜的言语,使这些东西显得格外贵重。现在它们的芳香已经消散,请您拿了回去吧,因为送礼的人要是变了心,礼物虽贵,也会失去了价值。拿去吧,殿下。

哈姆雷特 哈哈!你贞洁吗?

奥菲利娅 殿下!

哈姆雷特 你美丽吗?

奥菲利娅 殿下是什么意思?

哈姆雷特 要是你既贞洁又美丽,那么顶好不要让你的贞洁跟你的美丽来往。

奥菲利娅 殿下,美丽和贞洁相交,那不是再好没有吗?

哈姆雷特 嗯,真的。因为美丽可以使贞洁变成淫荡,贞洁却未必能使美丽受它自己的感化。这句话从前像是怪诞之谈,可是现在的时世已经把它证实了。我曾经爱过你。

奥菲利娅 真的,殿下,您曾经使我相信您爱我。

哈姆雷特 你当初就不应该相信我,因为美德不能熏陶我们罪恶的本性,我没有爱过你。

奥菲利娅　那么我真是受了骗了。

哈姆雷特　进尼姑庵去吧！为什么你要生养一群罪人出来呢？我自己还不算是一个顶坏的人,可是我可以指出我的许多过失,一个人有了那些过失,他的母亲还是不要生下他来的好。我很骄傲,使气,不安分,还有那么多的罪恶,连我的思想里也容纳不下,我的想象也不能给它们形象,甚至我都没有充分的时间可以把它们实行出来。像我这样的家伙,匍匐于天地之间,有什么用处呢?我们都是些十足的坏人,一个也不要相信我们。进尼姑庵去吧。你的父亲呢？

奥菲利娅　在家里,殿下。

哈姆雷特　把他关起来,让他在家里发发傻劲。再会！

奥菲利娅　哎哟,天哪！救救他！

哈姆雷特　要是你一定要嫁人,我就把这一个诅咒送给你做嫁妆:尽管你像冰一样坚贞,像雪一样纯洁,你还是逃不过谗人的诽谤。进尼姑庵去吧,去。再会！或者要是你必须嫁人的话,就嫁给一个傻瓜吧！因为聪明人都明白你们会叫他们变成怎样的怪物。进尼姑庵去吧！去,越快越好。再会！

奥菲利娅　天上的神明啊,让他清醒过来吧！

哈姆雷特　我也知道你们会怎样涂脂抹粉,上帝给了你们一张脸,你们又替自己另外造了一张。你们烟视媚行、淫声浪气,替上帝造下的生物乱取名字,卖弄你们不懂事的风骚。算了吧,我再也不敢领教了,它已经使我发了狂。我说,我们以后再不要结什么婚了,已经结过婚的,除了一个人以外,都可以让他们活下去。没有结婚的不准再结婚,进尼姑庵去吧,去。(下)

奥菲利娅 啊,一颗多么高贵的星是这样陨落了!朝臣的眼睛,学者的辩舌,军人的利剑,国家所瞩望的一朵娇花,时流的明镜,人伦的雅范,举世注目的中心,这样无可挽回地陨落了!我是一切妇女中间最伤心而不幸的,我曾经从他音乐一般的盟誓中吮吸芬芳的甘蜜,现在却眼看着他的高贵无上的理智,像一串美妙的银铃失去了谐和的音调,无比的青春美貌,在疯狂中凋谢!啊!我好苦,谁料过去的繁花,变作今朝的泥土!

【国王及波洛涅斯重上。

国王 恋爱!他的精神错乱不像是为了恋爱。他说的话虽然有些颠倒,也不像是疯狂。他有些什么心事盘踞在他的灵魂里,我怕它也许会产生危险的结果。为了防免万一起见,我已经当机立断,决定了一个办法:他必须立刻到英国去,向他们追索延宕未纳的贡物。也许他到海外各国游历一趟以后,时时变换的环境,可以替他排解这一桩使他神思恍惚的心事。你看怎么样?

波洛涅斯 那很好。可是我相信他的烦闷的根本原因,还是为了恋爱上的失意。啊,奥菲利娅!你不用告诉我们哈姆雷特殿下说些什么话,我们全都听见了。陛下,照您的意思办吧。可是您要是认为可以的话,不妨在戏剧终场以后,让他的母后独自一人跟他在一起,恳求他向她吐露他的心事。她必须很坦白地跟他谈谈,我就找一个所在听他们说些什么。要是她也探听不出他的秘密来,您就叫他到英国去,或者凭着您的高见,把他关禁在一个适当的地方。

国王　就是这样吧,大人物的疯狂是不能听其自然的。(同下)

第二场
城堡中的厅堂

【哈姆雷特及若干伶人上。

哈姆雷特　请你念这段剧词的时候,要照我刚才读给你听的那样子,一个字一个字打舌头上很轻快地吐出来。要是你也像多数的伶人一样,只会拉开了喉咙嘶叫,那么我宁愿叫那宣布告示的公差念我这几行词句。也不要老是把你的手在空中这么摇挥,一切动作都要温文,因为就是在洪水暴风一样的感情激发之中,你也必须取得一种节制,免得流于过火。啊!我顶不愿意听见一个披着满头假发的家伙在台上乱嚷乱叫,把一段感情片片撕碎,让那些只爱热闹的下层观众听得入神,他们中间的大部分是除了欣赏一些莫名其妙的手势以外,什么都不懂得的。我可以把这种家伙抓起来抽一顿鞭子,因为他把妥玛刚特形容过了分,希律王的凶暴也要对他甘拜下风。① 请你留心避免才好。

伶甲 我留心着就是了,殿下。

哈姆雷特 可是太平淡了也不对,你应该接受你自己的常识的指导,把动作和言语互相配合起来。特别要注意到这一点,你不能越过人情的常道,因为不近情理的过分描写是和演剧的原意相反的,自有戏剧以来,它的目的始终是反映人生,显示善恶的本来面目,给它的时代看一看它自己演变发展的模型。要是表演得过分了或者太懈怠了,虽然可以博外行的观众一笑,明眼之士却要因此而皱眉,你必须看重这样一个卓识者的批评甚于满场观众盲目的毁誉。啊! 我曾经看见有几个伶人演戏,而且也听见有人把他们极口捧场,说一句并不过分的话,他们既不会说基督徒的语言,又不会学着人的样子走路,瞧他们在台上大摇大摆,使劲叫喊的样子,我心里就想一定是什么造化的雇工把他们造了下来,造得这样拙劣,以至于全然失去了人类的面目。

---

① 妥玛刚特(Termagant),传说中残恶凶暴之回教女神。希律(Herod),耶稣时代统治伽利利之暴君。二者为往时教训剧(Morality)及神迹剧(Mystery)中常见之角色。

伶甲　我希望我们在这方面已经相当纠正过来了。

哈姆雷特　啊！你们必须彻底纠正这一种弊病。还有你们那些扮演小丑的,除了剧本上专为他们写下的台词以外,不要让他们临时编造一些话儿加上去。往往有许多小丑爱用自己的笑声,引起台下一些无知的观众的哄笑,虽然那时候全场的注意力应当集中在其他更重要的问题上。这种行为是不可恕的,它表示出那丑角的可鄙的野心。去,准备起来吧。(伶人等同下。)

【波洛涅斯、罗森格兰兹及吉尔登斯吞上。

哈姆雷特　啊,大人,王上愿意来听这一本戏吗?

波洛涅斯　他跟娘娘都就要来了。

哈姆雷特　叫那些戏子赶紧点儿。(波洛涅斯下)你们两人也去帮着催催他们。

罗森格兰兹
吉尔登斯吞　是,殿下。(罗森格兰兹、吉尔登斯吞下)

哈姆雷特　喂!霍拉旭!

【霍拉旭上。

霍拉旭　有,殿下。

哈姆雷特　霍拉旭,你是在我所交接的人们中间最正直的一个人。

霍拉旭　啊,殿下!——

哈姆雷特　不,不要以为我在恭维你,你除了你的善良的精神以外,身无长物,我恭维了你又有什么好处呢?为什么要向穷人恭维？不,让蜜糖一样的嘴唇去吮舐愚妄的荣华,在有利可图的所在弯下他们生财有道的膝盖来吧。听着。自从我能够辨别是非、察择贤愚以后,你就是我灵魂里选中的一个人,因为你虽然经历一切的颠沛,却不曾受到一点伤害,命运的虐待和恩宠,对于你都是一样。能够把感情和理智调整得那么适当,命运不能把他玩弄于指掌之间,那样的人是有福的。给我一个不为感情所奴役的人,我愿意把他珍藏在我的心坎、我的灵魂的深处,正像我对你一样。这些话现在也不必多说了。今晚我们要在国王面前表演一本戏剧,其中有一场的情节跟我告诉过你的我的父亲的死状颇相仿佛。当那幕戏正在串演的时候,我要请你集中你的全部精神,注视我的叔父,要是他在听到了那一段戏词以后,他的隐藏的罪恶还是不露出一丝痕迹来,那么我们所看见的那个鬼魂一定是个恶魔,我的幻想也就像铁匠的砧石那样黑漆一团了。留心看好他,我也要把我的眼睛看定他的脸上,过后我们再把各人观察到的结果综合起来,替他下一个判断。

霍拉旭　很好,殿下。在这本戏表演的时候,要是他在容色举止之间,有什么地方逃过了我们的注意,请您唯我是问。

哈姆雷特　他们来看戏了。我必须装作无所事事的神气。你去拣一个地方坐下。

【奏丹麦进行曲,喇叭奏花腔。国王、王后、波洛涅斯、奥菲利娅、罗森格兰兹、吉尔登斯吞及余人等上。

国王　你好吗,哈姆雷特贤侄?

哈姆雷特　很好,好极了。我吃的是变色蜥蜴的肉,喝的是充满着甜言蜜语的空气,你们的肥鸡还没有这样的味道哩。

国王　你这种话真是答非所问,哈姆雷特,我不是那个意思。

哈姆雷特　不,我现在也没有那个意思。(向波洛涅斯)大人,您说您在大学里念书的时候,曾经演过一回戏吗?

波洛涅斯　是的,殿下,他们都赞我是一个很好的演员哩。

哈姆雷特　您扮演什么角色呢?

波洛涅斯　我扮的是裘力斯·恺撒,勃鲁托斯在朱庇特神殿里把我杀死。

哈姆雷特　他在神殿里杀死了那么好的一头小牛,真是太残忍了。那班戏子已经预备好了吗?

罗森格兰兹　是,殿下,他们在等候您的旨意。

王后　过来,我的好哈姆雷特,坐在我的旁边。

哈姆雷特　不,好妈妈,这儿有一个更迷人的东西哩。

波洛涅斯　(向国王)啊哈!您看见吗?

哈姆雷特　小姐,我可以睡在您的怀里吗?

奥菲利娅　不,殿下。

哈姆雷特　我的意思是说,我可以把我的头枕在您的膝上吗?

奥菲利娅 嗯,殿下。

哈姆雷特 您以为我在转着下流的念头吗?

奥菲利娅 我没有想到,殿下。

哈姆雷特 睡在姑娘大腿的中间,想起来倒是很有趣的。

奥菲利娅 什么,殿下?

哈姆雷特 没有什么。

奥菲利娅 您在开玩笑哩,殿下。

哈姆雷特 谁?我吗?

奥菲利娅 嗯,殿下。

哈姆雷特 上帝啊!我不过是给您消遣消遣的。一个人为什么不说说笑笑呢?您瞧,我的母亲多么高兴,我的父亲还不过死了两个钟头。

奥菲利娅 不,已经四个月了,殿下。

哈姆雷特 这么久了吗?哎哟,那么让魔鬼去穿孝服吧,我可要去做一身貂皮的新衣啦。天啊!死了两个月,还没有把他忘记吗?那么也许一个大人物死了以后,他的记忆还可以保持半年之久。可是凭着圣母起誓,他必须造下几所教堂,否则他就要跟那被遗弃的木马一样,没有人再会想念他了。

【高音笛奏乐。哑剧登场。

一国王及一王后上,状极亲热、互相拥抱。后跪地,向王做宣誓状,王扶后起,俯首后颈上。王

79

就花坪上睡下;后见王睡熟离去。另一人上,自王头上去冠,吻冠,注毒药于王耳,下。后重上,见王死,做哀恸状。下毒者率其他二三人重上,伴作陪后悲哭状。从者舁王尸下。下毒者以礼物赠后,向其乞爱;后先做憎恶不愿状,卒允其请。同下。

奥菲利娅　这是什么意思,殿下?

哈姆雷特　呃,这是阴谋诡计的意思。

奥菲利娅　大概这一场哑剧就是全剧的本事了。

【致开场词者上。

哈姆雷特　这家伙可以告诉我们一切;演戏的都不能保守秘密,他们什么话都会说出来。

　　　　　　开场词

　　这悲剧要是演不好,

　　要请各位原谅指教,

　　小的在这厢有礼了。(致开场词者下)

哈姆雷特　这算开场词呢,还是指环上的诗铭?

奥菲利娅　它很短,殿下。

哈姆雷特　正像女人的爱情一样。

【二伶人扮国王王后上。

伶王　日轮已经盘绕三十春秋,

　　那茫茫海水和滚滚地球,

　　月亮吐耀着借来的晶光,

　　三百六十回向大地环航,

　　　　自从爱把我们缔结良姻，
　　　　许门替我们证下了鸳盟。
伶后　愿日月继续他们的周游，
　　　　让我们再厮守三十春秋！
　　　　可是，唉，你近来这样多病，
　　　　郁郁寡欢，失去旧时高兴，
　　　　好教我满心里为你忧惧。
　　　　可是，我的主，你不必疑虑，
　　　　女人的忧伤像她的爱一样，
　　　　不是太少，就是超过分量。
　　　　你知道我爱你是多么深，
　　　　所以才会如此地忧心。
　　　　越是相爱，越是挂肚牵胸，
　　　　不这样那显得你我情浓？
伶王　爱人，我不久必须离开你，
　　　　我的全身将要失去生机。
　　　　留下你在这繁华的世界
　　　　安享尊荣，
　　　　受人们的敬爱，
　　　　也许再嫁一位如意郎君，
伶后　啊！我断不是那样薄情人。
　　　　我倘忘旧迎新，难邀天恕，
　　　　再嫁的除非是杀夫淫妇。

81

哈姆雷特 （旁白）苦恼,苦恼!
伶后 妇人失节大半贪慕荣华,
多情女子决不另抱琵琶。
我要是与他人共枕同衾,
怎么对得起地下的先灵!
伶王 我相信你的话发自心田,
可是我们往往自食前言。
志愿不过是记忆的奴隶,
总是有始无终,虎头蛇尾,
像未熟的果子密布树梢,
一朝红烂就会离去枝条。
我们对自己所负的债务,
最好把它丢在脑后不顾。
一时的热情中发下誓愿,
心冷了,那意志也随云散。
过分的喜乐,剧烈的哀伤,
反会毁害了感情的本常。
人世间的哀乐变幻无端,
痛哭一转瞬早换了狂欢。
世界也会有毁灭的一天,
何怪爱情要随境遇变迁。
有谁能解答这一个哑谜,
境由爱造?爱逐境移?

　　　　失财势的伟人举目无亲，
　　　　走时运的穷酸仇敌逢迎。
　　　　这炎凉的世态古今一辙：
　　　　富有的门庭挤满了宾客。
　　　　要是你在穷途向人求助，
　　　　即使知交也要情同陌路。
　　　　把我们的谈话拉回本题，
　　　　意志命运往往背道而驰，
　　　　决心到最后会全部推倒，
　　　　事实的结果总难符预料。
　　　　你以为你自己不会再嫁，
　　　　只怕我一死你就要变卦。

伶后　地不要养我，天不要亮我！
　　　　昼不得游乐，夜不得安卧！
　　　　毁灭了我的希望和信心。
　　　　铁锁囚门把我监禁终生！
　　　　每一种恼人的飞来横逆，
　　　　把我一重重的心愿摧折！
　　　　我倘死了丈夫再做新人，
　　　　让我生前死后永陷沉沦！

哈姆雷特　要是她现在背了誓！

伶王　难为你发这样重的誓愿。
　　　　爱人，你且去，我神思昏倦，

　　　　　想要小睡片刻。(睡)

伶后　　　　　　　　愿你安睡；
　　　上天保佑我俩永无灾悔!(下)

哈姆雷特　母亲,您觉得这本戏怎样?

王后　我想那女人发的誓太重了。

哈姆雷特　啊,可是她会守约的。

国王　这本戏是怎么一个情节?里面没有什么要不得的地方吗?

哈姆雷特　不,不,他们不过开玩笑毒死了一个人;没有什么要不得的。

国王　戏名叫什么?

哈姆雷特　《捕鼠机》。呃,怎么,这是一个象征的名字?戏中的故事影射着维也纳的一件谋杀案。贡扎古是那公爵的名字,他的妻子叫作白普蒂丝妲。您看下去就知道是怎么一回事。这是一个很恶劣的作品,可是那有什么关系?它不会对您陛下跟我们这些灵魂清白的人有什么相干,让那有毛病的马儿去惊跳退缩吧,我们的肩背都是好好儿的。

【一伶人扮琉西安纳斯上。

哈姆雷特　这个人叫作琉西安纳斯,是那国王的侄子。

奥菲利娅　您很会解释剧情,殿下。

哈姆雷特　要是我看见傀儡戏搬演您跟您爱人的故事,我也会替你们解释的。动手吧,凶手!混账东西,别扮鬼

84　哈姆雷特

脸了,动手吧!来,哑哑的乌鸦发出复仇的啼声。

琉西安纳斯

>黑心快手,遇到妙药良机;
>
>趁着没人看见事不宜迟。
>
>你夜半采来的毒草炼成,
>
>赫卡忒①的咒语念上三巡,
>
>赶快发挥你凶恶的魔力,
>
>让他的生命速归于幻灭。(以毒药注入睡者耳中)

哈姆雷特 他为了觊觎权位,在花园里把他毒死。他的名字叫贡扎古。那故事原文还存在,是用很好的意大利文写成的。底下就要做到那凶手怎样得到贡扎古的妻子的爱了。

奥菲利娅 王上起来了!

哈姆雷特 什么!给一场假火吓怕了吗?

王后 陛下怎么样啦?

波洛涅斯 不要演下去了!

国王 给我点起火把来!去!

众人 火把!火把!火把!(除哈姆雷特、霍拉旭外均下)

哈姆雷特 嗨,让那中箭的母鹿掉泪,

>没有伤的公鹿自去游玩;
>
>有的人失眠,有的人酣睡,

---

① 赫卡忒(Hecate),黑夜及幽冥之女神。

　　　　　　　世界就是这样循环轮转。
　　　　　　老兄,要是我的命运跟我作起对来,
　　　　　　　凭着我这样的本领,
　　　　　　　再插上满头的羽毛,
　　　　　　　开缝的靴子上缀上两朵绢花,
　　　　　　　你想我能不能在戏班子里插足?

霍拉旭　也许他们可以让您领半额包银。

哈姆雷特　我可要领全额的。
　　　　　　　因为你知道,亲爱的台芒,
　　　　　　　这一个荒凉破碎的国土
　　　　　　　原本是乔武统治的雄邦,
　　　　　　　而今王位上却坐着——孔雀。

霍拉旭　您该把它押了韵才是。

哈姆雷特　啊,好霍拉旭!那鬼魂真的没有骗我。你看见吗?

霍拉旭　看见了,殿下。

哈姆雷特　当那演戏的一提到毒药的时候?

霍拉旭　我看得他很清楚。

哈姆雷特　啊哈!来,奏乐!来,那吹笛子的呢?
　　　　　　　要是国王不爱这本喜剧,
　　　　　　　那么他多分是不能赏识。
　　　　　　　来,奏乐!

【**罗森格兰兹及吉尔登斯吞重上。**

吉尔登斯吞 殿下,允许我跟您说句话。

哈姆雷特 好,你对我讲全部历史都可以。

吉尔登斯吞 殿下,王上——

哈姆雷特 嗯,王上怎么样?

吉尔登斯吞 他回去以后,非常不舒服。

哈姆雷特 喝醉酒了吗?

吉尔登斯吞 不,殿下,他在动脾气。

哈姆雷特 你应该把这件事告诉他的医生,才算你的聪明,因为叫我去替他诊视,恐怕反而更会激动他的脾气的。

吉尔登斯吞 好殿下,请您说话检点些,别这样拉扯开去。

哈姆雷特 好,我是听话的,你说吧。

吉尔登斯吞 您的母后心里很难过,所以叫我来。

哈姆雷特 欢迎得很。

吉尔登斯吞 不,殿下,这一种礼貌是用不到的。要是您愿意给我一个好好的回答,我就把您母亲的意旨向您传达;不然的话,请您原谅我,让我就这么回去,我的事情算是完了。

哈姆雷特 我不能。

吉尔登斯吞 您不能什么,殿下?

哈姆雷特 我不能给你一个好好的回答,因为我的脑子已经坏了;可是我所能够给你的回答,你——我应该说我的母亲——可以要多少有多少。所以别说废话,言归正传吧;你说我的母亲——

罗森格兰兹　她这样说：您的行为使她非常惊愕。

哈姆雷特　啊，好儿子，居然会叫一个母亲吃惊！可是在这母亲的惊愕的后面，还有些什么话呢？说吧。

罗森格兰兹　她请您在就寝以前，到她房间里去跟她谈谈。

哈姆雷特　即使她是我的十个母亲，我也一定服从她。你还有什么别的事情？

罗森格兰兹　殿下，我曾经蒙您错爱。

哈姆雷特　凭着我这双扒儿手起誓，我现在还是欢喜你的。

罗森格兰兹　好殿下，您心里这样不痛快，究竟是为了什么原因？要是您不肯把您的心事告诉您的朋友，那恐怕会害您自己失去自由的。

哈姆雷特　我不满足我现在的地位。

罗森格兰兹　怎么！王上自己已经亲口把您立为王位的继承者了，您还不能满足吗？

哈姆雷特　嗯，可是"草儿青青——"这句老古话也有点儿发了霉啦。

【乐工等持笛上。

哈姆雷特　啊！笛子来了，拿一支给我。跟你们退后一步说话，为什么你们这样千方百计地窥探我的隐私，好像一定要把我逼进你们的圈套？

吉尔登斯吞　啊！殿下，要是我有太冒昧、放肆的地方，那都是因为我对于您的忠诚太激切了。

哈姆雷特　我不大懂得你的话。你愿意吹吹这笛子吗？

吉尔登斯吞 殿下,我不会吹。

哈姆雷特 请你吹一吹。

吉尔登斯吞 我真的不会吹。

哈姆雷特 请你不要客气。

吉尔登斯吞 我真的一点不会,殿下。

哈姆雷特 那是跟说谎一样容易的;你只要用你的手指按着这些笛孔,把你的嘴放在上面一吹,它就会发出最好听的音乐来。瞧,这些是音栓。

吉尔登斯吞 可是我不会从它里面吹出谐和的曲调来,我没有懂得它的技巧。

哈姆雷特 哼,你把我看成了什么东西!你会玩弄我,你自以为摸得到我的心窍,你想要探出我的内心的秘密,你会从我的最低音试到我的最高音,可是在这支小小的乐器之内,藏着绝妙的音乐,你却不会使它发出声音来。哼,你以为玩弄我比玩弄一支笛子容易吗?无论你把我叫作什么乐器,我是不让你把我玩弄的。

【波洛涅斯重上。

哈姆雷特 上帝祝福你,先生!

波洛涅斯 殿下,娘娘请您立刻就去见她说话。

哈姆雷特 你看见那片像骆驼一样的云吗?

波洛涅斯 哎哟,它真的像一头骆驼。

哈姆雷特 我想它还是像一头鼬鼠。

波洛涅斯 它拱起了背,正像是一头鼬鼠。

哈姆雷特　还是像一条鲸鱼吧？

波洛涅斯　很像一条鲸鱼。

哈姆雷特　那么等一会儿我就去见我的母亲。(旁白)我给他们愚弄得再也忍不住了。(高声)我等一会儿就来。

波洛涅斯　我就去这么说。(下)

哈姆雷特　等一会儿是很容易说的。离开我,朋友们。(除哈姆雷特外均下)现在是一夜之中最阴森的时候,鬼魂都在此刻从坟墓里出来,地狱也要向人世吐放疠气;现在我可以痛饮热腾腾的鲜血,干那白昼所不敢正视的残忍的行为。且慢!我还要到我母亲那儿去一趟。心啊!不要失去你的天性之情,永远不要让尼禄的灵魂潜入我这坚定的胸怀①。让我做一个凶徒,可是不要做一个逆子。我要用利剑一样的说话刺痛她的心,可是决不伤害她身体上一根毛发。我的舌头和灵魂要在这一次学学伪善者的样子,无论在言语上给她多么严厉的谴责,在行动上却要做得丝毫不让人家指摘。(下)

---

①　尼禄(Nero),古罗马暴君。

第三场
城堡中的一室

【国王,罗森格兰兹及吉尔登斯吞上。

国王　我不喜欢他,纵容他这样疯闹下去,对于我是一个很大的威胁。所以你们快去准备起来吧;我马上就可以发表明令,派遣你们两人护送他到英国去。就我的地位而论,他的疯狂每小时都可以危害我的安全,我不能让他留在我的近旁。

吉尔登斯吞　我们就去准备起来;许多人的安危都寄托在陛下身上,这一种顾虑是最圣明不过的。

罗森格兰兹　每一个庶民都知道怎样远祸全身,一个身负天下重寄的人,尤其应该刻刻不懈地防备危害的袭击。君主的薨逝不仅是个人的死亡,它像一个旋涡一样,凡是在它近旁的东西,都要被它卷去同归于尽;又像一个矗立在最高山峰上的巨轮,它的轮辐上连附着无数的小物件,当巨轮轰然崩裂的时候,那些小物件也跟着它一齐粉碎。国王的一声叹气,总是随着全国的呻吟。

国王　请你们准备立刻出发,因为我们必须及早制止这一种公然的威胁。

罗森格兰兹　我们就去赶紧预备。(罗森格兰兹、吉尔登斯吞同下。)

【波洛涅斯上。

波洛涅斯 陛下,他到他母亲房间里去了。我现在就去躲在帷幕后面,听他们怎么说。我可以断定她一定会把他好好教训一顿的。您说得很不错,母亲对于儿子总有几分偏心,所以最好有一个第三者躲在旁边偷听他们的谈话。再会,陛下。在您未睡以前,我还要来看您一次,把我所探听到的事情告诉您。

国王 谢谢你,贤卿。(波洛涅斯下)啊!我的罪恶的戾气已经上达于天,我的灵魂上负着一个原始以来最初的咒诅,杀害兄弟的暴行!我不能祈祷,虽然我的愿望像决心一样强烈,我的更坚强的罪恶击败了我的坚强的意愿。像一个人同时要做两件事情,我因为不知道应该先从什么地方下手而徘徊歧途,结果反到弄得一事无成。要是这一只可咒诅的手上染满了一层比它本身还厚的兄弟的血,难道天上所有的甘霖,都不能把它洗涤得像雪一样洁白吗?慈悲的使命,不就是宽宥罪恶吗?祈祷的目的,不是一方面预防我们的堕落,一方面救拔我们于已堕落之后吗?那么我要仰望上天。我的过失已经消灭了。可是唉!哪一种祈祷才是我所适用的呢?"求上帝赦免我的杀人重罪"吗?那不能,因为我现在还占有着那些引起我的犯罪动机的目的物,我的王冠、我的野心和我的王后。非分攫取的利益还在手里,就可以幸邀宽恕吗?在这贪污的人世,罪恶的镀金的手也许可以把公道推开不顾,暴徒的赃物往往就是枉法的贿赂。可是天上却不是这样的,在那边一切都无可遁避,任何行动都要显现它的真相,我们必须当面为我们自己的罪恶做证。那么怎么办呢?还有什么法子好想呢?试一试忏悔的力量吧。什么事情是忏悔所不能做到的?可是对于一个不能忏悔的人,它又有什么用呢?啊,不幸的处境!啊,像死亡一样黑暗的心胸!啊,越是挣扎,越是不能脱身的胶住了的灵魂!救救我,天使们!试一试吧:弯下来,顽强的膝盖,钢丝一样的心弦,变得像新生之婴的筋肉一样柔嫩吧!但愿一切转祸为福!(退后跪祷)

【哈姆雷特上。

哈姆雷特 他现在正在祈祷,我正好动手;我决定现在就干,让他上天堂去,我也算报了仇了。不,那还要考虑一下:一个恶人杀死我的父亲,我,他的独生子,却把这个恶人送上天堂。啊,这简直是以恩报怨了。他用卑鄙的手段,在我父亲罪孽方中的时候趁其不备地把他杀死;虽然谁也不知道在上帝面前,他的生前的善恶如何相抵,可是照我们一般的推想,他的孽债多分是很重的。现在他正在洗涤他的灵魂,要是我在这时候结果了他的性命,那么天国的路是为他开放着,这样还算是复仇吗?不!收起来,我的剑,等候一个更惨酷的机会

93

吧。当他在酒醉以后,在愤怒之中,或是在荒淫纵欲的时候,有赌博、咒骂或是其他邪恶的行为的中间,我就要叫他颠踬在我的脚下,让他幽深黑暗不见天日的灵魂永堕地狱。我的母亲在等我,这一服续命的药剂不过延长了你临死的痛苦。(下)

【国王起立上前。

国王 我的言语高高飞起,我的思想滞留地下。没有思想的言语永远不会上升天界。(下)

第四场
王后寝宫

【王后及波洛涅斯上。

波洛涅斯 他就要来了。请您把他着实教训一顿,对他说他这种狂妄的态度,实在叫人忍无可忍,倘没有您娘娘替他居中回护,王上早已对他大发雷霆了。我就悄悄地躲在这儿。请您对他讲得着力一点。

哈姆雷特 (在内)母亲,母亲,母亲!

王后 都在我身上,你放心吧。退下去,我听见他来了。

(波洛涅斯匿帷后)

【哈姆雷特上。

哈姆雷特 母亲,您叫我有什么事?

王后　哈姆雷特,你已经大大得罪了你的父亲啦。

哈姆雷特　母亲,您已经大大得罪了我的父亲啦。

王后　来,来,不要用这种胡说八道的话回答我。

哈姆雷特　去,去,不要用这种胡说八道的话问我。

王后　啊,怎么,哈姆雷特!

哈姆雷特　现在又是什么事?

王后　你忘记我了吗?

哈姆雷特　不,凭着十字架起誓,我没有忘记你;你是王后,你的丈夫的兄弟的妻子,你又是我的母亲,——但愿你不是!

王后　哎哟,那么我要去叫那些会说话的人来跟你谈谈了。

哈姆雷特　来,来,坐下来,不要动。我要把一面镜子放在你的面前,让你看一看你自己的灵魂。

王后　你要干吗呀?你不是要杀我吗?救命!救命呀!

波洛涅斯　(在后)喂!救命!救命!救命!

哈姆雷特　(拔剑)怎么!是哪一个鼠贼?要钱不要命吗?我来结果你。(以剑刺穿帷幕)

波洛涅斯　(在后)啊!我死了!

王后　哎哟!你干了什么事啦?

哈姆雷特　我也不知道,那不是国王吗?

王后　啊,多么鲁莽残酷的行为!

哈姆雷特　残酷的行为!好妈妈,简直就跟杀了一个国王,再去嫁给他的兄弟一样坏。

王后　杀了一个国王!

哈姆雷特　嗯,母亲,我正是这样说。(揭帷见波洛涅斯)你这倒运的、粗心的、爱管闲事的傻瓜,再会!我还以为是一个在你上面的人哩。也是你命不该活,现在你可知道爱管闲事的危险了。——别尽扭着你的手。静一静,坐下来,让我扭你的心。你的心倘不是铁石打成的,万恶的习惯倘不曾把它硬化得透不进一点感情,那么我的话一定可以把它刺痛。

王后　我干了些什么错事,你才敢这样肆无忌惮地向我摇

96　哈姆雷特

唇弄舌呢?

哈姆雷特 你的行为可以使贞节蒙污,使美德得到了伪善的名称,从纯洁的恋情的额上取下娇艳的蔷薇,替它盖上一个烙印,使婚姻的盟约变成博徒的誓言一样虚伪。啊!这样一种行为,简直使盟约成为一个没有灵魂的躯壳,神圣的宗教变成一串谵妄的狂言。苍天的脸上也为它带上羞色,大地因为痛心这样的行为,也罩上满面的愁容,好像世界末日就要到来一般。

王后 唉!究竟是什么极恶重罪,你把它说得这样惊人呢?

哈姆雷特 瞧这一幅图画,再瞧这一幅——这是两个兄弟的肖像。你看这一个的相貌是多么高雅优美:太阳神的鬈发、天神的前额,像战神马斯一样威风凛凛的眼睛,像降落在高吻穹苍的山巅的传报神一样矫健的姿态。这一个完善卓越的仪表,真像每一个天神都曾在那上面打下印记,向世间证明这是一个男子的典型。这是你从前的丈夫。现在你再看这一个:这是你现在的丈夫,像一株霉烂的禾穗,损害了他的健硕的兄弟。你有眼睛吗?你甘心离开这一座大好的高山,靠着这荒野生活吗?吓!你有眼睛吗?你不能说那是爱情,因为在你的年纪,热情已经冷淡下来,它必须等候理智的判断。什么理智愿意从这么高的地方,降落到这么低的所在呢?知觉你当然是有的,否则你就不会有行动。可是你那知觉也一定已经麻木了。因为就是疯人也不会犯那样的错误,无论怎样丧心病狂,总不会连这样悬殊的差异都分辨不出来的。那么,是什么魔鬼蒙住了你的眼睛,把你这样欺骗呢?你的视觉、听觉、触觉、嗅觉,全都失去了交相为用的功能了吗?因为单单一个感官有了毛病,绝不会使人愚蠢到这步田地。羞啊!你不觉得惭愧吗?要是地狱中的孽火可以在一个中年妇人的骨髓里煽起了蠢动,那么在青春的烈焰中,让贞操像蜡一样融化了吧。在强力的威迫下失身,有什么可耻呢霜雪都会自动燃烧,理智都会做情欲的奴隶呢。

王后 啊,哈姆雷特!不要说下去了!你使我的眼睛看进了我自己灵魂的深处,看见我灵魂里那些洗拭不去的黑色的污点。

哈姆雷特 嘿,生活在汗臭垢腻的眠床上,让淫邪熏没了心窍,在污秽的猪圈里调情弄爱——

王后 啊,不要再对我说下去了!这些话像刀子一样戳进我的耳朵里。不要说下去了,亲爱的哈姆雷特!

哈姆雷特 一个杀人犯,一个恶徒,一个不及你前夫二百分之一的庸奴,一个戴王冠的丑角,一个盗国窃位的扒儿手!

王后 别说了!

哈姆雷特 一个下流无赖的国王——

【鬼上。

哈姆雷特　天上的神明啊,救救我,用你们的翅膀覆盖我的头顶!——陛下英灵不昧,有什么见教?

王后　哎哟,他疯了!

哈姆雷特　您不是来责备您的儿子不该消磨他的时间和感情,把您煌煌的命令搁在一旁,耽误了我所应该做的大事吗?啊,说吧!

鬼魂　不要忘记。我现在是来磨砺你的快要蹉跎下去的决心。可是瞧!你的母亲满身都是惊愕。啊,快去安慰安慰她的正在交战中的灵魂吧!最柔弱的人最容易受幻想的激动。对她说话去,哈姆雷特。

哈姆雷特　您怎么啦,母亲?

王后　唉!你怎么啦?为什么你把眼睛睁视着虚无?向空中喃喃说话?你的眼睛里射出狂乱的神情,像熟睡的军士突然听到警号一般,你的整齐的头发一根根都像有了生命似的竖立起来。啊,好儿子!在你的疯狂的热焰上,浇洒一些清凉的镇静吧!你在瞧什么?

哈姆雷特　他,他!您瞧,他的脸色多么惨白!看见了他这一种形状,要是再知道他所负的沉冤,即使石块也会感动的。——不要瞧着我,因为那不过徒然勾起我的哀感,也许反会妨碍我的冷酷的决心,也许我会因此而失去勇气,让挥泪代替了流血。

王后　你这番话是对谁说的?

哈姆雷特　您没有看见什么吗?

王后　什么也没有。要是有什么东西在那边,我不会不看见的。

哈姆雷特　您也没有听见什么吗?

王后　不,除了我们两人的说话以外,我什么也没有听见。

哈姆雷特　啊,您瞧!瞧,它悄悄儿去了!我的父亲,穿着他生前所穿的衣服!瞧!他就在这一刻,从门口走出去了!(鬼下)

王后　这是你脑中虚构的意象,一个人在心神恍惚的状态中,最容易发生这种幻妄的错觉。

哈姆雷特　心神恍惚!我的脉搏跟您的一样,在按着正常的节奏跳动哩。我所说的并不是疯话,要是您不信,我可以把我刚才说过的话一字不漏地复述一遍,一个疯人是不会记忆得那样清楚的。母亲,为了上帝的慈悲,不要自己安慰自己,以为我这一番说话,只是出于疯狂,不是真的对您的过失而发。那样的思想不过是骗人的油膏,只能使您溃烂的良心上结起一层薄膜,那内部的毒疮却在底下愈长愈大。向上天承认您的罪恶吧,忏悔过去、警戒未来。不要把肥料浇在莠草上,使它们格外蔓延起来。原谅我这一番正义的劝告,因为在这种万恶的时世,正义必须向罪恶乞恕,它必须俯首屈膝,要求人家接纳它的善意的箴规。

王后　啊,哈姆雷特!你把我的心劈为两半了!

哈姆雷特　啊!把那坏的一半丢掉,保留那另外的一半,让您的灵魂清净一些。晚安！可是不要上我叔父的床！即使您已经失节,也得勉力学做一个贞节妇人的样子。习惯虽然是一个可以使人失去羞耻的魔鬼,但是它也可以做一个天使,对于勉力为善的人,它会用潜移默化的手段,使他弃恶从善。您要是今天晚上自加抑制,下一次就会觉得这一种自制的功夫并不怎样为难,慢慢地就可以习以为常了。因为习惯简直有一种改变气质的神奇的力量,它可以使魔鬼主宰人类的灵魂,也可以把他从人们心里驱逐出去。让我再向您道一次晚安。当您希望得到上天祝福的时候,我将求您祝福我。至于这一位老人家,(指波洛涅斯)我很后悔自己一时鲁莽把他杀死。可是这是上天的意思,要借着他的死惩罚我,同时借着我的手惩罚他,使我一方面自己受到天谴,一方面又成为代天行刑的使者。我现在先去把他的尸体安顿好了,再来担承这一个杀人的过咎。晚安！为了顾全母子的恩慈,我不得不忍心暴戾。不幸已经开始,更大的灾祸还在接踵而至。再有一句话,母亲。

王后　我应当怎么做？

哈姆雷特　我不能禁止您不再让那骄淫的僭王引诱您和他同床,让他拧您的脸颊,叫您做他的小耗子。我也不能禁止您因为他给了您一两个恶臭的吻,或是用他万恶的手指抚摩您的颈项,就把您所知道的事情一起说了出来,告诉他我实在是装疯,不是真疯。您应该让他知道;因为那一个聪明懂事的王后,愿意隐藏着这样重大的消息,不去告诉一头蛤蟆、一头蝙蝠、一头老雄猫知道呢?不,虽然理性警告您保守秘密,您尽管学那寓言中的猴子,因为受了好奇心的驱使,到屋顶上去开了笼门,把鸟儿放走,自己钻进笼里去,结果连笼子一起掉下来跌死吧。

王后 你放心吧,要是言语是从呼吸里吐出来的,我决不会让我的呼吸泄漏了你对我所说的话。

哈姆雷特 我必须到英国去,您知道吗?

王后 唉!我忘了这事情已经这样决定了。

哈姆雷特 公文已经封好,打算交给我那两个同学带去,对这两个家伙我要像对待两条咬人的毒蛇一样随时提防;他们将要做我的先驱,引导我钻进什么圈套里去。我倒要瞧瞧他们的能耐。开炮的要是给炮轰了,也是一件好玩的事。他们会埋地雷,我要比他们埋得更深,把他们轰到月亮上去。啊!用诡计对付诡计,不是顶有趣的吗?这家伙一死,多半会提早了我的行期。让我把这尸体拖到隔壁去。母亲,晚安!这一位大臣生前是个愚蠢饶舌的家伙,现在却变成非常谨严庄重的人了。来,老先生,让我把您拖下您的坟墓里去。晚安,母亲!(各下。哈姆雷特曳波洛涅斯尸入内)

第四幕

第一场
城堡中的一室

【国王、王后、罗森格兰兹及吉尔登斯吞上。

国王 这些长吁短叹之中,都含着深长的意义,我们必须设法探索出来。你的儿子呢?

王后 （向罗森格兰兹、吉尔登斯吞）请你们暂时退开。（罗森格兰兹、吉尔登斯吞下）啊，陛下！今晚我看见了多么惊人的事情！

国王 什么？乔特鲁德。哈姆雷特怎么啦？

王后 疯狂得像彼此争强斗胜的天风和海浪一样。在他野性发作的时候，他听见帷幕后面有什么东西爬动的声音，就拔出剑来，嚷着，"有耗子！有耗子！"于是在一阵疯狂的恐惧之中，把那躲在幕后的好老人家杀死了。

国王 啊，罪过罪过！要是我在那儿，我也会照样死在他手里的；放任他这样胡作非为，对于你，对于我，对于每一个人，都是极大的威胁。唉！这一件流血的暴行应当由谁负责呢？我们是难辞其咎的，因为我们早该防患于未然，把这个发疯的孩子关禁起来，不让他到处乱走；可是我们太爱他了，以至于不愿想一个适当的方策，正像一个害着恶疮的人，因为不让它出毒的缘故，弄到毒气攻心，无法救治一样。他到哪儿去了？

王后 拖着那个被他杀死的尸体出去了。像一堆下贱的铅铁，掩不了真金的光彩一样，他知道他自己做错了事，他的纯良的本性就从他的疯狂里透露出来，他哭了。

国王 啊，乔特鲁德！来！太阳一到了山上，我们必须赶紧让他登船出发。对于这一次罪恶的行为，我们必须用最严正的态度，最巧妙的措辞，决定一个执法原情的措置。喂！吉尔登斯吞！

【罗森格兰兹及吉尔登斯吞重上。

国王 两位朋友,我们还要借用你们一下。哈姆雷特在疯狂之中,已经把波洛涅斯杀死;他现在把那尸体从他母亲的房间里拖出去了。你们去找他来,对他说话要和气一点;再把那尸体搬到教堂里去。请你们快去把这件事情办一办好。(罗森格兰兹、吉尔登斯吞下)来,乔特鲁德,我们要去召集我们那些最有见识的朋友,把我们的决定和这一件意外的变故告诉他们,免得外边无稽的谰言牵涉到我们身上,它的毒箭从低声的密语中间散放出去,是像弹丸从炮口里射出去一样每发必中的。啊,来吧!我的灵魂里充满着混乱和惊愕。(同下)

第二场
城堡中的另一室

【哈姆雷特上。

哈姆雷特　藏好了。

罗森格兰兹
吉尔登斯吞　（在内）哈姆雷特！哈姆雷特殿下！

哈姆雷特　什么声音？谁在叫哈姆雷特？啊,他们来了。

【罗森格兰兹及吉尔登斯呑上。

罗森格兰兹　殿下,您把那尸体怎么样啦?

哈姆雷特　它本来就是泥土,我仍旧让它回到泥土里去。

罗森格兰兹　告诉我们它在什么地方,让我们把它搬到教堂里去。

哈姆雷特　不要相信。

罗森格兰兹　相信什么?

哈姆雷特　相信我会放弃我自己的意见来听你的话。而且,一块海绵也敢问起我来!一个堂堂王子应该用什么话去回答它呢?

罗森格兰兹　您把我当作一块海绵吗,殿下?

哈姆雷特　嗯,先生,一块吸收君王的恩宠、利禄和官爵的海绵。可是这样的官员要到最后才会显出他们最大的用处来,像猴子吃硬壳果一般,他们的君王先把他们含在嘴里舐弄了好久,然后再一口咽了下去。当他需要被你们所吸收去的东西的时候,他只要把你们一挤,于是,海绵,你又是一块干干的海绵了。

罗森格兰兹　我不懂您的话,殿下。

哈姆雷特　那很好,一句下流的话睡在一个傻瓜的耳朵里。

罗森格兰兹　殿下,您必须告诉我们那尸体在什么地方?然后跟我们见王上去。

哈姆雷特　他的身体和国王同在,可是那国王并不和他的身体同在。国王是一件东西——

吉尔登斯吞 一件东西,殿下!

哈姆雷特 一件虚无的东西。带我去见他。狐狸躲起来,大家追上去。(同下)

第三场
同前,另一室

【国王上,侍从后随。

国王 我已经叫他们找他去了,并且叫他们把那尸体寻出来。让这家伙任意胡闹,是一件多么危险的事情!可是我们又不能把严刑峻法加在他的身上,他是为糊涂的群众所喜爱的,他们喜欢一个人,只凭眼睛,不凭理智。我要是处罚了他,他们只看见我的刑罚的苛酷,却不想到他犯的是什么重罪。为了顾全各方面的关系,叫他迅速离国,不失为一种最适宜的策略。应付非常的变故,必须用非常的手段。

【罗森格兰兹上。

国王 啊!事情怎样啦?

罗森格兰兹 陛下,他不肯告诉我们那尸体在什么地方。

国王 可是他人呢?

罗森格兰兹 在外面,陛下;我们把他看起来了,等候您的旨意。

国王　带他来见我。

罗森格兰兹　喂,吉尔登斯吞! 带殿下进来。

【哈姆雷特及吉尔登斯吞上。

国王　啊,哈姆雷特,波洛涅斯呢?

哈姆雷特　吃饭去了。

国王　吃饭去了! 什么地方?

哈姆雷特　不是在他吃饭的地方,是在人家吃他的地方;有一群精明的蛆虫正在他身上大吃特吃哩。蛆虫是全世界最大的饕餮家。我们喂肥了各种牲畜给自己受用,再喂肥了自己去给蛆虫受用。胖胖的国王跟瘦瘦的乞丐是一个桌子上两道不同的菜,不过是这么一回事。

国王　哎! 哎!

哈姆雷特　一个人可以拿一条吃过一个国王的蛆虫去钓鱼,再吃那吃过那条蛆虫的鱼。

国王　你这句话是什么意思?

哈姆雷特　没有什么意思,我不过指点你一个国王可以在一个乞丐的脏腑里经过一番什么变化。

国王　波洛涅斯呢?

哈姆雷特　在天上。你差人到那边去找他吧。要是你的使者在天上找不到他,那么你可以自己到另外一个所在地去找他。可是你们在这一个月里要是找不到他的话,你们只要跑上走廊的阶石,也就可以闻到他的气味了。

国王 （向若干侍从）到走廊里去找一找。

哈姆雷特 他在等着你们哩。（侍从等下）

国王 哈姆雷特，你干出这种事来，使我非常痛心。为了你自身的安全起见，你必须火速离开国境；所以快去自己预备预备。船已经整装待发，风势也很顺利，同行的人都在等着你，一切都已经准备好向英国出发。

哈姆雷特 到英国去！

国王 是的，哈姆雷特。

哈姆雷特 好。

国王 要是你明白我的用意，你应该知道这是为了你好。

哈姆雷特 我看见一个明白你的用意的天使。可是来，到英国去！再会，亲爱的母亲！

国王 你的慈爱的父亲，哈姆雷特。

哈姆雷特 我的母亲。父亲和母亲是夫妇两个，夫妇是一体之亲；所以再会吧，我的母亲！来，到英国去！（下）

国王 跟在他的后面，劝诱他赶快上船，不要耽误；我要叫他在今晚离开国境。去！这件事情一解决，什么问题都没有了。请你们赶快一点。（罗森格兰兹、吉尔登斯吞下）英格兰王啊，丹麦的宝剑在你的身上还留着鲜明的创痕，你向我纳款输诚的敬礼至今未减，要是你畏惧我的威力，重视我的友谊，你就不能忽视我的旨意；我已经在公函里要求你把哈姆雷特立即处死，照着我的意思做吧，英格兰王，因为他像是我深入膏肓的痼

疾,一定要借你的手把我医好。我必须知道他已经不在人世,我脸上才会有笑容浮起。(下)

第四场
丹麦原野

【福丁布拉斯;一队长及兵士等列队行进上。

福丁布拉斯 队长,你去替我问候丹麦国王,告诉他说福丁布拉斯因为得到他的允许,已经按照约定,率领一支军队通过他的国境。你知道我们在什么地方集合。要是丹麦王有什么话要跟我当面说的,我也可以入朝晋谒。你就这样对他说吧。

队长 是,主将。

福丁布拉斯 慢步前进。(福丁布拉斯及兵士等下)

【哈姆雷特,罗森格兰兹,吉尔登斯吞等同上。

哈姆雷特 官长,这些是什么人的军队?

队长 他们都是挪威的军队,先生。

哈姆雷特 请问他们是开到什么地方去的?

队长 到波兰的某一部分去。

哈姆雷特 谁是领兵的主将?

队长 挪威老王的侄儿福丁布拉斯。

哈姆雷特 他们是要向波兰本土进攻呢,还是去袭击边疆?

队长　不瞒您说,我们是要去夺一小块徒有虚名、毫无实利的土地。叫我出五块钱去把它买了下来,我也不要;无论挪威人波兰人,要是把它标卖起来,谁也不会付出比这大一点的价钱来的。

哈姆雷特　啊,那么波兰人一定不会防卫它的了。

队长　不,他们早已布防好了。

哈姆雷特　为了这一块荒瘠的土地,浪抛了两千人的生命、两千块的金币,谁也不对它表示一点疑问。这完全是因为国家太富足升平了,晏安的积毒蕴蓄于内,虽然已经到了溃烂的程度,外表上却还一点看不出将死的征象来。谢谢您,官长。

队长　上帝和您同在,先生。(下)

罗森格兰兹 我们去吧,殿下。

哈姆雷特 我就来,你们先走一步。(除哈姆雷特外均下)
我所见到听到的一切,都好像在对我谴责,鞭策我赶快进行我的蹉跎未就的复仇大愿!一个人要是在他生命的盛年,只知道吃吃睡睡,他还算是个什么东西?简直是一头畜生!上帝造下我们来,使我们能够这样高谈阔论、瞻前顾后,当然要我们利用他所赋予我们的这一种能力和灵明的理智,不让它们白白废掉。现在我明明有理由、有决心、有力量、有方法,可以动手干我所要干的事,可是我还是在说一些空话:"我要怎么怎么干。"而始终不曾在行动上表现出来。我不知道这是为了鹿豕一般的健忘呢,还是为了三分懦怯一分智慧的过于审慎的顾虑。像大地一样显明的榜样都在鼓励我:瞧这一支勇猛的大军,领队的是一个娇养的少年王子,勃勃的雄心振起了他的精神,使他蔑视不可知的结果,为了区区弹丸大小的一块不毛之地,拼着血肉之躯,去向命运、死亡和危险挑战。真正的伟大不是轻举妄动,而是在荣誉遭遇危险的时候,即使为了一根稻秆之微,也要慷慨力争。可是我的父亲给人惨杀,我的母亲给人污辱,我的理智和感情都被这种不共戴天的大仇所激动,我却因循隐忍,一切听其自然,看着这两千个人为了博取一个空虚的名声,视死如归地走下他们的坟墓里去,目的只是争夺一方还不够作为他们埋骨

之所的土地,相比之下,我将何地自容呢?啊!从这一刻起,让我屏除一切的疑虑妄念,把流血的思想充满在我的脑际!(下)

第五场
艾尔西诺;城堡中一室

【王后,霍拉旭及一侍臣上。
王后 我不愿意跟她说话。
侍臣 她一定要见您;她的神情疯疯癫癫,瞧着怪可怜的。
王后 她要什么?
侍臣 她不断提起她的父亲;她说她听见这世上到处是诡计,一边呻吟,一边搥她的心,对一些琐琐屑屑的事情痛骂,讲的都是些很玄妙的话,好像有意思好像又没有意思。她的话虽然不知所云,可是却能在听见的人心中发生反应,而企图从它里面找出意义来。他们妄加猜测,把她的话断章取义,用自己的思想附会上去。当她讲那些话的时候,有时眨眼,有时点头,做着种种的手势,的确使人相信在她的言语之间,含蓄着什么意思,虽然不能确定,却可以做一些很不好听的解释。
霍拉旭 最好有什么人跟她谈谈,因为也许她会在愚妄的脑筋里散布一些危险的猜测。

王后　让她进来。(侍臣下)

　　　我负疚的灵魂惴惴惊惶,
　　　琐琐细事也像预兆灾殃;
　　　罪恶是这样充满了疑猜,
　　　越小心越容易流露鬼胎。

【侍臣率奥菲利娅重上。

奥菲利娅　丹麦的美丽的王后陛下呢?

王后　啊,奥菲利娅!

奥菲利娅　(唱)

　　　张三李四满街走,
　　　谁是你情郎?
　　　毡帽在头杖在手,
　　　草鞋穿一双。

王后　唉!好姑娘,这支歌是什么意思呢?

奥菲利娅　您说?请您听好了。(唱)

　　　姑娘,姑娘,他死了,
　　　一去不复来;
　　　头上盖着青青草,
　　　脚下石生苔。
　　　嗄呵!

王后　嗳,可是,奥菲利娅——

奥菲利娅　请您听好了。(唱)

　　　殓衾遮体白如雪——

115

【国王上。

王后　唉！陛下，您瞧。

奥菲利娅

　　　　鲜花红似雨；

　　　　花上盈盈有泪滴，

　　　　伴郎坟墓去。

国王　你好，美丽的姑娘？

奥菲利娅　好，上帝保佑您！他们说猫头鹰是一个面包司务的女儿变成的。主啊！我们谁也不知道自己将来会变成什么。愿上帝在您的食桌上！

国王　她父亲的死激成了她这种幻想。

奥菲利娅　对不起，我们以后再别提这件事了。要是有人问您这是什么意思，您就这样对他说：（唱）

　　　　情人佳节就在明天，

　　　　我要一早起身，

　　　　梳洗齐整到你窗前，

　　　　来做你的恋人。

　　　　他下了床披了衣裳，

　　　　他开了房门；

　　　　她进去时是个女郎，

　　　　出来变了妇人。

国王　美丽的奥菲利娅！

奥菲利娅　真的，不用发誓，我会把它唱完：（唱）

> 凭着神圣慈悲名字,
> 这种事太丢脸!
> 少年男子不知羞耻,
> 一味无赖纠缠。
> 她说你曾答应婚嫁,
> 然后再同枕席。
> 谁料如今被你欺诈,
> 懊悔万千无及!

国王 她这个样子已经多久了?

奥菲利娅 我希望一切转祸为福!我们必须忍耐。可是我一想到他们把他放下寒冷的泥土里去,我就禁不住掉泪。我的哥哥必须知道这件事。谢谢你们很好的劝告。来,我的马车!晚安,太太们!晚安,可爱的小姐们!晚安,晚安!(下)

国王 紧紧跟住她,留心不要让她闹出乱子来。(霍拉旭下)啊!深心的忧伤把她害成了这样子,这完全是为了她父亲的死。啊,乔特鲁德,乔特鲁德!不幸的事情总是接踵而来:第一是她父亲的被杀,然后是你儿子的远别,他闯了这样大祸,不得不亡命异国,也是自取其咎。人民对于善良的波洛涅斯的暴死,已经群疑蜂起、议论纷纷。我们这样匆匆忙忙地把他秘密安葬,更加引起了外间的疑窦。可怜的奥菲利娅也因此而悲伤得失去了她的正常的理智,我们人类没有了理智,不过是画上的图形、无知的禽兽。最后,跟这些事情同样使我不安的,她的哥哥已经从法国秘密回来,行动诡异、居心叵测,他的耳中所听到的,都是那些搬弄是非的人所散播的关于他父亲死状的恶意的谣言。少不得牵涉到我们身上。啊,我的亲爱的乔特鲁德!这种消息像一尊杀人的巨炮,到处都在危害我的生命。(内喧呼声)

王后 哎哟!这是什么声音?

【一侍臣上。

国王 我的瑞士卫队呢?叫他们把守宫门。什么事?

侍臣 赶快避一避吧,陛下。比大洋中的怒潮冲决堤岸还要汹汹其势,年轻的雷欧提斯带领着一队叛军,打败了您的卫士,冲进宫里来了。这一群暴徒把他称为主上。就像世界还不过刚才开始一般,他们推翻了一切的传统和习惯,高喊着,"我们推举雷欧提斯做国王!"他们掷帽举手,呕喝的声音响彻云霄,"让雷欧提斯做国王,让雷欧提斯做国王!"

王后 他们这样兴高采烈,却不知道已经误入歧途!啊,你们干了错事了,你们这些不忠的丹麦狗!(内喧呼声)

国王 宫门都已打破了。

【雷欧提斯戎装上;一群丹麦人随上。

雷欧提斯 这国王在那儿?弟兄们,大家站在外面。

众人 不,让我们进来。

雷欧提斯 对不起,请你们让我一个人在这儿。

众人 好,好。(众人退立门外)

雷欧提斯 谢谢你们,把门看守好了。啊,你这万恶的奸王!还我的父亲来!

王后 安静一点,好雷欧提斯。

雷欧提斯 我身上要是有一点血安静下来,我就是个野生的杂种,我父亲是个王八,我母亲的贞洁的额角上,也要雕上娼妓的恶名。

国王 雷欧提斯,你这样大张声势,兴兵犯上,究竟什么原因?——放了他,乔特鲁德,不要担心他会伤害我的身体,一个君王是有神圣呵护的,他的威严可以吓退叛逆。——告诉我,雷欧提斯,你有什么气恼不平的事?——放了他,乔特鲁德。——你说吧。

雷欧提斯 我的父亲呢?

国王 死了。

王后 但是并不是他杀死的。

国王 尽他问下去。

雷欧提斯 他怎么会死?我可不能受人家的愚弄。忠心,到地狱里去吧!让最黑暗的魔鬼把一切誓言抓了去!什么良心,什么礼貌,都给我滚下无底的深渊里去!我要向永劫挑战。我的立场已经决定:死也好,活也好,我什么都不管,只要痛痛快快地为我的父亲复仇。

国王 谁可以阻止你?

雷欧提斯 除了我自己的意志以外,全世界也不能阻止我。

我不费吹灰之力,就可以达到我的目标。

国王　好雷欧提斯,要是你想知道你的亲爱的父亲究竟是怎样死去的话,你还是先认清楚谁是友人谁是敌人呢,还是不分青红皂白把他们一概作为你复仇的对象?

雷欧提斯　冤有头,债有主,我只要找我父亲的敌人算账。

国王　那么你要知道谁是他的敌人吗?

雷欧提斯　对于他的好朋友,我愿意张开我的手臂拥抱他们,像舍身的企鹅一样,把我的血供他们喝饮①。

国王　啊,现在你才说得像一个孝顺的儿子和真正的绅士。我不但对于令尊的死不曾有份,而且为此也感觉到非常悲痛。这一个事实将会透过你的心,正像白昼的阳光照射你的眼睛一样。

众人　(在内)放她进去!

雷欧提斯　怎么!那是什么声音?

【奥菲利娅重上。

雷欧提斯　啊,赤热的烈焰,炙枯了我的脑浆吧!七倍辛酸的眼泪,灼伤了我的视觉吧!天日在上,我一定要叫那害你疯狂的仇人重重地抵偿他的罪恶。啊,五月的玫瑰!亲爱的女郎,好妹妹,奥菲利娅!天啊!一个少女的理智,也会像一个老人的生命一样受不起打击吗?

奥菲利娅　(唱)

---

① 昔人误信企鹅以其血哺雏,故云。

>   他们把他抬上柩架,
>
>   哎呀,哎呀,哎哎呀。
>
>   在他坟上泪如雨下——
>
>   再会,我的鸽子!

雷欧提斯 要是你没有发疯,你会激励我复仇,你的言语也不会比你现在这样子更使我感动了。

奥菲利娅 啊,这纺轮转动的声音多么好听!是那坏良心的管家把主人的女儿拐了去了。

雷欧提斯 这一种无意识的话,比正言危论还要有力得多。

奥菲利娅 这是表示记忆的迷迭香;爱人,请你记着吧,这是表示思想的三色堇。

雷欧提斯 她在疯话中把思想和记忆混杂在一起了。

奥菲利娅 这是给您的茴香和漏斗花,这是给您的芸香,这儿还留着一些给我自己。啊!您可以把您的芸香插戴得别致点儿。这儿是一枝雏菊,我想要给您几朵紫罗兰,可是我父亲一死,它们全都谢了。他们说他死得很好——(唱)

>   可爱的罗宾是我的宝贝。

雷欧提斯 忧愁、痛苦、悲哀和地狱中的磨难,在她身上都变成了可怜可爱。

奥菲利娅 (唱)

>   他会不会再回来?
>
>   他会不会再回来?

不,不,他死了。
你的命难保,
他再也不会回来。
他的胡须像白银,
满头黄发乱纷纷。
人死不能活,
且把悲声歇,
上帝饶赦他灵魂!

求上帝饶赦一切基督徒的灵魂!上帝和你们同在!(下)

雷欧提斯 上帝啊,你看见这种惨事吗?

国王　雷欧提斯,我必须跟你详细谈谈关于你所遭逢的不幸。你不能拒绝我这个权利。你不妨先去选择几个你的最有见识的朋友,请他们在你我两人之间做公证人:要是他们评断的结果,认为是我主动或同谋杀害你的父亲,我愿意放弃我的国土,我的王冠,我的生命以及我所有的一切,作为对你的补偿。可是他们假如认为我是无罪的,那么你必须答应帮助我一臂之力,让我们两人开诚合作,定出一个惩凶的方策来。

雷欧提斯　就是这样吧。他死得这样不明不白,他的下葬又是这样偷偷摸摸的,他的尸体上没有一些战士的荣饰,也不曾替他举行一些哀祭的仪式,从天上到地下都在发出愤懑不平的呼声,我不能不问一个明白。

国王　你可以明白一切。谁是真有罪的,让斧钺加在他的头上吧。请你跟我来。(同下)

第六场
同前另一室

【霍拉旭及一仆人上。

霍拉旭　要来见我说话的是些什么人?

仆人　是几个水手,主人,他们说他们有信要交给您。

霍拉旭　叫他们进来。(仆人下)倘不是哈姆雷特殿下差来的人,我不知道在这世上的哪些人来看我。

【水手等上。

水手甲　上帝祝福您,先生!

霍拉旭　愿他也祝福你。

水手乙　他要是高兴,先生,他会祝福我们的。这儿有一封信给您,先生——它是从那位到英国去的钦使寄来的。要是您的名字是霍拉旭的话。

霍拉旭　"霍拉旭,你把这封信看过以后,请把来人领去见一见国王;他们还有信要交给他。我们在海上的第二天,就有一艘很凶猛的海盗船向我们追击。我们因为船行太慢,只好勉力迎敌;在彼此相持的时候,我跳上了盗船,他们就立刻抛下我们的船,扬帆而去,剩下我一个人做他们的俘虏。他们对待我很是有礼,可是他们知道他们所做的事,我还要重谢他们哩。把我给国王的信交给他以后,请你就像逃命一般火速来见我。我有一些可以使你听了咋舌不下的话要在你的耳边说,可是事实的本身比这些话还要严重得多。来人可以把你带到我现在所在的地方。罗森格兰兹和吉尔登斯吞到英国去了,关于他们我还有许多话要告诉你。再会。你的哈姆雷特。"来,让我立刻就带你们去把你们的信送出,然后请你们领我到那把这些信交给你们的那个人的地方去。(同下)

第七场
同前；另一室

【国王及雷欧提斯上。

国王　你已经用你同情的耳朵，听见我告诉你那杀死令尊的人，也在图谋我的生命。现在你必须明白我的无罪，并且把我当作你的一个心腹的友人了。

雷欧提斯　听您所说，果然像是真的。可是告诉我，为了您自己的安全起见，为什么您对于这样罪大恶极的暴行，不采取严厉的手段呢？

国王　啊！那是因为有两个理由，也许在你看来是不称其为理由的，可是对于我却有很大的关系。王后，他的母亲，差不多一天不看见他就不能生活；至于我自己，那么不管这是我的好处或是我的致命的弱点，我的生命和灵魂是这样跟她联结在一起，正像星球不能跳出轨道一样，我也不能没有她而生活。而且我之所以不能把这件案子公开，还有一个重要的顾虑：一般民众对他都有很大的好感，他们盲目的崇拜像一道使树木变成石块的魔泉一样，把他所有的错处都变成了优点。我的箭太轻，太没有力了，遇到这样的狂风，一定不能射中目的，反而给吹了转来。

雷欧提斯 那么难道我高贵的父亲就是这样白白死去,一个好好的妹妹就是这样白白疯了不成?她的完美卓越的姿容才德,是可以傲视一世、睥睨古今的。可是我的报仇的机会总有一天会到来。

国王 不要让这件事扰乱了你的睡眠。你不要以为我是这样一个麻木不仁的人,会让人家揪着我的胡须,还以为不过是开开玩笑。不久你就可以听到消息。我爱你父亲,我也爱我自己。那我希望可以使你想到——

【一使者上。

国王 啊！什么消息？

使者 启禀陛下,是哈姆雷特寄来的信,这一封是给陛下的,这一封是给王后的。

国王 哈姆雷特寄来的！是谁把它们送到这儿来？

使者 他们说是几个水手,陛下,我没有看见他们。这两封信是克劳狄奥交给我的,他们把信送在他手里。

国王 雷欧提斯,你可以听一听这封信。出去！（使者下）
"陛下,我已经光着身子回到您的国土上来了。明天我就要请您允许我拜谒御容。让我先向您告我的不召而返之罪,然后再禀告您我这次突然而意外回国的原因。哈姆雷特敬上。"
这是什么意思？同去的人也都一起回来了吗？还是什么人在捣鬼,并没有这么一回事？

雷欧提斯 您认识这笔迹吗？

国王 这确实是哈姆雷特的亲笔。"光着身子"！这儿还附着一笔,说是"一个人回来"。你看他是什么用意？

雷欧提斯 我可弄不明白,陛下。可是他来得正好；我一想到我能够有这样一天当面申斥他的罪状,我的郁闷的心也热起来了。

国王 要是果然这样的话,雷欧提斯,你愿意听我的吩咐吗？

雷欧提斯 愿意,陛下,只要您不勉强我跟他和解。

国王　我是要使你自己心里得到平安。要是他现在中途而返,不预备再做这样的航行,那么我已经想好了一个计策,激他去干一件事情,一定可以叫他自投罗网。而且他死了以后,谁也不能讲一句闲话,即使他的母亲也不能觉察我们的计谋,只好认为是一件意外的灾祸。

雷欧提斯　陛下,我愿意服从您的指挥,最好请您设法让他死在我的手里。

国王　我正是这样计划。自从你到国外游学以后,人家常常说起你有一种特长的本领,这种话哈姆雷特也是早有耳闻;虽然在我的意见之中,这不过是你所有的才艺中间最不足道的一种,可是你的一切才艺的总和,都不及这一种本领更能挑起他的妒忌。

雷欧提斯　是什么本领呢,陛下?

国王　它虽然不过是装饰在少年人帽上的一条缎带,但也是少不了的。因为年轻人应该装束得华丽潇洒一些,表示他的健康活泼,正像老年人应该装束得朴素大方一些,表示他的矜严庄重一样。两个月以前,这儿来了一个诺曼的绅士,我自己曾经和法国人在马上比过武艺,他们都是很精于骑术的,可是这位好汉简直有不可思议的魔力,他骑在马上,好像他和他的坐骑化成了一体似的,随意驰骤,出神入化。他的技术是那样远超过我的预料,无论我杜撰一些怎样夸大的词句,都不够形容它的奇妙。

雷欧提斯 是个诺曼人吗？

国王 是诺曼人。

雷欧提斯 那么一定是拉摩德了。

国王 正是他。

雷欧提斯 我认识他；他的确是全国知名的勇士。

国王 他承认你的武艺很了不得，对于你的剑术尤其极口称赞，说是倘有人能够和你对敌，那一定大有可观；他发誓说他们国里的剑士要是跟你交起手来，一定会眼花缭乱，全然失去招架之功。他对你的这一番夸奖，使哈姆雷特妒恼交集，一心希望你快些回来，跟他比赛一下。从这一点上——

雷欧提斯 从这一点上怎么，陛下？

国王 雷欧提斯，你是真爱你的父亲吗？还是不过是做作出来的悲哀，只有表面，没有真心吗？

雷欧提斯 您为什么这样问我？

国王 我不是以为你不爱你的父亲；可是我知道爱不过起于一时感情的冲动，经验告诉我，经过了相当时间，它是会逐渐冷淡下去的。爱像一盏油灯，灯芯烧枯以后，它的火焰也会由微暗而至于消灭。一切事情都不能永远保持良好，因为过度的善反会摧毁它的本身，正像一个人因充血而死去一样。我们所要做的事，应该一想到就做；因为一个人的心理是会随时变化的，一迟疑就会遭遇种种的阻碍。可是回到我们所要谈论的中心问题上来吧。哈姆雷特回来了,你预备怎样用行动代替言语,表明你自己的确是你父亲的孝子呢?

雷欧提斯 我要在教堂里割破他的喉咙。

国王 无论什么所在都不能庇护一个杀人的凶手,复仇不应该在碍手碍脚的地方。可是,好雷欧提斯,你要是志在复仇,还是住在自己家里不要出来。哈姆雷特回来以后,我们可以让他知道你也回来,叫几个人在他的面前夸奖你的本领,把你说得比那法国人所讲的还要了得,怂恿他和你来一次比赛。他是个粗心的人,一点不想到人家在算计他,一定不会仔细检视比赛用的刀剑的利钝;你只要预先把一柄利剑混杂在里面,趁他没有注意的时候不动声色地自己拿了,在比赛之际,看准他的要害刺了过去,就可以替你的父亲报了仇了。

雷欧提斯 我愿意这样做;为了达到复仇的目的,我还要在我的剑上涂一些毒药。我已经从一个卖药人手里买到一种致命的药油,只要在剑头上沾上一滴,刺到人身上,它一碰到血,即使只是擦破了一些皮肤,也会毒性发作,无论什么灵丹仙草,都不能挽救他的性命。

国王 让我们再考虑考虑,看时间和机会能够给我们什么方便。要是这一个计策会失败,要是我们会在行动之间露出破绽,那么还是不要尝试的好。为了预防失败,我们应该另外再想一个万全之策。且慢!让我想来,我们可以对你们两人的胜负打赌;啊,有了,你在跟他交手的时候,必须使出你全副的精神,使他疲于奔命,等他口干舌燥,要讨水喝的当儿,我就为他预备好一杯毒酒,万一他逃过了你的毒剑,也逃不过我们这一着。且慢!什么声音?

【王后上。

国王 啊,亲爱的王后!

王后 一桩祸事刚刚到来,又有一桩接踵而至。雷欧提斯,你的妹妹掉在水里溺死了。

雷欧提斯 溺死了!啊!在哪儿?

王后 在小溪之旁,斜生着一株杨柳,它的毵毵的枝叶倒映在明镜一样的水流之中。她一个人到那边去,用毛茛、荨麻、雏菊和长颈兰编成了一个个花圈,替她自己做成了奇异的装饰。她爬上一根横垂的树枝,想要把她的花冠挂在上面。就在这时候,树枝折断了,连人带花一起落下呜咽的溪水里。她的衣服四散展开,使她暂时像人鱼一样漂浮于水上。她嘴里还断断续续唱着古旧的谣曲,好像一点不感觉到什么痛苦,又好像她本来就是生长在水中的一般。可是不多一会儿,她的衣服给水浸得重起来了,这可怜的人儿歌还没有唱完,就已经沉了下去。

雷欧提斯 唉!那么她溺死了吗?

王后 溺死了!溺死了!

雷欧提斯 太多的水淹没了你的身体,可怜的奥菲利娅,所以我必须忍住我的眼泪。可是人类的常情是不能遏阻的,我掩饰不了心中的悲哀,只好顾不得惭愧了。当我们的眼泪干了以后,我们的妇人之仁也是会随着消灭的。再会,陛下!我有一段炎炎欲焚的烈火般的说话,可是我的傻气的眼泪把它浇熄了。(下)

国王 让我们跟上去,乔特鲁德。我好容易才把他的怒气平息了一下,现在我怕又要把它挑起来了。快让我们跟上去吧。(同下)

第五幕

第一场
墓　地

【二小丑携锄锹等上。

小丑甲　她存心自己脱离人世,却要照基督徒的仪式下葬吗?

小丑乙　我对你说是的,所以你赶快把她的坟掘好了吧;验尸官已经验明她的死状,宣布应该按照基督徒的仪式把她下葬。

小丑甲 这可怪了,难道她是因为自卫而跳下水里的吗?

小丑乙 他们验明是这样的。

小丑甲 那么故意杀人也可以罪从末减了。因为问题是这样的:要是我有意投水自杀,那必须成立一个行为。一个行为可以分为三部分,那就是干、行,做。所以,她是有意投水自杀的。

小丑乙 哎,你听我说——

小丑甲 对不起。这儿是水。好,这儿站着人。好,要是这个人跑到这个水里,把他自己淹死了,那么,不管他自己愿不愿意,总是他自己跑下去的。你听好了没有?可是要是那水走到他的身上把他淹死了,那就不是他自己把自己淹死。所以,对于他自己的死无罪的人,并没有杀害他自己的生命。

小丑乙 法律上是这样说的吗?

小丑甲 嗯,是的,这是验尸官的验尸法。

小丑乙 说一句老实话,要是这个死的不是一位贵家女子,他们绝不会按照基督徒的仪式把她下葬的。

小丑甲 对了,你说得有理。有财有势的人,就是要投河上吊,比起他们同教的基督徒来也可以格外通融,世上的事情真是太不公平! 来,我的锄头。古时候没有什么绅士,只有一些种地的、开沟的、掘坟的人。他们都继承着亚当的行业。

小丑乙 他是一个绅士吗?

小丑甲　什么？你是个异教徒吗？你有没有读过《圣经》？《圣经》上说"亚当掘地"。让我再问你一个问题；要是你回答得不对，那么你就承认你自己——

小丑乙　你问吧。

小丑甲　谁造得比泥水匠、船匠或是木匠更坚固？

小丑乙　造绞架的人。因为一千个寄寓在这屋子里的人都已经先后死去，它还是站在那儿动都不动。

小丑甲　我很欢喜你的聪明，真的。绞架是很合适的，可是它怎么是合适的？它对于那些有罪的人是合适的。你说绞架造得比教堂还坚固，说这样的话是罪过的，所以，绞架对于你是合适的。来，重新说过。

小丑乙　谁造得比泥水匠、船匠或是木匠更坚固？

小丑甲　嗯，你回答了这个问题，我就让你下工。

小丑乙　呃，现在我知道了。

小丑甲　说吧。

小丑乙　真的,我可回答不出来。

【哈姆雷特及霍拉旭上,立远处。

小丑甲　别绞尽你的脑筋了,懒驴子是打杀也走不快的。下回有人问你这个问题的时候,你就对他说,"掘坟的人",因为他造的房子是可以一直住到世界末日的。去,到酒店里去给我倒一杯酒来。(小丑乙下;小丑甲且掘且歌。)

　　　年轻时候最爱偷情,
　　　　　觉得那事很有趣味;
　　　规规矩矩学做好人,
　　　　　在我看来太无意义。

哈姆雷特　这家伙难道对于他的工作一点没有什么感觉?在掘坟的时候还会唱歌吗?

霍拉旭　他做惯了这种事,所以不以为意。

哈姆雷特　正是。不大劳动的手,它的感觉要比较灵敏一些。

小丑甲　(唱)

　　谁料如今岁月潜移,

　　老景催人急于星火,

　　两腿挺直,一命归西,

　　世上原来不曾有我。(掷起一骷髅)

哈姆雷特　那个骷髅里面曾经有一条舌头,它还会唱歌哩;瞧这家伙把它摔在地上,好像它是第一个杀人凶手该隐的颚骨似的[①]!它也许是一个政客的头颅,现在却让这蠢货把它丢来踢去。也许他生前是个偷天换日的好手,你看是不是?

霍拉旭　也许是的,殿下。

哈姆雷特　也许是一个朝臣,他会说,"早安,大人!您好,大人"!也许他就是某大人,嘴里称赞某大人的马好,心里却想把它讨了来,你看是不是?

霍拉旭　是,殿下。

哈姆雷特　啊,正是。现在却让蛆虫伴寝,他的下巴也脱掉了,一柄工役的锄头可以在他头上敲来敲去。从这种

[①]　该隐(Cain),亚当之长子,杀其弟亚伯(Abel),见《旧约·创世记》。

变化上,我们大可看透生命无常的消息。难道这些枯骨生前受了那么多的教养,死后却只好给人家当木块一般抛着玩吗?想起来真是怪不好受的。

小丑甲 (唱)

锄头一柄,铁铲一把,

殓衾一方掩面遮身;

挖松泥土深深掘下,

掘了个坑招待客人。(掷起另一骷髅)

哈姆雷特 又是一个。谁知道那不会是一个律师的骷髅?他的舞文弄法的手段、颠倒黑白的雄辩,现在都到哪儿去了?为什么他让这个放肆的家伙用龌龊的铁铲敲他的脑壳,不去控告他一个殴打罪?哼!这家伙生前也许曾经买下许多的地产,开口闭口用那些条文、具结、罚款、证据、赔偿一类的名词吓人,现在他的脑壳里塞满了泥土,这就算是他所取得的最后的赔偿了吗?除了两张契约大小的一方地面以外,谁能替他证明他究竟有多少地产?这一抔黄土,就是他所有的一切了吗?哈?

霍拉旭 这就是他所有的一切了,殿下。

哈姆雷特 我要去跟这家伙谈谈。喂,这是谁的坟墓?

小丑甲 我的,先生,——

挖松泥土深深掘下,

掘了个坑招待客人。

哈姆雷特 胡说！坟墓是死人睡的，怎么说是你的？你给什么人掘这坟墓？是个男人吗？

小丑甲 不是男人，先生。

哈姆雷特 那么是什么女人？

小丑甲 也不是女人。

哈姆雷特 不是男人，也不是女人，那么谁葬在这里面？

小丑甲 先生，她本来是一个女人，可是上帝安息她的灵魂，她已经死了。

哈姆雷特 这混蛋倒会分辨得这样清楚！我们讲话必须直接痛快，要是这样含含糊糊的，那可把人烦死了。凭着上帝发誓，霍拉旭，我觉得这三年来，时世变得越发不成样子了，一个平民也敢用他的脚指头去踢痛贵人的后跟。——你做这掘墓的营生，已经多久了？

小丑甲 我开始干这营生，是在我们的老王爷哈姆雷特打败福丁布拉斯那一天。

哈姆雷特 那是多少时候以前的事？

小丑 你不知道吗？每一个傻子都知道的，那正是小哈姆雷特出世的那一天，就是那个发了疯给他们送到英国去的。

哈姆雷特 嗯，对了，为什么他们叫他到英国去？

小丑甲 就是因为他发了疯呀。他到了英国去，他的疯病就会好的，即使疯病不会好，在那边也没有什么关系。

哈姆雷特 为什么？

小丑甲　英国人不会把他当作疯子；他们都是跟他一样疯的。

哈姆雷特　他怎么会发疯？

小丑甲　人家说得很奇怪。

哈姆雷特　怎么奇怪？

小丑甲　他们说他神经有了毛病。

哈姆雷特　一个人埋在地下，要经过多少时候才会腐烂？

小丑甲　假如他不是在未死以前就已经腐烂——现在多的是害杨梅疮死去的尸体，简直抬都抬不下去——他可以过八九年，一个硝皮匠在九年以内不会腐烂。

哈姆雷特　为什么他要比别人长久一些？

小丑甲　因为，先生，他的皮硝得比人家的硬，可以长久不透水。尸体一碰到水，是最会腐烂的。这儿又是一个骷髅，这骷髅已经埋在地下二十三年了。

哈姆雷特　它是谁的骷髅？

小丑甲　是个婊子养的疯小子，你猜是谁？

哈姆雷特　不，我猜不出。

小丑甲　这个遭瘟的疯小子！他有一次把一瓶葡萄酒倒在我的头上。这一个骷髅，先生，是国王的弄人郁利克的骷髅。

哈姆雷特　这就是他！

小丑甲　正是他。

哈姆雷特　让我看。（取骷髅）唉，可怜的郁利克！霍拉旭，我认识他,他是一个最会开玩笑,非常富于想象力的家伙。他曾经把我负在背上一千次;现在我一想起来,却忍不住胸头作恶。这儿本来有两片嘴唇,我不知吻过它们多少次。——现在你还会把人挖苦吗?你还会蹦蹦跳跳、逗人发笑吗?你还会唱歌吗?你还会随口编造一些笑话,说得一座人捧腹吗?你没有留下一个笑话,讥笑你自己吗?这样垂头丧气了吗?现在你给我到小姐的闺房里去,对她说,凭她脸上的脂粉搽得一寸厚,到后来总是要变成这个样子的。你用这样的话告诉她,看她笑不笑吧。霍拉旭,请你告诉我一件事情。

霍拉旭 什么事情,殿下?

哈姆雷特 你想亚历山大在地下也是这一副形状吗?

霍拉旭 也是这样。

哈姆雷特 也是有同样的臭味吗?呸!(掷下骷髅)

霍拉旭 也是有同样的臭味的,殿下。

哈姆雷特 谁知道我们将来会变成一些什么下贱的东西,霍拉旭!要是我们用想象推测下去,谁知道亚历山大的高贵的尸体,不就是塞在酒桶口上的泥土?

霍拉旭 那未免太想入非非了。

哈姆雷特 不,一点不,这是很可能的我们可以这样想:亚历山大死了,亚历山大埋葬了,亚历山大化为尘土,人们把尘土做成烂泥,那么为什么亚历山大所变成的烂泥,不会被人家拿来塞在啤酒桶的口上呢?

恺撒死了,你尊严的尸体

　　也许变了泥把破墙填砌;

　　啊! 他从前是何等的英雄,

　　现在只好替人挡雨遮风!

可是不要作声! 不要作声! 站开。国王来了。

【教士等列队上;众舁奥菲利娅尸体前行;雷欧提斯及诸送葬者、国王、王后及侍从等随后。

哈姆雷特　王后和朝臣们也都来了,他们是送什么人下葬呢? 仪式又是这样草率的? 瞧上去好像他们所送葬的那个人,是自杀而死的,同时又是个很有身份的人,让我们躲在一旁瞧瞧他们。(与霍拉旭退后)

雷欧提斯　还有些什么仪式?

哈姆雷特　(向霍拉旭旁白)那是雷欧提斯,一个很高贵的青年。听好。

雷欧提斯　还有些什么仪式?

教士甲　她的葬礼已经超过了她所应得的名分。她的死状很是可疑,倘不是因为我们迫于权力,按例就该把她安葬在圣地以外,直到最后审判的喇叭吹召她起来。我们不但不应该替她念祷告,并且还要用砖瓦、碎石丢在她坟上。可是现在我们已经允许给她处女的葬礼,用花圈盖在她的身上,替她撒播鲜花,鸣钟送她入土,这还不够吗?

雷欧提斯 难道不能再有其他的仪式了吗?

教士甲 不能再有其他的仪式了。要是我们为她奏安灵乐,就像对于一般平安死去的灵魂一样,那就要亵渎了教规。

雷欧提斯 把她放到泥土里去。愿她的娇美无瑕的肉体上,生出芬芳馥郁的紫罗兰来!我告诉你,你这下贱的教士,我的妹妹将要做一个天使,你死了却要在地狱里呼号。

哈姆雷特 什么!美丽的奥菲利娅吗?

王后 好花是应当撒在美人身上的;永别了!(撒花)我本来希望你做我的哈姆雷特的妻子;这些鲜花本来要铺在你的新床上,亲爱的女郎,谁想得到我要把它们撒在你的坟上!

雷欧提斯 啊!但愿千百重的灾祸,降临在害得你精神错乱的那个该死的恶人的头上!等一等,不要就把泥土盖上去,让我再把她拥抱一次。(跳下墓中)现在把你们的泥土倒下来,把死的和活的一起掩埋了吧,让这块平地上堆起一座高山,那古老的丕利恩和苍秀插天的俄林波斯都要俯伏在它的足下①。

哈姆雷特 (上前)哪一个人的心里装载得下这样沉重的悲伤?哪一个人的哀恸的词句,可以使天上的流星惊疑

---

① 丕利恩(Pelion)、俄林波斯(Olympus),均为希腊北境山名。

止步？那是我，丹麦王子哈姆雷特！（跳下墓中。）
雷欧提斯　魔鬼抓了你的灵魂去！（将哈姆雷特揪住。）
哈姆雷特　你祷告错了。请你不要拉住我的头颈，因为我虽然不是一个暴躁易怒的人，可是我的火性发作起来，是很危险的，你还是不要激恼我吧。放开你的手！
国王　把他们扯开！
王后　哈姆雷特！哈姆雷特！
众人　殿下，公子——
霍拉旭　好殿下，安静点儿。（侍从等分开二人，二人自墓中出）

哈姆雷特　嘿，我愿意为了这个题目跟他决斗，直到我的眼皮不再眨动。
王后　啊，我的孩子！什么题目？

哈姆雷特 我爱奥菲利娅,四万个兄弟的爱合起来,还抵不过我对她的爱。你愿意为她干些什么事情?

国王 啊!他是个疯人,雷欧提斯。

王后 看在上帝的情分上,不要跟他教真。

哈姆雷特 哼,让我瞧瞧你会干些什么事。你会哭吗?你会打架吗?你会绝食吗?你会撕破你自己的身体吗?你会喝一大缸醋吗?你会吃一条鳄鱼吗?我都做得到。你是到这儿来哭泣的吗?你跳下她的坟墓里,是要当面羞辱我吗?你跟她活埋在一起,我也会跟她活埋在一起;要是你还要夸说什么高山大岭,那么让他们把几百万亩的泥土堆在我们身上,直到我们的地面深陷到赤热的地心,让巍峨的奥萨山在相形之下变得只像一个瘤那么大小吧①!嘿,你会吹,我就不会吹吗?

王后 这不过是他一时的疯话。他的疯病一发作起来,总是这个样子的;可是等一会儿他就会安静下来,正像母鸽孵育它那一双金羽的雏鸽的时候一样温和了。

哈姆雷特 听我说,老兄;你为什么这样对待我?我一向都是爱你的。可是这些都不用说了,有本领的,随他干什么事吧;猫总是要叫,狗总是要闹的。(下)

国王 好霍拉旭,请你跟住他。(霍拉旭下)(向雷欧提斯)记着我们昨天晚上所说的话,格外忍耐点儿吧;我们马

---

① 奥萨(Ossa),亦希腊山名,与丕利恩及俄林波斯相近。

上就可以实行我们的办法。好乔特鲁德,叫几个人好好看守你的儿子。这一个坟上将要植立一块永久的墓碑。平静的时间不久就会到来,现在我们必须耐着心把一切安排。(同下)

第二场
城堡中的厅堂

【哈姆雷特及霍拉旭上。

哈姆雷特　这个题目已经讲完,现在我可以让你知道另外一段事情。你还记得当初的一切经过情形吗?

霍拉旭　记得,殿下!

哈姆雷特　在我的心里有一种战争,使我不能睡眠;我觉得我的处境比套在脚镣里的叛变的水手还要难堪。我们应该知道,我们乘着一时的猛浪,往往反而可以做出一些为我们的深谋密虑所做不成功的事。从这一点上,我们可以看出来,无论我们怎样辛苦图谋,我们的结果却早已有一种冥冥中的力量把它布置好了。

霍拉旭　这是毋庸置疑的。

哈姆雷特　从我的舱里起来,一件航海的宽衣罩在我的身上,我在黑暗之中摸索着找寻他们的所在,果然给我达到目的,摸到了他们的包裹。拿着它回到我自己的地方,疑心使我忘记了礼貌,我大胆地拆开了他们的公文,在那里面,霍拉旭,——啊,堂皇的诡计!——我发现一道切实的命令,借了许多好听的理由为名,掩藏着狰狞丑恶的鬼蜮的面貌,说是为了丹麦和英国双方的利益,必须不等磨好利斧,立即枭下我的首级。

霍拉旭 有这等事?

哈姆雷特 这一封就是原来的国书,你有空的时候可以仔细读一下。可是你愿意听我告诉你后来我怎么办吗?

霍拉旭 请您告诉我。

哈姆雷特 在这样重重诡计的包围之中,我的脑筋不等我定下心来思索,就开始活动起来了。我坐下来另外写了一通官样文章的国书。从前我曾经抱着跟我们那些政治家同样的意见,认为文章写得好是一件有失体面的事,总是想竭力忘记这一种学问,可是现在它却对我有了大大的用处。你知道我写些什么话吗?

霍拉旭 嗯,殿下。

哈姆雷特 我以国王的名义,向英王提出恳切的要求,因为英国是他忠心的藩属,因为两国之间的友谊,必须让它像棕榈树一样发荣繁茂,因为和平的女神必须永远戴着她的荣冠,沟通彼此的情感,以及许许多多诸如此类的重要理由,请他在读完这一封信以后,不要有任何的迟疑,立刻把那两个传书的来使处死,不让他们有从容忏悔的时间。

霍拉旭　可是国书上没有盖印,那怎么办呢?

哈姆雷特　啊,就在这件事上,也可以看出一切都是上天预先注定。我的衣袋里恰巧藏着我父亲的私印,它跟丹麦的国玺是一个式样的;我把伪造的国书照着原来的样子折好,签上名字,盖上印玺,把它小心封好,归还原处,一点不露出破绽来。下一天就遇见了海盗,那以后的情形,你早已知道了。

霍拉旭　这样说来,吉尔登斯吞和罗森格兰兹是去送死的了?

哈姆雷特　哎,朋友,他们本来是自己钻求这件差使的。我在良心上没有对不起他们的地方,是他们自己的阿谀献媚断送了他们的生命。两个强敌猛烈争斗的时候,不自量力的微弱之辈,却去插身在他们的中间,这样的事情是最危险不过的。

霍拉旭　嘿,这是一个什么国王!

哈姆雷特　你想,我是不是应该——他杀死了我的父王,奸污了我的母亲,篡夺了我的嗣位的权利,用这种诡计谋害我的生命,凭良心说我是不是应该亲手向他报仇雪恨?上天会不会嘉许我替世上剪除这一个戕害天性的蟊贼,不让他继续为非作歹?

霍拉旭　他不久就会从英国得到消息,知道这一回事情产生了怎样的结果。

哈姆雷特　时间虽然很局促,可是我已经抓住眼前这一刻工夫;一个人的生命可以在说一个"一"字的一刹那之间了结。可是我很后悔,好霍拉旭,不该在雷欧提斯之前失去了自制;因为他所遭遇的惨痛,正是我自己的怨愤的影子。我要取得他的好感。可是他倘不是那样夸大他的悲哀,我也绝不会动起那么大的火性来的。

霍拉旭　不要作声!谁来了?

【奥斯里克上。

奥斯里克　殿下,欢迎您回到丹麦来!

哈姆雷特　谢谢您,先生。(向霍拉旭旁白)你认识这头水苍蝇吗?

霍拉旭 （向哈姆雷特旁白）不，殿下。

哈姆雷特 （向霍拉旭旁白）那是你的运气，因为认识他是一件丢脸的事。他有许多肥田美壤，要是一头畜生做了万兽之王，他也会在御座之前低头吃草。他是个满身泥土气的伧夫。

奥斯里克 殿下，您要是有空的话，我奉陛下之命，要来告诉您一件事情。

哈姆雷特 先生，我愿意恭聆大教。您的帽子是应该戴在头上的，您还是戴上去吧。

奥斯里克 谢谢殿下，天气真热。

哈姆雷特 不，相信我，天冷得很，在吹北风哩。

奥斯里克 真的有点儿冷，殿下。

哈姆雷特 可是对于像我这样的体质，我觉得这一种天气却是闷热得厉害。

奥斯里克 对了，殿下。真是说不出来的闷热。可是，殿下，陛下叫我来通知您一声，他已经为您下了一个很大的赌注了。殿下，事情是这样的——

哈姆雷特 请您不要忘记了您的帽子。

奥斯里克 不，殿下，我还是这样舒服些，真的。殿下，雷欧提斯新近到我们的宫廷里来。相信我，他是一位完善的绅士，充满着最卓越的特点，他的礼貌非常温雅，他的谈吐又是非常渊博。说一句发自内心的话，他是上流社会的指南针，因为在他身上可以找到一个绅士所应有的品性的总汇。

哈姆雷特　先生,他对于您这一番描写,的确可以当之无愧。虽然我知道,要是把他的好处一件一件列举出来,不但我们的记忆将要因此而淆乱,交不出一篇正确的账目来,而且他这一艘满帆的快船,也绝不是我们失舵之舟所能追及。可是,凭着真诚的赞美而言,我认为他是一个才德优异的人,他的高超的禀赋是那样稀有而罕见,说一句真心的话,除了在他的镜子里以外,再也找不到第二个跟他同样的人,纷纷追踪稀迹之辈,不过是他的影子而已。

奥斯里克　殿下把他说得一点不错。

哈姆雷特　您的用意呢?为什么我们要用尘俗的呼吸,嘘在这位绅士的身上呢?

奥斯里克　殿下?

霍拉旭　就是您自己所用的语言,到了别人嘴里,您就听不懂了吗?

哈姆雷特　您向我提起这位绅士的名字,是什么意思?

奥斯里克　雷欧提斯吗?

霍拉旭　他的嘴里已经变得空空洞洞,因为他的那些好听话都说完了。

哈姆雷特　正是雷欧提斯。

奥斯里克　我知道您不是不知道——

哈姆雷特　您既然知道,那就很好。虽然,即使你不知道对我也没有什么不好。好,您怎么说?

奥斯里克 您不是不知道雷欧提斯有些什么特长——

哈姆雷特 那我可不敢说,因为也许人家会疑心我有意跟他比并高下。可是要知道一个人的底细,应该先知道他自己。

奥斯里克 殿下,我的意思是说他的武艺。人家都称赞他的本领一时无两。

哈姆雷特 他会使些什么武器?

奥斯里克 长剑和短刀。

哈姆雷特 他会使这两种武器吗?很好。

奥斯里克 殿下,王上已经用六匹巴巴里的骏马跟他打赌。在他的一方面,照我所知道的,是六柄法国的宝剑和好刀,连同一切鞘带之类的附件,其中有三柄的革绶尤其珍奇可爱,跟剑柄配得非常合适,式样非常精致,花纹非常富丽。

哈姆雷特 您所说的革绶是什么东西?

霍拉旭 我知道您要听懂他的说话,非得翻查一下注解不可。

奥斯里克 殿下,革绶就是剑柄上的皮带。

哈姆雷特 好,说下去。六匹巴巴里骏马对六柄法国宝剑,附件在内,外加三条花纹富丽的革绶。为什么两方面要下这样的赌注呢?

奥斯里克 殿下,王上跟他打赌,要是你们两人交手起来,在十二个回合之中,他至多不过有三个回合占据到您的上风。殿下要是答应的话,马上就可以试一试。

哈姆雷特 要是我不答应呢?

奥斯里克 殿下,我的意思是说,王上要请您去跟他当面比较高低。

哈姆雷特 先生,我还要在这儿厅堂里散散步。您去回陛下说,现在是我一天之中休息的时间。叫他们把比赛用的钝剑预备好了,要是这位绅士愿意,王上也不改变他的意见的话,我愿意尽力为他博取一次胜利。万一不幸失败,那我也不过丢了一次脸,给他剁了两下。

奥斯里克 我就是照这样去回话吗?

哈姆雷特 您就照这个意思去说,随便您再加上一些什么花巧的句子都行。

奥斯里克 那么,殿下,我告辞了。

哈姆雷特 再见,再见。(奥斯里克下)

霍拉旭 这一头小鸭子顶着壳儿逃走了。

哈姆雷特 他在母亲怀抱里的时候,也要先把他母亲的奶头恭维了几句,然后吮吸。像他这一类靠着一些繁文缛节撑撑场面的家伙,正是愚妄的世人所醉心的。他们的浅薄的牙慧使傻瓜和聪明人同样受他们的欺骗,可是一经试验,他们的水泡就爆破了。

【一贵族上。

贵族 殿下,陛下刚才叫奥斯里克来向您传话,知道您在这儿厅上等候他的旨意。他叫我再来问您一声,您是仍旧愿意跟雷欧提斯比剑,还是慢慢再说?

哈姆雷特 我没有改变我的初心,一切服从王上的旨意。现在也好,无论什么时候都好,只要他方便,我总是随时准备着,除非我丧失了现在所有的力气。

贵族 王上、娘娘,跟其他的人都要到这儿来了。

哈姆雷特 他们来得正好。

贵族 娘娘请您在开始比赛以前,对雷欧提斯客气点儿。

哈姆雷特 我愿意服从她的教诲。(贵族下)

霍拉旭 殿下,您在这一回打赌中间,多半要失败的。

哈姆雷特 我想我不会失败。自从他到法国去了以后,我练习得很勤。我一定可以把他打败。可是你不知道我的心里是多么不舒服,那也不用说了。

霍拉旭 啊,我的好殿下——

哈姆雷特 那不过是一种傻气的心理;可是一个女人也许会因为这种莫名其妙的疑虑而惶惑。

霍拉旭 要是您心里不愿意做一件事,那么就不要做吧。我可以去通知他们不用到这儿来,说您现在不能比赛。

哈姆雷特 不,我们不要害怕什么预兆,一头雀子的生死,都是命运预先注定的。注定在今天,就不会是明天;不是明天,就是今天;逃过了今天,明天还是逃不了,随时准备着就是了。一个人既然不知道他会留下些什么,那么早早脱身而去,不好吗?随它去。

【国王、王后、雷欧提斯、众贵族、奥斯里克及侍从等持钝剑等上。

国王 来,哈姆雷特,来,让我替你们两人和解和解。(牵雷欧提斯、哈姆雷特二人手使相握)

哈姆雷特 原谅我,雷欧提斯;我得罪了你,可是你是个堂堂男子,请你原谅我吧。这儿在场的众人都知道,你也一定听见人家说起,我是怎样为疯狂所害苦。凡是我的所作所为,足以伤害你的感情和荣誉,挑起你的愤激来的,我现在声明都是我在疯狂中犯下的过失。难道哈姆雷特会做对不起雷欧提斯的事吗?哈姆雷特不会做这种事。要是哈姆雷特在丧失他自己的心神的时候,做了对不起雷欧提斯的事,那样的事不是哈姆雷特做的,哈姆雷特不能承认。那么是谁做的呢?是他的疯狂。既然是这样,那么哈姆雷特也是属于受害的一方,他的疯狂是可怜的哈姆雷特的敌人。当着在座众人之前,我承认我在无心中射出的箭,误伤了我的兄弟;我现在要向他请求大度包涵,宽恕我的不是出于故意的罪恶。

雷欧提斯　我的气愤虽然已经平息,可是几句道歉的说话,却不能使我抛弃我的复仇的誓愿;除非有什么为众人所敬仰的长者,告诉我可以跟你捐除宿怨,指出这样的事是有前例可援的,不至于损害我的名誉,那时我才可以跟你归言于好。可是现在我愿意抛弃一切的猜疑,诚心接受你的友好的表示。

哈姆雷特　我绝对信任你的诚意,愿意奉陪你举行这一次友谊的比赛。把钝剑给我们。来。

雷欧提斯　来,给我一柄。

哈姆雷特　雷欧提斯,我的剑术荒疏已久,不是你的对手。正像最黑暗的夜里一颗吐耀的明星一般,彼此相形之下,一定更显得你的本领的高强。

雷欧提斯　殿下不要取笑。

哈姆雷特　不,我可以举手起誓,这不是取笑。

国王　奥斯里克,把钝剑分给他们。哈姆雷特侄儿,你知道我们怎样打赌吗?

哈姆雷特　我知道,陛下;您把赌注下在实力较弱的一方了。

国王 我想我的判断不会有错。你们两人的技术我都领教过;现在我们不过要看看他比从前进步得怎么样。

雷欧提斯 这一柄太重了,换一柄给我。

哈姆雷特 这一柄我很满意。这些钝剑都是同样长短的吗?

奥斯里克 是,殿下。(二人准备比剑)

国王 替我在那桌子上斟下几杯酒。要是哈姆雷特击中了第一剑或是第二剑,或者在第三次交锋的时候争得上风,让所有的碉堡上一齐鸣起炮来;国王将要饮酒慰劳哈姆雷特,他还要拿一颗比丹麦四代国王戴在王冠上的更贵重的珍珠丢在酒杯里。把杯子给我;鼓声一起,喇叭就接着吹响,通知外面的炮手,让炮声震彻天地,报告这一个消息,"现在国王为哈姆雷特祝饮了"!来,开始比赛吧;你们在场裁判的都要留心看好。

哈姆雷特 请了。

雷欧提斯 请了,殿下。(二人比赛)

哈姆雷特 一剑。

雷欧提斯 不,没有击中。

哈姆雷特 请裁判员公断。

奥斯里克 中了,很明显的一剑。

雷欧提斯 好,再来。

国王 且慢,拿酒来。哈姆雷特,这一颗珍珠是你的,祝你

健康!把这一杯酒给他。(喇叭齐奏。内鸣炮)

哈姆雷特 让我先赛完这一局。暂时把它放在一旁。来。(二人比赛)又是一剑。你怎么说?

雷欧提斯 我承认给你碰着了。

国王 我们的孩子一定会胜利。

王后 他身体太胖,有些喘不过气来。来,哈姆雷特,把我的手巾拿去,揩干你额上的汗。王后为你饮下这一杯酒,祝你的胜利了,哈姆雷特。

哈姆雷特 好妈妈!

国王 乔特鲁德,不要喝。

王后 我要喝的,陛下。请您原谅我。

国王 (旁白)这一杯酒里有毒。太迟了!

哈姆雷特 母亲,我现在还不敢喝酒。等一等再喝吧。

王后 来,让我揩揩干净你的脸孔。

雷欧提斯 陛下,现在我一定要击中他了。

国王 我怕你击不中他。

雷欧提斯 (旁白)可是我的良心却不赞成我干这件事。

哈姆雷特 来,再受我一剑,雷欧提斯。你怎么一点不上劲的?请你使出你全身本领来吧;我怕你在开我的玩笑哩。

雷欧提斯 你这样说吗?来。(二人比剑)

奥斯里克 两边都没有中。

雷欧提斯 受我这一剑!(雷欧提斯挺剑刺伤哈姆雷特;二

人在争夺中彼此手中之剑各为对方夺去,哈姆雷特以夺来之剑刺雷欧提斯,雷欧提斯亦受伤)

国王 分开他们!他们动起火性来了。

哈姆雷特 来,再试一下。(王后倒地)

奥斯里克 哎哟,瞧王后怎么样啦!

霍拉旭 他们两人都在流血。您怎么啦,殿下?

奥斯里克 您怎么啦,雷欧提斯?

雷欧提斯 唉,奥斯里克,正像一头自投罗网的山鹬,我用诡计害人,反而害了自己,这也是我应得的报应。

哈姆雷特 王后怎么样啦?

国王 她看见他们流血,昏了过去了。

王后 不,不,那杯酒,那杯酒,——啊,我的亲爱的哈姆雷特!那杯酒,那杯酒;我中毒了。(死)

哈姆雷特 啊,奸恶的阴谋!喂!把门锁上了!阴谋!查出来是哪一个干的。(雷欧提斯倒地)

雷欧提斯 凶手就在这儿,哈姆雷特。哈姆雷特,你已经不能活命了;世上没有一种药可以救治你,不到半小时,你就要死去。那杀人的凶器就在你的手里,它的锋利的刃上还涂着毒药。这奸恶的诡计已经回转来害了我自己;瞧!我躺在这儿,再也不会站起来了。你的母亲也中了毒。我说不下去了。国王——国王——都是他一个人的罪恶。

哈姆雷特 锋利的刃上还涂着毒药!——好,毒药,发挥你

的力量吧!(刺国王)

众人 反了!反了!

国王 啊!帮帮我,朋友们。我不过受了点伤。

哈姆雷特 好,你这败坏伦常,嗜杀贪淫,万恶不赦的丹麦奸王!喝干了这杯毒药——你那颗珍珠是在这儿吗?——跟我的母亲一道去吧!(国王死)

雷欧提斯 他死得应该,这毒药是他亲手调下的。尊贵的哈姆雷特,让我们互相宽恕。我不怪你杀死我和我的父亲,你也不要怪我杀死你!(死)

哈姆雷特 愿上天赦免你的错误!我也跟着你来了。我死了,霍拉旭。不幸的王后,别了!你们这些看见这一幕意外的惨变而战栗失色的无言的观众,倘不是因为死神的拘捕不给人片刻的留滞,啊!我可以告诉你们——可是随它去吧。霍拉旭,我死了,你还活在世上。请你把我的行事的始末根由昭告世人,解除他们的疑惑。

霍拉旭 不,我虽然是个丹麦人,可是在精神上我却更是个古代的罗马人。这儿还留剩着一些毒药。

哈姆雷特 你是个汉子,把那杯子给我。放手!凭着上天起誓,你必须把它给我。啊,上帝!霍拉旭,我一死之后,要是世人不明白这一切事情的真相,我的名誉将要永远蒙着怎样的损伤!你倘然爱我,请你暂时牺牲一下天堂上的幸福,留在这一个冷酷的世间,替我传述我的故事吧。(内军队自远处行进及鸣炮声)这是哪儿来的战场上的声音?

奥斯里克 年轻的福丁布拉斯从波兰奏凯班,这是他对英国来的钦使所发的礼炮。

哈姆雷特 啊!我死了,霍拉旭。猛烈的毒药已经克服了我的精神,我不能活着听见英国来的消息。可是我可以预言福丁布拉斯将被推戴为王,他已经得到我这临死之人的同意。你可以把这儿所发生的一切事实告诉他。此外唯余沉默。(死)

霍拉旭 一颗高贵的心现在碎裂了!晚安,亲爱的王子,愿成群的天使们用歌唱抚慰你安息!——为什么鼓声越来越近了?(内军队行进声)

【福丁布拉斯、英国使臣及余人等上。

福丁布拉斯 这一场比赛在什么地方举行?

霍拉旭 你们要看些什么?要是你们想知道一些惊人的惨事,那么不用再到别处找了。

福丁布拉斯 好一场惊心动魄的屠杀!啊,骄傲的死神!你用这样残忍的手腕,一下子杀死了这许多王裔贵胄,在你的永久的幽窟里,将要有一席多么丰美的盛宴!

使臣甲 这一个景象太惨了。我们从英国奉命来此,本来是要回复这儿的王上,告诉他我们已经遵从他的命令,把罗森格兰兹和吉尔登斯吞两人处死。不幸我们来迟了一步,那应该听我们说话的耳朵已经没有知觉了,我们还希望从谁的嘴里得到一声感谢呢?

霍拉旭　即使他能够向你们开口说话,他也不会感谢你们,他从来不曾命令你们把他们处死。可是既然你们都来得这样凑巧,有的刚从波兰回来,有的刚从英国到来,恰好看见这一幕流血的惨剧,那么请你们叫人把这几个尸体抬起来放在高台上面,让大家可以看见,让我向那懵懂无所知的世人报告这些事情的发生经过。你们可以听到奸淫残杀,反常悖理的行为,冥冥中的判决,意外的屠戮,借手杀人的狡计,以及陷入自害的结局。这一切我都可以确确实实地告诉你们。

福丁布拉斯　让我们赶快听你说,所有最尊贵的人,都叫他们一起来吧。我在这一个国内本来也有继承王位的权利,现在国中无主,正是我要求这一个权利的机会。可是我虽然准备接受我的幸运,我的心里却充满了悲哀。

霍拉旭　关于那一点,我受死者的嘱托,也有一句话要说,他的意见是可以影响许多人的。可是在这人心惶惶的时候,让我还是先把这一切解释明白了,免得引起更多的不幸、阴谋和错误来。

福丁布拉斯　让四个将士把哈姆雷特像一个军人似的扛到台上,因为要是他能够践登王位,一定会成为一个贤明的君主的。为了表示对他的悲悼,我们要用军乐和战地的仪式,向他致敬。把这些尸体一起抬起来。这一种情形在战场上是不足为奇的,可是在宫廷之内,却是

非常的变故。去,叫兵士放起炮来。(奏丧礼进行曲。众舁尸同下。内鸣炮)

The Tragedy of Hamlet, Prince of Denmark

Characters

Claudius	King of Danmark
Hamlet	Son to the former King, and nephew to Claudius
Fortinbras	Prince of Norway
Horatio	Friend to Hamlet
Polonius	Lord Chamberlain
Laertes	Son to Polonius
Voltimand	Courtier
Cornelius	Courtier
Rosencrantz	Courtier
Guildenstern	Courtier
Osric	Courtier
Marcellus	Officer
Bernardo	Officer
Francisco	a Soldier
Reynaldo	Servant to Polonius
Lords	
Attendants	
Two Clowns	Grave-maker
Gertrude	Queen of Denmark, and mother to Hamlet
Ophelia	Daughter to Polonius

Lords, Ladies, Officers, Soldiers, Sailors, Messengers, and other Attendants. Ghost of Hamlet's Father

SCENE

Elsinore.

ACT1.

SCENE I.
Elsinore. A platform before the castle.

[*FRANCISCO at his post. Enter to him BERNARDO*]

BERNARDO:

Who's there?

BERNARDO:

Nay, answer me; stand, and unfold yourself.

BERNARDO:

Long live the king!

BERNARDO:

Bernardo?

BERNARDO:

He.

BERNARDO:

You come most carefully upon your hour.

BERNARDO:

'Tis now struck twelve; get thee to bed, Francisco.

BERNARDO:

For this relief much thanks; 'tis bitter cold,

And I am sick at heart.

BERNARDO:

Have you had quiet guard?

BERNARDO:

Not a mouse stirring.

BERNARDO:

Well, good night.

If you do meet Horatio and Marcellus,

The rivals of my watch, bid them make haste.

BERNARDO:

I think I hear them. Stand, ho! Who's there?

[*Enter HORATIO and MARCELLUS*]

HORATIO:

Friends to this ground.

MARCELLUS:

And liegemen to the Dane.

BERNARDO:

Give you good night.

MARCELLUS:

O, farewell, honest soldier;

Who hath relieved you?

BERNARDO:

Bernardo has my place.

Give you good night.

[*Exit*]

MARCELLUS:

Holla! Bernardo!

BERNARDO:

Say,

What, is Horatio there?

HORATIO:

A piece of him.

BERNARDO:

Welcome, Horatio; welcome, good Marcellus.

MARCELLUS:

What, has this thing appear'd again to-night?

BERNARDO:

I have seen nothing.

MARCELLUS:

Horatio says 'tis but our fantasy,

And will not let belief take hold of him

Touching this dreaded sight, twice seen of us.

Therefore I have entreated him along

With us to watch the minutes of this night;

That if again this apparition come,

He may approve our eyes and speak to it.

HORATIO:

Tush, tush, 'twill not appear.

BERNARDO:

Sit down awhile;

And let us once again assail your ears,

That are so fortified against our story

What we have two nights seen.

HORATIO:

Well, sit we down,

And let us hear Bernardo speak of this.

BERNARDO:

Last night of all,

When yond same star that's westward from the pole
Had made his course to illume that part of heaven
Where now it burns, Marcellus and myself,
The bell then beating one,—

Enter Ghost

MARCELLUS:

Peace, break thee off; look, where it comes again!

BERNARDO:

In the same figure, like the king that's dead.

MARCELLUS:

Thou art a scholar; speak to it, Horatio.

BERNARDO:

Looks it not like the king? mark it, Horatio.

HORATIO:

Most like; it harrows me with fear and wonder.

BERNARDO:

It would be spoke to.

MARCELLUS:

Question it, Horatio.

HORATIO:

What art thou that usurp'st this time of night,
Together with that fair and warlike form
In which the majesty of buriedDenmark

Did sometimes march? by heaven I charge thee, speak!

MARCELLUS:

It is offended.

BERNARDO:

See, it stalks away!

HORATIO:

Stay! speak, speak! I charge thee, speak!

[*Exit Ghost*]

MARCELLUS:

'Tis gone, and will not answer.

BERNARDO:

How now, Horatio! you tremble and look pale.

Is not this something more than fantasy?

What think you on't?

HORATIO:

Before my God, I might not this believe

Without the sensible and true avouch

Of mine own eyes.

MARCELLUS:

Is it not like the king?

HORATIO:

As thou art to thyself.

Such was the very armour he had on

When he the ambitiousNorway combated;

So frown'd he once, when, in an angry parle,

He smote the sledded Polacks on the ice.

'Tis strange.

MARCELLUS:

Thus twice before, and jump at this dead hour,

With martial stalk hath he gone by our watch.

HORATIO:

In what particular thought to work I know not;

But in the gross and scope of my opinion,

This bodes some strange eruption to our state.

MARCELLUS:

Good now, sit down, and tell me, he that knows,

Why this same strict and most observant watch

So nightly toils the subject of the land,

And why such daily cast of brazen cannon,

And foreign mart for implements of war;

Why such impress of shipwrights, whose sore task

Does not divide the Sunday from the week;

What might be toward, that this sweaty haste

Doth make the night joint-labourer with the day.

Who is't that can inform me?

HORATIO:

That can I;

At least, the whisper goes so. Our last king,
Whose image even but now appear'd to us,
Was, as you know, by Fortinbras of Norway,
Thereto prick'd on by a most emulate pride,
Dared to the combat; in which our valiant Hamlet—
For so this side of our known world esteem'd him—
Did slay this Fortinbras; who by a seal'd compact,
Well ratified by law and heraldry,
Did forfeit, with his life, all those his lands
Which he stood seized of, to the conqueror.
Against the which, a moiety competent
Was gaged by our king; which had return'd
To the inheritance of Fortinbras,
Had he been vanquisher; as, by the same covenant,
And carriage of the article design'd,
His fell to Hamlet. Now, sir, young Fortinbras,
Of unimproved mettle hot and full,
Hath in the skirts ofNorway here and there
Shark'd up a list of lawless resolutes,
For food and diet, to some enterprise

That hath a stomach in't; which is no other—
As it doth well appear unto our state—
But to recover of us, by strong hand
And terms compulsatory, those foresaid lands
So by his father lost; and this, I take it,
Is the main motive of our preparations,
The source of this our watch and the chief head
Of this post-haste and romage in the land.

BERNARDO:

I think it be no other but e'en so.
Well may it sort that this portentous figure
Comes armed through our watch; so like the king
That was and is the question of these wars.

HORATIO:

A mote it is to trouble the mind's eye.
In the most high and palmy state ofRome,
A little ere the mightiest Julius fell,
The graves stood tenantless and the sheeted dead
Did squeak and gibber in the Roman streets.
As stars with trains of fire and dews of blood,
Disasters in the sun; and the moist star
Upon whose influenceNeptune's empire stands
Was sick almost to doomsday with eclipse.

And even the like precurse of fierce events,
As harbingers preceding still the fates
And prologue to the omen coming on,
Have heaven and earth together demonstrated
Unto our climatures and countrymen. —
But soft, behold! lo, where it comes again!
Re-enter Ghost
I'll cross it, though it blast me. Stay, illusion!
If thou hast any sound, or use of voice,
Speak to me.
If there be any good thing to be done,
That may to thee do ease and grace to me,
Speak to me.

[*Cock crows*]

If thou art privy to thy country's fate,
Which, happily, foreknowing may avoid, O, speak!
Or if thou hast uphoarded in thy life
Extorted treasure in the womb of earth,
For which, they say, you spirits oft walk in death,
Speak of it; stay, and speak! Stop it, Marcellus.
MARCELLUS:

Shall I strike at it with my partisan?

HORATIO:

Do, if it will not stand.

BERNARDO:

'Tis here!

HORATIO:

'Tis here!

MARCELLUS:

'Tis gone!

[*Exit Ghost*]

We do it wrong, being so majestical,

To offer it the show of violence;

For it is, as the air, invulnerable,

And our vain blows malicious mockery.

BERNARDO:

It was about to speak, when the cock crew.

HORATIO:

And then it started like a guilty thing

Upon a fearful summons. I have heard,

The cock, that is the trumpet to the morn,

Doth with his lofty and shrill-sounding throat

Awake the god of day; and, at his warning,
Whether in sea or fire, in earth or air,
The extravagant and erring spirit hies
To his confine; and of the truth herein
This present object made probation.

MARCELLUS:

It faded on the crowing of the cock.
Some say that ever 'gainst that season comes
Wherein our Saviour's birth is celebrated,
The bird of dawning singeth all night long.
And then, they say, no spirit dares stir abroad;
The nights are wholesome; then no planets strike,
No fairy takes, nor witch hath power to charm,
So hallow'd and so gracious is the time.

HORATIO:

So have I heard and do in part believe it.
But, look, the morn, in russet mantle clad,
Walks o'er the dew of yon high eastward hill.
Break we our watch up; and by my advice,
Let us impart what we have seen to-night
Unto young Hamlet; for, upon my life,
This spirit, dumb to us, will speak to him.
Do you consent we shall acquaint him with it,

As needful in our loves, fitting our duty?

MARCELLUS:

Let's do't, I pray; and I this morning know
Where we shall find him most conveniently.

[*Exeunt*]

SCENE II.
A room of state in the castle.

[*Enter KING CLAUDIUS, QUEEN GERTRUDE, HAMLET, POLONIUS, LAERTES, VOLTIMAND, CORNELIUS, Lords, and Attendants*]

KING CLAUDIUS:

Though yet of Hamlet our dear brother's death
The memory be green, and that it us befitted
To bear our hearts in grief and our whole kingdom
To be contracted in one brow of woe,
Yet so far hath discretion fought with nature
That we with wisest sorrow think on him,

Together with remembrance of ourselves.
Therefore our sometime sister, now our queen,
The imperial jointress to this warlike state,
Have we, as 'twere with a defeated joy,—
With an auspicious and a dropping eye,
With mirth in funeral and with dirge in marriage,
In equal scale weighing delight and dole,—
Taken to wife; nor have we herein barr'd
Your better wisdoms, which have freely gone
With this affair along. For all, our thanks.
Now follows, that you know, young Fortinbras,
Holding a weak supposal of our worth,
Or thinking by our late dear brother's death
Our state to be disjoint and out of frame,
Colleagued with the dream of his advantage,
He hath not fail'd to pester us with message,
Importing the surrender of those lands
Lost by his father, with all bonds of law,
To our most valiant brother. So much for him.
Now for ourself and for this time of meeting.
Thus much the business is; we have here writ
ToNorway, uncle of young Fortinbras,—
Who, impotent and bed-rid, scarcely hears

Of this his nephew's purpose,—to suppress
His further gait herein; in that the levies,
The lists and full proportions, are all made
Out of his subject; and we here dispatch
You, good Cornelius, and you, Voltimand,
For bearers of this greeting to oldNorway;
Giving to you no further personal power
To business with the king, more than the scope
Of these delated articles allow.
Farewell, and let your haste commend your duty.

CORNELIUS VOLTIMAND:

In that and all things will we show our duty.

KING CLAUDIUS:

We doubt it nothing; heartily farewell.

[Exeunt VOLTIMAND and CORNELIUS]

And now, Laertes, what's the news with you?
You told us of some suit; what is't, Laertes?
You cannot speak of reason to the Dane,
And loose your voice; what wouldst thou beg, Laertes,
That shall not be my offer, not thy asking?
The head is not more native to the heart,

The hand more instrumental to the mouth,

Than is the throne ofDenmark to thy father.

What wouldst thou have, Laertes?

LAERTES:

My dread lord,

Your leave and favour to return toFrance;

From whence though willingly I came toDenmark,

To show my duty in your coronation,

Yet now, I must confess, that duty done,

My thoughts and wishes bend again towardFrance

And bow them to your gracious leave and pardon.

KING CLAUDIUS:

Have you your father's leave? What says Polonius?

LORD POLONIUS:

He hath, my lord, wrung from me my slow leave

By laboursome petition, and at last

Upon his will I seal'd my hard consent.

I do beseech you, give him leave to go.

KING CLAUDIUS:

Take thy fair hour, Laertes; time be thine,

And thy best graces spend it at thy will!

But now, my cousin Hamlet, and my son,—

HAMLET:

[*Aside*] A little more than kin, and less than kind.

KING CLAUDIUS:

How is it that the clouds still hang on you?

HAMLET:

Not so, my lord; I am too much i' the sun.

QUEEN GERTRUDE:

Good Hamlet, cast thy nighted colour off,

And let thine eye look like a friend onDenmark.

Do not for ever with thy vailed lids

Seek for thy noble father in the dust.

Thou know'st 'tis common; all that lives must die,

Passing through nature to eternity.

HAMLET:

Ay, madam, it is common.

QUEEN GERTRUDE:

If it be,

Why seems it so particular with thee?

HAMLET:

Seems, madam! nay it is; I know not 'seems.'

'Tis not alone my inky cloak, good mother,

Nor customary suits of solemn black,

Nor windy suspiration of forced breath,

No, nor the fruitful river in the eye,

Nor the dejected 'havior of the visage,
Together with all forms, moods, shapes of grief,
That can denote me truly; these indeed seem,
For they are actions that a man might play.
But I have that within which passeth show;
These but the trappings and the suits of woe.

KING CLAUDIUS:

'Tis sweet and commendable in your nature, Hamlet,
To give these mourning duties to your father.
But, you must know, your father lost a father;
That father lost, lost his, and the survivor bound
In filial obligation for some term
To do obsequious sorrow; but to persever
In obstinate condolement is a course
Of impious stubbornness; 'tis unmanly grief;
It shows a will most incorrect to heaven,
A heart unfortified, a mind impatient,
An understanding simple and unschool'd.
For what we know must be and is as common
As any the most vulgar thing to sense,
Why should we in our peevish opposition
Take it to heart? Fie! 'tis a fault to heaven,
A fault against the dead, a fault to nature,

To reason most absurd; whose common theme
Is death of fathers, and who still hath cried,
From the first corse till he that died to-day,
'This must be so.' We pray you, throw to earth
This unprevailing woe, and think of us
As of a father; for let the world take note,
You are the most immediate to our throne;
And with no less nobility of love
Than that which dearest father bears his son,
Do I impart toward you. For your intent
In going back to school inWittenberg,
It is most retrograde to our desire.
And we beseech you, bend you to remain
Here, in the cheer and comfort of our eye,
Our chiefest courtier, cousin, and our son.

QUEEN GERTRUDE:

Let not thy mother lose her prayers, Hamlet.
I pray thee, stay with us; go not toWittenberg.

HAMLET:

I shall in all my best obey you, madam.

KING CLAUDIUS:

Why, 'tis a loving and a fair reply.
Be as ourself inDenmark. Madam, come;

This gentle and unforced accord of Hamlet
Sits smiling to my heart; in grace whereof,
No jocund health thatDenmark drinks to-day,
But the great cannon to the clouds shall tell,
And the king's rouse the heavens all bruit again,
Re-speaking earthly thunder. Come away.

[*Exeunt all but HAMLET*]

HAMLET:
O, that this too too solid flesh would melt
Thaw and resolve itself into a dew!
Or that the Everlasting had not fix'd
His canon 'gainst self-slaughter! O God! God!
How weary, stale, flat and unprofitable,
Seem to me all the uses of this world!
Fie on't! ah fie! 'tis an unweeded garden,
That grows to seed; things rank and gross in nature
Possess it merely. That it should come to this!
But two months dead; nay, not so much, not two;
So excellent a king; that was, to this,
Hyperion to a satyr; so loving to my mother
That he might not beteem the winds of heaven

Visit her face too roughly. Heaven and earth!
Must I remember? why, she would hang on him,
As if increase of appetite had grown
By what it fed on; and yet, within a month—
Let me not think on't—Frailty, thy name is woman! —
A little month, or ere those shoes were old
With which she follow'd my poor father's body,
Like Niobe, all tears:—why she, even she—
O, God! a beast, that wants discourse of reason,
Would have mourn'd longer—married with my uncle,
My father's brother, but no more like my father
Than I to Hercules; within a month;
Ere yet the salt of most unrighteous tears
Had left the flushing in her galled eyes,
She married. O, most wicked speed, to post
With such dexterity to incestuous sheets!
It is not nor it cannot come to good;
But break, my heart; for I must hold my tongue.

[*Enter HORATIO, MARCELLUS, and BERNARDO*]

HORATIO:

Hail to your lordship!

HAMLET:

I am glad to see you well;

Horatio,—or I do forget myself.

HORATIO:

The same, my lord, and your poor servant ever.

HAMLET:

Sir, my good friend; I'll change that name with you;

And what make you from Wittenberg, Horatio? Marcellus?

MARCELLUS:

My good lord—

HAMLET:

I am very glad to see you. Good even, sir.

But what, in faith, make you from Wittenberg?

HORATIO:

A truant disposition, good my lord.

HAMLET:

I would not hear your enemy say so,

Nor shall you do mine ear that violence,

To make it truster of your own report

Against yourself; I know you are no truant.

But what is your affair in Elsinore?

We'll teach you to drink deep ere you depart.

HORATIO:

My lord, I came to see your father's funeral.

HAMLET:

I pray thee, do not mock me, fellow-student;

I think it was to see my mother's wedding.

HORATIO:

Indeed, my lord, it follow'd hard upon.

HAMLET:

Thrift, thrift, Horatio! the funeral baked meats

Did coldly furnish forth the marriage tables.

Would I had met my dearest foe in heaven

Or ever I had seen that day, Horatio!

My father! —methinks I see my father.

HORATIO:

Where, my lord?

HAMLET:

In my mind's eye, Horatio.

HORATIO:

I saw him once; he was a goodly king.

HAMLET:

He was a man, take him for all in all,

I shall not look upon his like again.

HORATIO:

My lord, I think I saw him yesternight.

HAMLET:

Saw? who?

HORATIO:

My lord, the king your father.

HAMLET:

The king my father!

HORATIO:

Season your admiration for awhile

With an attent ear, till I may deliver,

Upon the witness of these gentlemen,

This marvel to you.

HAMLET:

For God's love, let me hear.

HORATIO:

Two nights together had these gentlemen,

Marcellus and Bernardo, on their watch,

In the dead vast and middle of the night,

Been thus encounter'd. A figure like your father,

Armed at point exactly, cap-a-pe,

Appears before them, and with solemn march

Goes slow and stately by them; thrice he walk'd

By their oppress'd and fear-surprised eyes,

Within his truncheon's length; whilst they, distilled

Almost to jelly with the act of fear,

Stand dumb and speak not to him. This to me

In dreadful secrecy impart they did;

And I with them the third night kept the watch;

Where, as they had deliver'd, both in time,

Form of the thing, each word made true and good,

The apparition comes; I knew your father;

These hands are not more like.

HAMLET:

But where was this?

MARCELLUS:

My lord, upon the platform where we watch'd.

HAMLET:

Did you not speak to it?

HORATIO:

My lord, I did;

But answer made it none; yet once methought

It lifted up its head and did address

Itself to motion, like as it would speak;

But even then the morning cock crew loud,

And at the sound it shrunk in haste away,

And vanish'd from our sight.

HAMLET:

'Tis very strange.

HORATIO:

As I do live, my honour'd lord, 'tis true;

And we did think it writ down in our duty

To let you know of it.

HAMLET:

Indeed, indeed, sirs, but this troubles me.

Hold you the watch to-night?

MARCELLUS   BERNARDO:

We do, my lord.

HAMLET:

Arm'd, say you?

MARCELLUS   BERNARDO:

Arm'd, my lord.

HAMLET:

From top to toe?

MARCELLUS   BERNARDO:

My lord, from head to foot.

HAMLET:

Then saw you not his face?

HORATIO:

O, yes, my lord; he wore his beaver up.

HAMLET:

What, look'd he frowningly?

HORATIO:

A countenance more in sorrow than in anger.

HAMLET:

Pale or red?

HORATIO:

Nay, very pale.

HAMLET:

And fix'd his eyes upon you?

HORATIO:

Most constantly.

HAMLET:

I would I had been there.

HORATIO:

It would have much amazed you.

HAMLET:

Very like, very like. Stay'd it long?

HORATIO:

While one with moderate haste might tell a hundred.

MARCELLUS **BERNARDO**:

Longer, longer.

HORATIO:

Not when I saw't.

HAMLET:

His beard was grizzled—no?

HORATIO:

It was, as I have seen it in his life,

A sable silver'd.

HAMLET:

I will watch to-night;

Perchance 'twill walk again.

HORATIO:

I warrant it will.

HAMLET:

If it assume my noble father's person,

I'll speak to it, though hell itself should gape

And bid me hold my peace. I pray you all,

If you have hitherto conceal'd this sight,

Let it be tenable in your silence still;

And whatsoever else shall hap to-night,

Give it an understanding, but no tongue;

I will requite your loves. So, fare you well;

Upon the platform, 'twixt eleven and twelve,

I'll visit you.

All:

Our duty to your honour.

HAMLET:

Your loves, as mine to you; farewell.

[*Exeunt all but HAMLET*]

My father's spirit in arms! all is not well;
I doubt some foul play; would the night were come!
Till then sit still, my soul; foul deeds will rise,
Though all the earth o'erwhelm them, to men's eyes.

[*Exit*]

SCENE III.
A room in Polonius' house.

[*Enter LAERTES and OPHELIA*]

LAERTES:

My necessaries are embark'd; farewell;
And, sister, as the winds give benefit
And convoy is assistant, do not sleep,

But let me hear from you.

OPHELIA:

Do you doubt that?

LAERTES:

For Hamlet and the trifling of his favour,

Hold it a fashion and a toy in blood,

A violet in the youth of primy nature,

Forward, not permanent, sweet, not lasting,

The perfume and suppliance of a minute; No more.

OPHELIA:

No more but so?

LAERTES:

Think it no more;

For nature, crescent, does not grow alone

In thews and bulk, but, as this temple waxes,

The inward service of the mind and soul

Grows wide withal. Perhaps he loves you now,

And now no soil nor cautel doth besmirch

The virtue of his will; but you must fear,

His greatness weigh'd, his will is not his own;

For he himself is subject to his birth;

He may not, as unvalued persons do,

Carve for himself; for on his choice depends

The safety and health of this whole state;
And therefore must his choice be circumscribed
Unto the voice and yielding of that body
Whereof he is the head. Then if he says he loves you,
It fits your wisdom so far to believe it
As he in his particular act and place
May give his saying deed; which is no further
Than the main voice ofDenmark goes withal.
Then weigh what loss your honour may sustain,
If with too credent ear you list his songs,
Or lose your heart, or your chaste treasure open
To his unmaster'd importunity.
Fear it, Ophelia, fear it, my dear sister,
And keep you in the rear of your affection,
Out of the shot and danger of desire.
The chariest maid is prodigal enough,
If she unmask her beauty to the moon;
Virtue itself 'scapes not calumnious strokes;
The canker galls the infants of the spring,
Too oft before their buttons be disclosed,
And in the morn and liquid dew of youth
Contagious blastments are most imminent.
Be wary then; best safety lies in fear;

Youth to itself rebels, though none else near.
OPHELIA:
I shall the effect of this good lesson keep,
As watchman to my heart. But, good my brother,
Do not, as some ungracious pastors do,
Show me the steep and thorny way to heaven;
Whiles, like a puff'd and reckless libertine,
Himself the primrose path of dalliance treads,
And recks not his own rede.
LAERTES:
O, fear me not.

I stay too long; but here my father comes.

[*Enter*]

POLONIUS
A double blessing is a double grace,
Occasion smiles upon a second leave.
LORD POLONIUS:
Yet here, Laertes! aboard, aboard, for shame!
The wind sits in the shoulder of your sail,
And you are stay'd for. There; my blessing with thee!
And these few precepts in thy memory

See thou character. Give thy thoughts no tongue,
Nor any unproportioned thought his act.
Be thou familiar, but by no means vulgar.
Those friends thou hast, and their adoption tried,
Grapple them to thy soul with hoops of steel;
But do not dull thy palm with entertainment
Of each new-hatch'd, unfledged comrade. Beware
Of entrance to a quarrel, but being in,
Bear't that the opposed may beware of thee.
Give every man thy ear, but few thy voice;
Take each man's censure, but reserve thy judgment.
Costly thy habit as thy purse can buy,
But not express'd in fancy; rich, not gaudy;
For the apparel oft proclaims the man,
And they inFrance of the best rank and station
Are of a most select and generous chief in that.
Neither a borrower nor a lender be;
For loan oft loses both itself and friend,
And borrowing dulls the edge of husbandry.
This above all; to thine ownself be true,
And it must follow, as the night the day,
Thou canst not then be false to any man.
Farewell; my blessing season this in thee!

LAERTES:

Most humbly do I take my leave, my lord.

LORD POLONIUS:

The time invites you; go; your servants tend.

LAERTES:

Farewell, Ophelia; and remember well

What I have said to you.

OPHELIA:

'Tis in my memory lock'd,

And you yourself shall keep the key of it.

LAERTES:

Farewell.

[*Exit*]

LORD POLONIUS:

What is't, Ophelia, be hath said to you?

OPHELIA:

So please you, something touching the Lord Hamlet.

LORD POLONIUS:

Marry, well bethought;

'Tis told me, he hath very oft of late

Given private time to you; and you yourself

Have of your audience been most free and bounteous;
If it be so, as so 'tis put on me,
And that in way of caution, I must tell you,
You do not understand yourself so clearly
As it behoves my daughter and your honour.
What is between you? give me up the truth.

OPHELIA:

He hath, my lord, of late made many tenders
Of his affection to me.

LORD POLONIUS:

Affection! pooh! you speak like a green girl,
Unsifted in such perilous circumstance.
Do you believe his tenders, as you call them?

OPHELIA:

I do not know, my lord, what I should think.

LORD POLONIUS:

Marry, I'll teach you; think yourself a baby;
That you have ta'en these tenders for true pay,
Which are not sterling. Tender yourself more dearly;
Or—not to crack the wind of the poor phrase,
Running it thus—you'll tender me a fool.

OPHELIA:

My lord, he hath importuned me with love

In honourable fashion.

LORD POLONIUS:

Ay, fashion you may call it; go to, go to.

OPHELIA:

And hath given countenance to his speech, my lord,
With almost all the holy vows of heaven.

LORD POLONIUS:

Ay, springes to catch woodcocks. I do know,
When the blood burns, how prodigal the soul
Lends the tongue vows; these blazes, daughter,
Giving more light than heat, extinct in both,
Even in their promise, as it is a-making,
You must not take for fire. From this time
Be somewhat scanter of your maiden presence;
Set your entreatments at a higher rate
Than a command to parley. For Lord Hamlet,
Believe so much in him, that he is young
And with a larger tether may he walk
Than may be given you; in few, Ophelia,
Do not believe his vows; for they are brokers,
Not of that dye which their investments show,
But mere implorators of unholy suits,
Breathing like sanctified and pious bawds,

The better to beguile. This is for all;
I would not, in plain terms, from this time forth,
Have you so slander any moment leisure,
As to give words or talk with the Lord Hamlet.
Look to't, I charge you; come your ways.

OPHELIA:

I shall obey, my lord.

[*Exeunt*]

SCENE IV.
The platform.

[*Enter HAMLET, HORATIO, and MARCELLUS*]

HAMLET:

The air bites shrewdly; it is very cold.

HORATIO:

It is a nipping and an eager air.

HAMLET:

What hour now?

HORATIO:

I think it lacks of twelve.

HAMLET:

No, it is struck.

HORATIO:

Indeed? I heard it not; then it draws near the season
Wherein the spirit held his wont to walk.

A flourish of trumpets, and ordnance shot off, within

What does this mean, my lord?

HAMLET:

The king doth wake to-night and takes his rouse,
Keeps wassail, and the swaggering up-spring reels;
And, as he drains his draughts of Rhenish down,
The kettle-drum and trumpet thus bray out
The triumph of his pledge.

HORATIO:

Is it a custom?

HAMLET:

Ay, marry, is't;
But to my mind, though I am native here
And to the manner born, it is a custom
More honour'd in the breach than the observance.
This heavy-headed revel east and west

Makes us traduced and tax'd of other nations;
They clepe us drunkards, and with swinish phrase
Soil our addition; and indeed it takes
From our achievements, though perform'd at height,
The pith and marrow of our attribute.
So, oft it chances in particular men,
That for some vicious mole of nature in them,
As, in their birth—wherein they are not guilty,
Since nature cannot choose his origin—
By the o'ergrowth of some complexion,
Oft breaking down the pales and forts of reason,
Or by some habit that too much o'er-leavens
The form of plausive manners, that these men,
Carrying, I say, the stamp of one defect,
Being nature's livery, or fortune's star,—
Their virtues else—be they as pure as grace,
As infinite as man may undergo—
Shall in the general censure take corruption
From that particular fault; the dram of eale
Doth all the noble substance of a doubt
To his own scandal.

HORATIO:

Look, my lord, it comes!

Enter Ghost

HAMLET:

Angels and ministers of grace defend us!
Be thou a spirit of health or goblin damn'd,
Bring with thee airs from heaven or blasts from hell,
Be thy intents wicked or charitable,
Thou comest in such a questionable shape
That I will speak to thee; I'll call thee Hamlet,
King, father, royal Dane; O, answer me!
Let me not burst in ignorance; but tell
Why thy canonized bones, hearsed in death,
Have burst their cerements; why the sepulchre,
Wherein we saw thee quietly inurn'd,
Hath oped his ponderous and marble jaws,
To cast thee up again. What may this mean,
That thou, dead corse, again in complete steel
Revisit'st thus the glimpses of the moon,
Making night hideous; and we fools of nature
So horridly to shake our disposition
With thoughts beyond the reaches of our souls?
Say, why is this? wherefore? what should we do?

[*Ghost beckons HAMLET*]

HORATIO:

It beckons you to go away with it,

As if it some impartment did desire

To you alone.

MARCELLUS:

Look, with what courteous action

It waves you to a more removed ground;

But do not go with it.

HORATIO:

No, by no means.

HAMLET:

It will not speak; then I will follow it.

HORATIO:

Do not, my lord.

HAMLET:

Why, what should be the fear?

I do not set my life in a pin's fee;

And for my soul, what can it do to that,

Being a thing immortal as itself?

It waves me forth again; I'll follow it.

HORATIO:

What if it tempt you toward the flood, my lord,

Or to the dreadful summit of the cliff
That beetles o'er his base into the sea,
And there assume some other horrible form,
Which might deprive your sovereignty of reason
And draw you into madness? think of it;
The very place puts toys of desperation,
Without more motive, into every brain
That looks so many fathoms to the sea
And hears it roar beneath.

HAMLET:

It waves me still.
Go on; I'll follow thee.

MARCELLUS:

You shall not go, my lord.

HAMLET:

Hold off your hands.

HORATIO:

Be ruled; you shall not go.

HAMLET:

My fate cries out,
And makes each petty artery in this body
As hardy as the Nemean lion's nerve.
Still am I call'd. Unhand me, gentlemen.

By heaven, I'll make a ghost of him that lets me!
I say, away! Go on; I'll follow thee.

[*Exeunt Ghost and HAMLET*]

HORATIO:

He waxes desperate with imagination.

MARCELLUS:

Let's follow; 'tis not fit thus to obey him.

HORATIO:

Have after. To what issue will this come?

MARCELLUS:

Something is rotten in the state of Denmark.

HORATIO:

Heaven will direct it.

MARCELLUS:

Nay, let's follow him.

[*Exeunt*]

SCENE V.
Another part of the platform.

[*Enter GHOST and HAMLET*]

HAMLET:

Where wilt thou lead me? speak; I'll go no further.

Ghost:

Mark me.

HAMLET:

I will.

Ghost:

My hour is almost come,

When I to sulphurous and tormenting flames

Must render up myself.

HAMLET:

Alas, poor ghost!

Ghost:

Pity me not, but lend thy serious hearing

To what I shall unfold.

HAMLET:

Speak; I am bound to hear.

Ghost:

So art thou to revenge, when thou shalt hear.

HAMLET:

What?

Ghost:

I am thy father's spirit,

Doom'd for a certain term to walk the night,

And for the day confined to fast in fires,

Till the foul crimes done in my days of nature

Are burnt and purged away. But that I am forbid

To tell the secrets of my prison-house,

I could a tale unfold whose lightest word

Would harrow up thy soul, freeze thy young blood,

Make thy two eyes, like stars, start from their spheres,

Thy knotted and combined locks to part

And each particular hair to stand on end,

Like quills upon the fretful porpentine;

But this eternal blazon must not be

To ears of flesh and blood. List, list, O, list!

If thou didst ever thy dear father love—

HAMLET:

O God!

Ghost:

Revenge his foul and most unnatural murder.

HAMLET:

Murder!

Ghost:

Murder most foul, as in the best it is;

But this most foul, strange and unnatural.

HAMLET:

Haste me to know't, that I, with wings as swift

As meditation or the thoughts of love,

May sweep to my revenge.

Ghost:

I find thee apt;

And duller shouldst thou be than the fat weed

That roots itself in ease on Lethe wharf,

Wouldst thou not stir in this. Now, Hamlet, hear;

'Tis given out that, sleeping in my orchard,

A serpent stung me; so the whole ear ofDenmark

Is by a forged process of my death

Rankly abused; but know, thou noble youth,

The serpent that did sting thy father's life

Now wears his crown.

HAMLET:

O my prophetic soul! My uncle!

Ghost:

Ay, that incestuous, that adulterate beast,
With witchcraft of his wit, with traitorous gifts,—
O wicked wit and gifts, that have the power
So to seduce! —won to his shameful lust
The will of my most seeming-virtuous queen;
O Hamlet, what a falling-off was there!
From me, whose love was of that dignity
That it went hand in hand even with the vow
I made to her in marriage, and to decline
Upon a wretch whose natural gifts were poor
To those of mine!
But virtue, as it never will be moved,
Though lewdness court it in a shape of heaven,
So lust, though to a radiant angel link'd,
Will sate itself in a celestial bed,
And prey on garbage.
But, soft! methinks I scent the morning air;
Brief let me be. Sleeping within my orchard,
My custom always of the afternoon,
Upon my secure hour thy uncle stole,
With juice of cursed hebenon in a vial,

And in the porches of my ears did pour
The leperous distilment; whose effect
Holds such an enmity with blood of man
That swift as quicksilver it courses through
The natural gates and alleys of the body,
And with a sudden vigour doth posset
And curd, like eager droppings into milk,
The thin and wholesome blood; so did it mine;
And a most instant tetter bark'd about,
Most lazar-like, with vile and loathsome crust,
All my smooth body.
Thus was I, sleeping, by a brother's hand
Of life, of crown, of queen, at once dispatch'd;
Cut off even in the blossoms of my sin,
Unhousel'd, disappointed, unanel'd,
No reckoning made, but sent to my account
With all my imperfections on my head;
O, horrible! O, horrible! most horrible!
If thou hast nature in thee, bear it not;
Let not the royal bed ofDenmark be
A couch for luxury and damned incest.
But, howsoever thou pursuest this act,
Taint not thy mind, nor let thy soul contrive

Against thy mother aught; leave her to heaven
And to those thorns that in her bosom lodge,
To prick and sting her. Fare thee well at once!
The glow-worm shows the matin to be near,
And 'gins to pale his uneffectual fire;
Adieu, adieu! Hamlet, remember me.

[*Exit*]

HAMLET:

O all you host of heaven! O earth! what else?
And shall I couple hell? O, fie! Hold, hold, my heart;
And you, my sinews, grow not instant old,
But bear me stiffly up. Remember thee!
Ay, thou poor ghost, while memory holds a seat
In this distracted globe. Remember thee!
Yea, from the table of my memory
I'll wipe away all trivial fond records,
All saws of books, all forms, all pressures past,
That youth and observation copied there;
And thy commandment all alone shall live
Within the book and volume of my brain,
Unmix'd with baser matter; yes, by heaven!

O most pernicious woman!

O villain, villain, smiling, damned villain!

My tables,—meet it is I set it down,

That one may smile, and smile, and be a villain;

At least I'm sure it may be so inDenmark;

Writing

So, uncle, there you are. Now to my word;

It is 'Adieu, adieu! remember me.'

I have sworn 't.

MARCELLUS   HORATIO:

[*Within*] My lord, my lord,—

MARCELLUS:

[*Within*] Lord Hamlet,—

HORATIO:

[*Within*] Heaven secure him!

HAMLET:

So be it!

HORATIO:

[*Within*] Hillo, ho, ho, my lord!

HAMLET:

Hillo, ho, ho, boy! come, bird, come.

[*Enter HORATIO and MARCELLUS*]

MARCELLUS:

How is't, my noble lord?

HORATIO:

What news, my lord?

HAMLET:

O, wonderful!

HORATIO:

Good my lord, tell it.

HAMLET:

No; you'll reveal it.

HORATIO:

Not I, my lord, by heaven.

MARCELLUS:

Nor I, my lord.

HAMLET:

How say you, then; would heart of man once think it?

But you'll be secret?

HORATIO   MARCELLUS:

Ay, by heaven, my lord.

HAMLET:

There's ne'er a villain dwelling in all Denmark

But he's an arrant knave.

HORATIO:

There needs no ghost, my lord, come from the grave
To tell us this.

HAMLET:

Why, right; you are i' the right;
And so, without more circumstance at all,
I hold it fit that we shake hands and part;
You, as your business and desire shall point you;
For every man has business and desire,
Such as it is; and for mine own poor part,
Look you, I'll go pray.

HORATIO:

These are but wild and whirling words, my lord.

HAMLET:

I'm sorry they offend you, heartily;
Yes, 'faith heartily.

HORATIO:

There's no offence, my lord.

HAMLET:

Yes, by Saint Patrick, but there is, Horatio,
And much offence too. Touching this vision here,
It is an honest ghost, that let me tell you;
For your desire to know what is between us,

O'ermaster 't as you may. And now, good friends,

As you are friends, scholars and soldiers,

Give me one poor request.

HORATIO:

What is't, my lord? we will.

HAMLET:

Never make known what you have seen to-night.

HORATIO MARCELLUS:

My lord, we will not.

HAMLET:

Nay, but swear't.

HORATIO:

In faith,

My lord, not I.

MARCELLUS:

Nor I, my lord, in faith.

HAMLET:

Upon my sword.

MARCELLUS:

We have sworn, my lord, already.

HAMLET:

Indeed, upon my sword, indeed.

Ghost:

[*Beneath*] Swear.

HAMLET:

Ah, ha, boy! say'st thou so? art thou there,

truepenny?

Come on—you hear this fellow in the cellarage—

Consent to swear.

HORATIO:

Propose the oath, my lord.

HAMLET:

Never to speak of this that you have seen,

Swear by my sword.

Ghost:

[*Beneath*] Swear.

HAMLET:

Hic et ubique? then we'll shift our ground.

Come hither, gentlemen,

And lay your hands again upon my sword;

Never to speak of this that you have heard,

Swear by my sword.

Ghost:

[*Beneath*] Swear.

HAMLET:

Well said, old mole! canst work i' the earth so fast?

A worthy pioner! Once more remove, good friends.

HORATIO:

O day and night, but this is wondrous strange!

HAMLET:

And therefore as a stranger give it welcome.
There are more things in heaven and earth, Horatio,
Than are dreamt of in your philosophy. But come;
Here, as before, never, so help you mercy,
How strange or odd soe'er I bear myself,
As I perchance hereafter shall think meet
To put an antic disposition on,
That you, at such times seeing me, never shall,
With arms encumber'd thus, or this headshake,
Or by pronouncing of some doubtful phrase,
As 'Well, well, we know,' or 'We could, an if we would,'
Or 'If we list to speak,' or 'There be, an if they might,'
Or such ambiguous giving out, to note
That you know aught of me; this not to do,
So grace and mercy at your most need help you, Swear.

Ghost:

[*Beneath*] Swear.

HAMLET:

Rest, rest, perturbed spirit!

They swear

So, gentlemen,

With all my love I do commend me to you;

And what so poor a man as Hamlet is

May do, to express his love and friending to you,

God willing, shall not lack. Let us go in together;

And still your fingers on your lips, I pray.

The time is out of joint; O cursed spite,

That ever I was born to set it right!

Nay, come, let's go together.

[*Exeunt*]

ACT2.

SCENE Ⅰ.
A room in **POLONIUS'** house.

[*Enter POLONIUS and REYNALDO*]

LORD POLONIUS:

Give him this money and these notes, Reynaldo.

REYNALDO:

I will, my lord.

LORD POLONIUS:

You shall do marvellous wisely, good Reynaldo,

Before you visit him, to make inquire

Of his behavior.

REYNALDO:

My lord, I did intend it.

LORD POLONIUS:

Marry, well said; very well said. Look you, sir,
Inquire me first what Danskers are inParis;
And how, and who, what means, and where they keep,
What company, at what expense; and finding
By this encompassment and drift of question
That they do know my son, come you more nearer
Than your particular demands will touch it;
Take you, as 'twere, some distant knowledge of him;
As thus, 'I know his father and his friends,
And in part him; ' do you mark this, Reynaldo?

REYNALDO:

Ay, very well, my lord.

LORD POLONIUS:

'And in part him; but' you may say 'not well;
But, if't be he I mean, he's very wild;
Addicted so and so;' and there put on him
What forgeries you please; marry, none so rank
As may dishonour him; take heed of that;
But, sir, such wanton, wild and usual slips
As are companions noted and most known
To youth and liberty.

REYNALDO:

As gaming, my lord.

LORD POLONIUS:

Ay, or drinking, fencing, swearing, quarrelling,

Drabbing; you may go so far.

REYNALDO:

My lord, that would dishonour him.

LORD POLONIUS:

'Faith, no; as you may season it in the charge

You must not put another scandal on him,

That he is open to incontinency;

That's not my meaning; but breathe his faults so quaintly

That they may seem the taints of liberty,

The flash and outbreak of a fiery mind,

A savageness in unreclaimed blood,

Of general assault.

REYNALDO:

But, my good lord,—

LORD POLONIUS:

Wherefore should you do this?

REYNALDO:

Ay, my lord,

I would know that.

LORD POLONIUS:

Marry, sir, here's my drift;
And I believe, it is a fetch of wit;
You laying these slight sullies on my son,
As 'twere a thing a little soil'd i' the working, Mark you,
Your party in converse, him you would sound,
Having ever seen in the prenominate crimes
The youth you breathe of guilty, be assured
He closes with you in this consequence;
'Good sir,' or so, or 'friend,' or 'gentleman,'
According to the phrase or the addition
Of man and country.

REYNALDO:

Very good, my lord.

LORD POLONIUS:

And then, sir, does he this—he does—what was I about to say? By the mass, I was about to say something; where did I leave?

REYNALDO:

At 'closes in the consequence,' at 'friend or so,' and 'gentleman.'

LORD POLONIUS:

At 'closes in the consequence,' ay, marry;

He closes thus; 'I know the gentleman;

I saw him yesterday, or t' other day,

Or then, or then; with such, or such; and, as you say,

There was a' gaming; there o'ertook in's rouse;

There falling out at tennis;' or perchance,

'I saw him enter such a house of sale,'

Videlicet, a brothel, or so forth.

See you now;

Your bait of falsehood takes this carp of truth;

And thus do we of wisdom and of reach,

With windlasses and with assays of bias,

By indirections find directions out;

So by my former lecture and advice,

Shall you my son. You have me, have you not?

REYNALDO:

My lord, I have.

LORD POLONIUS:

God be wi' you; fare you well.

REYNALDO:

Good my lord!

LORD POLONIUS:

Observe his inclination in yourself.

REYNALDO:

I shall, my lord.

LORD POLONIUS:

And let him ply his music.

REYNALDO:

Well, my lord.

LORD POLONIUS:

Farewell!

[*Exit REYNALDO*]
[*Enter OPHELIA*]

How now, Ophelia! what's the matter?

OPHELIA:

O, my lord, my lord, I have been so affrighted!

LORD POLONIUS:

With what, i' the name of God?

OPHELIA:

My lord, as I was sewing in my closet,
Lord Hamlet, with his doublet all unbraced;
No hat upon his head; his stockings foul'd,
Ungarter'd, and down-gyved to his ancle;
Pale as his shirt; his knees knocking each other;
And with a look so piteous in purport

As if he had been loosed out of hell

To speak of horrors,—he comes before me.

LORD POLONIUS:

Mad for thy love?

OPHELIA:

My lord, I do not know;

But truly, I do fear it.

LORD POLONIUS:

What said he?

OPHELIA:

He took me by the wrist and held me hard;

Then goes he to the length of all his arm;

And, with his other hand thus o'er his brow,

He falls to such perusal of my face

As he would draw it. Long stay'd he so;

At last, a little shaking of mine arm

And thrice his head thus waving up and down,

He raised a sigh so piteous and profound

As it did seem to shatter all his bulk

And end his being; that done, he lets me go;

And, with his head over his shoulder turn'd,

He seem'd to find his way without his eyes;

For out o' doors he went without their helps,

And, to the last, bended their light on me.

LORD POLONIUS:

Come, go with me; I will go seek the king.

This is the very ecstasy of love,

Whose violent property fordoes itself

And leads the will to desperate undertakings

As oft as any passion under heaven

That does afflict our natures. I am sorry.

What, have you given him any hard words of late?

OPHELIA:

No, my good lord, but, as you did command,

I did repel his fetters and denied

His access to me.

LORD POLONIUS:

That hath made him mad.

I am sorry that with better heed and judgment

I had not quoted him; I fear'd he did but trifle,

And meant to wreck thee; but, beshrew my jealousy!

By heaven, it is as proper to our age

To cast beyond ourselves in our opinions

As it is common for the younger sort

To lack discretion. Come, go we to the king;

This must be known; which, being kept close, might move

More grief to hide than hate to utter love.

[*Exeunt*]

SCENE II.
A room in the castle.

[*Enter KING CLAUDIUS, QUEEN GERTRUDE, ROSENCRA-NTZ, GUILDENSTERN, and Attendants*]

KING CLAUDIUS:

Welcome, dear Rosencrantz and Guildenstern!
Moreover that we much did long to see you,
The need we have to use you did provoke
Our hasty sending. Something have you heard
Of Hamlet's transformation; so call it,
Sith nor the exterior nor the inward man
Resembles that it was. What it should be,
More than his father's death, that thus hath put him
So much from the understanding of himself,
I cannot dream of; I entreat you both,

That, being of so young days brought up with him,
And sith so neighbour'd to his youth and havior,
That you vouchsafe your rest here in our court
Some little time; so by your companies
To draw him on to pleasures, and to gather,
So much as from occasion you may glean,
Whether aught, to us unknown, afflicts him thus,
That, open'd, lies within our remedy.

QUEEN GERTRUDE:

Good gentlemen, he hath much talk'd of you;
And sure I am two men there are not living
To whom he more adheres. If it will please you
To show us so much gentry and good will
As to expend your time with us awhile,
For the supply and profit of our hope,
Your visitation shall receive such thanks
As fits a king's remembrance.

ROSENCRANTZ:

Both your majesties
Might, by the sovereign power you have of us,
Put your dread pleasures more into command
Than to entreaty.

GUILDENSTERN:

But we both obey,

And here give up ourselves, in the full bent

To lay our service freely at your feet,

To be commanded.

KING CLAUDIUS:

Thanks, Rosencrantz and gentle Guildenstern.

QUEEN GERTRUDE:

Thanks, Guildenstern and gentle Rosencrantz;

And I beseech you instantly to visit

My too much changed son. Go, some of you,

And bring these gentlemen where Hamlet is.

GUILDENSTERN:

Heavens make our presence and our practises

Pleasant and helpful to him!

QUEEN GERTRUDE:

Ay, amen!

[*Exeunt ROSENCRANTZ, GUILDENSTERN, and some Attendants*]

[*Enter POLONIUS*]

LORD POLONIUS:

The ambassadors from Norway, my good lord,

Are joyfully return'd.

KING CLAUDIUS:

Thou still hast been the father of good news.

LORD POLONIUS:

Have I, my lord? I assure my good liege,
I hold my duty, as I hold my soul,
Both to my God and to my gracious king;
And I do think, or else this brain of mine
Hunts not the trail of policy so sure
As it hath used to do, that I have found
The very cause of Hamlet's lunacy.

KING CLAUDIUS:

O, speak of that; that do I long to hear.

LORD POLONIUS:

Give first admittance to the ambassadors;
My news shall be the fruit to that great feast.

KING CLAUDIUS:

Thyself do grace to them, and bring them in.

[*Exit POLONIUS*]

He tells me, my dear Gertrude, he hath found
The head and source of all your son's distemper.

QUEEN GERTRUDE:

I doubt it is no other but the main;

His father's death, and our o'erhasty marriage.

KING CLAUDIUS:

Well, we shall sift him.

Re-enter POLONIUS, with VOLTIMAND and CORNELIUS

Welcome, my good friends!

Say, Voltimand, what from our brotherNorway?

VOLTIMAND:

Most fair return of greetings and desires.

Upon our first, he sent out to suppress

His nephew's levies; which to him appear'd

To be a preparation 'gainst the Polack;

But, better look'd into, he truly found

It was against your highness; whereat grieved,

That so his sickness, age and impotence

Was falsely borne in hand, sends out arrests

On Fortinbras; which he, in brief, obeys;

Receives rebuke fromNorway, and in fine

Makes vow before his uncle never more

To give the assay of arms against your majesty.

Whereon oldNorway, overcome with joy,

Gives him three thousand crowns in annual fee,

And his commission to employ those soldiers,
So levied as before, against the Polack;
With an entreaty, herein further shown,

[*Giving a paper*]

That it might please you to give quiet pass
Through your dominions for this enterprise,
On such regards of safety and allowance
As therein are set down.

KING CLAUDIUS:

It likes us well;
And at our more consider'd time well read,
Answer, and think upon this business.
Meantime we thank you for your well-took labour;
Go to your rest; at night we'll feast together;
Most welcome home!

[*Exeunt VOLTIMAND and CORNELIUS*]

LORD POLONIUS:

This business is well ended.
My liege, and madam, to expostulate

What majesty should be, what duty is,
Why day is day, night night, and time is time,
Were nothing but to waste night, day and time.
Therefore, since brevity is the soul of wit,
And tediousness the limbs and outward flourishes,
I will be brief; your noble son is mad;
Mad call I it; for, to define true madness,
What is't but to be nothing else but mad?
But let that go.

QUEEN GERTRUDE:

More matter, with less art.

LORD POLONIUS:

Madam, I swear I use no art at all.
That he is mad, 'tis true; 'tis true 'tis pity;
And pity 'tis 'tis true; a foolish figure;
But farewell it, for I will use no art.
Mad let us grant him, then; and now remains
That we find out the cause of this effect,
Or rather say, the cause of this defect,
For this effect defective comes by cause;
Thus it remains, and the remainder thus. Perpend.
I have a daughter—have while she is mine—
Who, in her duty and obedience, mark,

Hath given me this; now gather, and surmise.

[*Reads*] 'To the celestial and my soul's idol, the most beautified Ophelia,'—

That's an ill phrase, a vile phrase; 'beautified' is a vile phrase; but you shall hear. Thus:

[*Reads*] 'In her excellent white bosom, these, etc.'

QUEEN GERTRUDE:

Came this from Hamlet to her?

LORD POLONIUS:

Good madam, stay awhile; I will be faithful.

[*Reads*]

'Doubt thou the stars are fire;

Doubt that the sun doth move;

Doubt truth to be a liar;

But never doubt I love.

'O dear Ophelia, I am ill at these numbers;

I have not art to reckon my groans; but that

I love thee best, O most best, believe it. Adieu.

'Thine evermore most dear lady, whilst

this machine is to him, HAMLET.'

This, in obedience, hath my daughter shown me,

And more above, hath his solicitings,

As they fell out by time, by means and place,

All given to mine ear.

KING CLAUDIUS:

But how hath she

Received his love?

LORD POLONIUS:

What do you think of me?

KING CLAUDIUS:

As of a man faithful and honourable.

LORD POLONIUS:

I would fain prove so. But what might you think,

When I had seen this hot love on the wing—

As I perceived it, I must tell you that,

Before my daughter told me—what might you,

Or my dear majesty your queen here, think,

If I had play'd the desk or table-book,

Or given my heart a winking, mute and dumb,

Or look'd upon this love with idle sight;

What might you think? No, I went round to work,

And my young mistress thus I did bespeak;

'Lord Hamlet is a prince, out of thy star;

This must not be:' and then I precepts gave her,

That she should lock herself from his resort,

Admit no messengers, receive no tokens.

Which done, she took the fruits of my advice;
And he, repulsed—a short tale to make—
Fell into a sadness, then into a fast,
Thence to a watch, thence into a weakness,
Thence to a lightness, and, by this declension,
Into the madness wherein now he raves,
And all we mourn for.

KING CLAUDIUS:

Do you think 'tis this?

QUEEN GERTRUDE:

It may be, very likely.

LORD POLONIUS:

Hath there been such a time—I'd fain know that—
That I have positively said 'Tis so,'
When it proved otherwise?

KING CLAUDIUS:

Not that I know.

LORD POLONIUS:

[*Pointing to his head and shoulder*]
Take this from this, if this be otherwise;
If circumstances lead me, I will find
Where truth is hid, though it were hid indeed
Within the centre.

KING CLAUDIUS:

How may we try it further?

LORD POLONIUS:

You know, sometimes he walks four hours together

Here in the lobby.

QUEEN GERTRUDE:

So he does indeed.

LORD POLONIUS:

At such a time I'll loose my daughter to him;

Be you and I behind an arras then;

Mark the encounter; if he love her not

And be not from his reason fall'n thereon,

Let me be no assistant for a state,

But keep a farm and carters.

KING CLAUDIUS:

We will try it.

QUEEN GERTRUDE:

But, look, where sadly the poor wretch comes reading.

LORD POLONIUS:

Away, I do beseech you, both away;

I'll board him presently.

[*Exeunt KING CLAUDIUS, QUEEN GERTRUDE, and Attend-*

ants

Enter HAMLET, reading]

O, give me leave;

How does my good Lord Hamlet?

HAMLET:

Well, God-a-mercy.

LORD POLONIUS:

Do you know me, my lord?

HAMLET:

excellent well; you are a fishmonger.

LORD POLONIUS:

Not I, my lord.

HAMLET:

Then I would you were so honest a man.

LORD POLONIUS:

Honest, my lord!

HAMLET:

Ay, sir; to be honest, as this world goes, is to be one man picked out of ten thousand.

LORD POLONIUS:

That's very true, my lord.

HAMLET:

For if the sun breed maggots in a dead dog, being a god kissing carrion,—Have you a daughter?

LORD POLONIUS:

I have, my lord.

HAMLET:

Let her not walk i' the sun; conception is a blessing; but not as your daughter may conceive.

Friend, look to 't.

LORD POLONIUS:

[*Aside*] How say you by that? Still harping on my daughter; yet he knew me not at first; he said I was a fishmonger; he is far gone, far gone; and truly in my youth I suffered much extremity for love; very near this. I'll speak to him again.

What do you read, my lord?

HAMLET:

Words, words, words.

LORD POLONIUS:

What is the matter, my lord?

HAMLET:

Between who?

LORD POLONIUS:

I mean, the matter that you read, my lord.

HAMLET:

Slanders, sir; for the satirical rogue says here that old men have grey beards, that their faces are wrinkled, their eyes purging thick amber and plum-tree gum and that they have a plentiful lack of wit, together with most weak hams; all which, sir, though I most powerfully and potently believe, yet I hold it not honesty to have it thus set down, for yourself, sir, should be old as I am, if like a crab you could go backward.

LORD POLONIUS:

[*Aside*] Though this be madness, yet there is method in 't. Will you walk out of the air, my lord?

HAMLET:

Into my grave.

LORD POLONIUS:

Indeed, that is out o' the air. —

[*Aside*] How pregnant sometimes his replies are! a happiness that often madness hits on, which reason and sanity could not so prosperously be delivered of. I will leave him, and suddenly contrive the means of meeting between him and my daughter. —My honourable lord, I will most humbly take my leave of you.

HAMLET:

You cannot, sir, take from me any thing that I will more willingly part withal; except my life, except my life, except my life.

LORD POLONIUS:

Fare you well, my lord.

HAMLET:

These tedious old fools!

[*Enter ROSENCRANTZ and GUILDENSTERN*]

LORD POLONIUS:

You go to seek the Lord Hamlet; there he is.

ROSENCRANTZ:

[*To POLONIUS*] God save you, sir!

[*Exit POLONIUS*]

GUILDENSTERN:

My honoured lord!

ROSENCRANTZ:

My most dear lord!

HAMLET:

My excellent good friends! How dost thou, Guildenstern?

Ah, Rosencrantz! Good lads, how do ye both?

ROSENCRANTZ:

As the indifferent children of the earth.

GUILDENSTERN:

Happy, in that we are not over-happy;

On fortune's cap we are not the very button.

HAMLET:

Nor the soles of her shoe?

ROSENCRANTZ:

Neither, my lord.

HAMLET:

Then you live about her waist, or in the middle of her favours?

GUILDENSTERN:

'Faith, her privates we.

HAMLET:

In the secret parts of fortune? O, most true; she is a strumpet. What's the news?

ROSENCRANTZ:

None, my lord, but that the world's grown honest.

HAMLET:

Then is doomsday near; but your news is not true.

Let me question more in particular; what have you,

my good friends, deserved at the hands of fortune, that she sends you to prison hither?

GUILDENSTERN:

Prison, my lord!

HAMLET:

Denmark's a prison.

ROSENCRANTZ:

Then is the world one.

HAMLET:

A goodly one; in which there are many confines, wards and dungeons, Denmark being one o' the worst.

ROSENCRANTZ:

We think not so, my lord.

HAMLET:

Why, then, 'tis none to you; for there is nothing either good or bad, but thinking makes it so; to me it is a prison.

ROSENCRANTZ:

Why then, your ambition makes it one; 'tis too narrow for your mind.

HAMLET:

O God, I could be bounded in a nut shell and count myself a king of infinite space, were it not that I have bad dreams.

GUILDENSTERN:

Which dreams indeed are ambition, for the very substance of the ambitious is merely the shadow of a dream.

HAMLET:

A dream itself is but a shadow.

ROSENCRANTZ:

Truly, and I hold ambition of so airy and light a quality that it is but a shadow's shadow.

HAMLET:

Then are our beggars bodies, and our monarchs and outstretched heroes the beggars' shadows. Shall we to the court? for, by my fay, I cannot reason.

ROSENCRANTZ GUILDENSTERN:

We'll wait upon you.

HAMLET:

No such matter; I will not sort you with the rest of my servants, for, to speak to you like an honest man, I am most dreadfully attended. But, in the beaten way of friendship, what make you atElsinore?

ROSENCRANTZ:

To visit you, my lord; no other occasion.

HAMLET:

Beggar that I am, I am even poor in thanks; but I thank you; and sure, dear friends, my thanks are too dear a halfpenny.

Were you not sent for? Is it your own inclining? Is it a free visitation? Come, deal justly with me; come, come; nay, speak.

GUILDENSTERN:

What should we say, my lord?

HAMLET:

Why, any thing, but to the purpose. You were sent for; and there is a kind of confession in your looks which your modesties have not craft enough to colour; I know the good king and queen have sent for you.

ROSENCRANTZ:

To what end, my lord?

HAMLET:

That you must teach me. But let me conjure you, by the rights of our fellowship, by the consonancy of our youth, by the obligation of our ever-preserved love, and by what more dear a better proposer could charge you withal, be even and direct with me, whether you were sent for, or no?

ROSENCRANTZ:

[*Aside to GUILDENSTERN*] What say you?

HAMLET:

[*Aside*] Nay, then, I have an eye of you. —If you love me, hold not off.

GUILDENSTERN:

My lord, we were sent for.

HAMLET:

I will tell you why; so shall my anticipation prevent your discovery, and your secrecy to the king and queen moult no feather. I have of late—but wherefore I know not—lost all my mirth, forgone all custom of exercises; and indeed it goes so heavily with my disposition that this goodly frame, the earth, seems to me a sterile promontory, this most excellent canopy, the air, look you, this brave o'erhanging firmament, this majestical roof fretted with golden fire, why, it appears no other thing to me than a foul and pestilent congregation of vapours. What a piece of work is a man! how noble in reason! how infinite in faculty! in form and moving how express and admirable! in action how like an angel! in apprehension how like a god! the beauty of the world! the paragon of animals! And yet, to me, what is this quintessence of dust? man delights not me; no, nor woman neither, though by your smiling you seem to say so.

ROSENCRANTZ:

My lord, there was no such stuff in my thoughts.

HAMLET:

Why did you laugh then, when I said 'man delights not me'?

ROSENCRANTZ:

To think, my lord, if you delight not in man, what lenten entertainment the players shall receive from you; we coted them on the way; and hither are they coming, to offer you service.

HAMLET:

He that plays the king shall be welcome; his majesty shall have tribute of me; the adventurous knight shall use his foil and target; the lover shall not sigh gratis; the humourous man shall end his part in peace; the clown shall make those laugh whose lungs are tickled o' the sere; and the lady shall say her mind freely, or the blank verse shall halt for't. What players are they?

ROSENCRANTZ:

Even those you were wont to take delight in, the tragedians of the city.

HAMLET:

How chances it they travel? their residence, both in reputation and profit, was better both ways.

ROSENCRANTZ:

I think their inhibition comes by the means of the late innovation.

HAMLET:

Do they hold the same estimation they did when I was in the

city? are they so followed?

ROSENCRANTZ:

No, indeed, are they not.

HAMLET:

How comes it? do they grow rusty?

ROSENCRANTZ:

Nay, their endeavour keeps in the wonted pace; but there is, sir, an aery of children, little eyases, that cry out on the top of question, and are most tyrannically clapped for't; these are now the fashion, and so berattle the common stages—so they call them—that many wearing rapiers are afraid of goose-quills and dare scarce come thither.

HAMLET:

What, are they children? who maintains 'em? how are they escoted? Will they pursue the quality no longer than they can sing? will they not say afterwards, if they should grow themselves to common players—as it is most like, if their means are no better—their writers do them wrong, to make them exclaim against their own succession?

ROSENCRANTZ:

'Faith, there has been much to do on both sides; and the nation holds it no sin to tarre them to controversy; there was, for a while, no money bid for argument, unless the poet and the player went to cuffs in the question.

HAMLET:

Is't possible?

GUILDENSTERN:

O, there has been much throwing about of brains.

HAMLET:

Do the boys carry it away?

ROSENCRANTZ:

Ay, that they do, my lord; Hercules and his load too.

HAMLET:

It is not very strange; for mine uncle is king of Denmark, and those that would make mows at him while my father lived, give twenty, forty, fifty, an hundred ducats a-piece for his picture in little.

'Sblood, there is something in this more than natural, if philosophy could find it out.

[*Flourish of trumpets within*]

GUILDENSTERN:

There are the players.

HAMLET:

Gentlemen, you are welcome to Elsinore. Your hands, come

then; the appurtenance of welcome is fashion and ceremony; let me comply with you in this garb, lest my extent to the players, which, I tell you,

must show fairly outward, should more appear like entertainment than yours. You are welcome; but my uncle-father and aunt-mother are deceived.

GUILDENSTERN:

In what, my dear lord?

HAMLET:

I am but mad north-north-west; when the wind is southerly I know a hawk from a handsaw.

[*Enter POLONIUS*]

LORD POLONIUS:

Well be with you, gentlemen!

HAMLET:

Hark you, Guildenstern; and you too; at each ear a hearer; that great baby you see there is not yet out of his swaddling-clouts.

ROSENCRANTZ:

Happily he's the second time come to them; for they say an old man is twice a child.

HAMLET:

I will prophesy he comes to tell me of the players;
mark it. You say right, sir; o' Monday morning;
'twas so indeed.

LORD POLONIUS:

My lord, I have news to tell you.

HAMLET:

My lord, I have news to tell you.

When Roscius was an actor inRome,—

LORD POLONIUS:

The actors are come hither, my lord.

HAMLET:

Buz, buz!

LORD POLONIUS:

Upon mine honour,—

HAMLET:

Then came each actor on his ass,—

LORD POLONIUS:

The best actors in the world, either for tragedy, comedy, history, pastoral, pastoral-comical, historical-pastoral, tragical-historical, tragical- comical-historical-pastoral, scene individable, or poem unlimited; Seneca cannot be too heavy, nor Plautus too light. For the law of writ and the liberty, these are the only men.

HAMLET:

O Jephthah, judge of Israel, what a treasure hadst thou!

LORD POLONIUS:

What a treasure had he, my lord?

HAMLET:

Why,

'One fair daughter and no more,

The which he loved passing well.'

LORD POLONIUS:

[*Aside*] Still on my daughter.

HAMLET:

Am I not i' the right, old Jephthah?

LORD POLONIUS:

If you call me Jephthah, my lord, I have a daughter that I love passing well.

HAMLET:

Nay, that follows not.

LORD POLONIUS:

What follows, then, my lord?

HAMLET:

Why,

'As by lot, God wot,'

and then, you know,

'It came to pass, as most like it was,'—the first row of the pious chanson will show you more; for look, where my abridgement comes.

[*Enter four or five Players*]

You are welcome, masters; welcome, all. I am glad to see thee well. Welcome, good friends. O, my old friend! thy face is valenced since I saw thee last; comest thou to beard me inDenmark? What, my young lady and mistress! By'r lady, your ladyship is nearer to heaven than when I saw you last, by the altitude of a chopine. Pray God, your voice, like apiece of uncurrent gold, be not cracked within the ring. Masters, you are all welcome. We'll e'en to't like French falconers, fly at any thing we see; we'll have a speech straight; come, give us a taste of your quality; come, a passionate speech.

First Player:

What speech, my lord?

HAMLET:

I heard thee speak me a speech once, but it was never acted; or, if it was, not above once; for the play, I remember, pleased not the million; 'twas caviare to the general; but it was—as I received it, and others, whose judgments in such matters cried in the top of mine—an excellent play, well digested in the scenes, set down with as much modesty as cunning. I remember, one said there were no sallets in the lines to make the matter savoury, nor no matter in the phrase that might indict the author of affectation; but called it an honest method, as wholesome as sweet, and by very much more handsome than fine. One speech in it I chiefly loved; 'twas Aeneas' tale to Dido; and thereabout of it especially, where he speaks of Priam's slaughter; if it live in your memory, begin at this line; let me see, let me see—

'The rugged Pyrrhus, like the Hyrcanian beast,'— it is not so:—it begins with Pyrrhus:—

'The rugged Pyrrhus, he whose sable arms,
Black as his purpose, did the night resemble
When he lay couched in the ominous horse,
Hath now this dread and black complexion smear'd
With heraldry more dismal; head to foot
Now is he total gules; horridly trick'd
With blood of fathers, mothers, daughters, sons,
Baked and impasted with the parching streets,
That lend a tyrannous and damned light
To their lord's murder; roasted in wrath and fire,
And thus o'er-sized with coagulate gore,

With eyes like carbuncles, the hellish Pyrrhus

Old grandsire Priam seeks. '

So, proceed you.

LORD POLONIUS:

'Fore God, my lord, well spoken, with good accent and good discretion.

First Player:

'Anon he finds him

Striking too short at Greeks; his antique sword,

Rebellious to his arm, lies where it falls,

Repugnant to command; unequal match'd,

Pyrrhus at Priam drives; in rage strikes wide;

But with the whiff and wind of his fell sword

The unnerved father falls. Then senselessIlium,

Seeming to feel this blow, with flaming top

Stoops to his base, and with a hideous crash

Takes prisoner Pyrrhus' ear; for, lo! his sword,

Which was declining on the milky head

Of reverend Priam, seem'd i' the air to stick;

So, as a painted tyrant, Pyrrhus stood,

And like a neutral to his will and matter,

Did nothing.

But, as we often see, against some storm,

A silence in the heavens, the rack stand still,
The bold winds speechless and the orb below
As hush as death, anon the dreadful thunder
Doth rend the region, so, after Pyrrhus' pause,
Aroused vengeance sets him new a-work;
And never did the Cyclops' hammers fall
On Mars's armour forged for proof eterne
With less remorse than Pyrrhus' bleeding sword
Now falls on Priam.
Out, out, thou strumpet, Fortune! All you gods,
In general synod 'take away her power;
Break all the spokes and fellies from her wheel,
And bowl the round nave down the hill of heaven,
As low as to the fiends! '

LORD POLONIUS:

This is too long.

HAMLET:

It shall to the barber's, with your beard. Prithee, say on; he's for a jig or a tale of bawdry, or he sleeps; say on: come to Hecuba.

First Player:

'But who, O, who had seen the mobled queen—'

HAMLET:

'The mobled queen? '

LORD POLONIUS:

That's good; 'mobled queen' is good.

First Player:

'Run barefoot up and down, threatening the flames
With bisson rheum; a clout upon that head
Where late the diadem stood, and for a robe,
About her lank and all o'er-teemed loins,
A blanket, in the alarm of fear caught up;
Who this had seen, with tongue in venom steep'd,
'Gainst Fortune's state would treason have pronounced;
But if the gods themselves did see her then
When she saw Pyrrhus make malicious sport
In mincing with his sword her husband's limbs,
The instant burst of clamour that she made,
Unless things mortal move them not at all,
Would have made milch the burning eyes of heaven,
And passion in the gods. '

LORD POLONIUS:

Look, whether he has not turned his colour and has tears in's eyes. Pray you, no more.

HAMLET:

'Tis well; I'll have thee speak out the rest soon.

Good my lord, will you see the players well bestowed? Do you hear, let them be well used; for they are the abstract and brief chronicles of the time; after your death you were better have a bad epitaph than their ill report while you live.

LORD POLONIUS:

My lord, I will use them according to their desert.

HAMLET:

God's bodykins, man, much better; use every man after his desert, and who should 'scape whipping? Use them after your own honour and dignity; the less they deserve, the more merit is in your bounty.

Take them in.

LORD POLONIUS:

Come, sirs.

HAMLET:

Follow him, friends; we'll hear a play to-morrow.

[*Exit POLONIUS with all the Players but the First*]

Dost thou hear me, old friend; can you play the Murder of Gonzago?

First Player:

Ay, my lord.

HAMLET:

We'll ha't to-morrow night. You could, for a need, study a speech of some dozen or sixteen lines, which I would set down and insert in't, could you not?

First Player:

Ay, my lord.

HAMLET:

Very well. Follow that lord; and look you mock him not. [*Exit First Player*] My good friends, I'll leave you till night; you are welcome toElsinore.

ROSENCRANTZ:

Good my lord!

HAMLET:

Ay, so, God be wi' ye;
[*Exeunt ROSENCRANTZ and GUILDENSTERN*]
Now I am alone.
O, what a rogue and peasant slave am I!
Is it not monstrous that this player here,
But in a fiction, in a dream of passion,
Could force his soul so to his own conceit
That from her working all his visage wann'd,
Tears in his eyes, distraction in's aspect,
A broken voice, and his whole function suiting

With forms to his conceit? and all for nothing!
For Hecuba!
What's Hecuba to him, or he to Hecuba,
That he should weep for her? What would he do,
Had he the motive and the cue for passion
That I have? He would drown the stage with tears
And cleave the general ear with horrid speech,
Make mad the guilty and appal the free,
Confound the ignorant, and amaze indeed
The very faculties of eyes and ears. Yet I,
A dull and muddy-mettled rascal, peak,
Like John-a-dreams, unpregnant of my cause,
And can say nothing; no, not for a king,
Upon whose property and most dear life
A damn'd defeat was made. Am I a coward?
Who calls me villain? breaks my pate across?
Plucks off my beard, and blows it in my face?
Tweaks me by the nose? gives me the lie i' the throat,
As deep as to the lungs? who does me this?
Ha!
'Swounds, I should take it; for it cannot be
But I am pigeon-liver'd and lack gall
To make oppression bitter, or ere this

I should have fatted all the region kites
With this slave's offal; bloody, bawdy villain!
Remorseless, treacherous, lecherous, kindless villain!
O, vengeance!
Why, what an ass am I! This is most brave,
That I, the son of a dear father murder'd,
Prompted to my revenge by heaven and hell,
Must, like a whore, unpack my heart with words,
And fall a-cursing, like a very drab,
A scullion!
Fie upon't! foh! About, my brain! I have heard
That guilty creatures sitting at a play
Have by the very cunning of the scene
Been struck so to the soul that presently
They have proclaim'd their malefactions;
For murder, though it have no tongue, will speak
With most miraculous organ. I'll have these players
Play something like the murder of my father
Before mine uncle; I'll observe his looks;
I'll tent him to the quick; if he but blench,
I know my course. The spirit that I have seen
May be the devil; and the devil hath power
To assume a pleasing shape; yea, and perhaps

Out of my weakness and my melancholy,
As he is very potent with such spirits,
Abuses me to damn me; I'll have grounds
More relative than this; the play 's the thing
Wherein I'll catch the conscience of the king.

[*Exit*]

ACT 3

SCENE I.
A room in the castle.

[Enter KING CLAUDIUS, QUEEN GERTRUDE, POLONIUS, OPHELIA, ROSENCRANTZ, and GUILDENSTERN]

KING CLAUDIUS:

And can you, by no drift of circumstance,
Get from him why he puts on this confusion,
Grating so harshly all his days of quiet
With turbulent and dangerous lunacy?

ROSENCRANTZ:

He does confess he feels himself distracted;
But from what cause he will by no means speak.

GUILDENSTERN:

Nor do we find him forward to be sounded,
But, with a crafty madness, keeps aloof,
When we would bring him on to some confession
Of his true state.

QUEEN GERTRUDE:

Did he receive you well?

ROSENCRANTZ:

Most like a gentleman.

GUILDENSTERN:

But with much forcing of his disposition.

ROSENCRANTZ:

Niggard of question; but, of our demands,
Most free in his reply.

QUEEN GERTRUDE:

Did you assay him?
To any pastime?

ROSENCRANTZ:

Madam, it so fell out, that certain players
We o'er-raught on the way; of these we told him;
And there did seem in him a kind of joy
To hear of it; they are about the court,
And, as I think, they have already order

This night to play before him.
LORD POLONIUS:
'Tis most true;

And he beseech'd me to entreat your majesties

To hear and see the matter.
KING CLAUDIUS:
With all my heart; and it doth much content me

To hear him so inclined.

Good gentlemen, give him a further edge,

And drive his purpose on to these delights.
ROSENCRANTZ:
We shall, my lord.

[*Exeunt ROSENCRANTZ and GUILDENSTERN*]

KING CLAUDIUS:
Sweet Gertrude, leave us too;

For we have closely sent for Hamlet hither,

That he, as 'twere by accident, may here

Affront Ophelia;

Her father and myself, lawful espials,

Will so bestow ourselves that, seeing, unseen,

We may of their encounter frankly judge,

And gather by him, as he is behaved,
If 't be the affliction of his love or no
That thus he suffers for.

QUEEN GERTRUDE:

I shall obey you.
And for your part, Ophelia, I do wish
That your good beauties be the happy cause
Of Hamlet's wildness; so shall I hope your virtues
Will bring him to his wonted way again,
To both your honours.

OPHELIA:

Madam, I wish it may.

[*Exit QUEEN GERTRUDE*]

LORD POLONIUS:

Ophelia, walk you here. Gracious, so please you,
We will bestow ourselves.

[*To OPHELIA*]

Read on this book;
That show of such an exercise may colour

Your loneliness. We are oft to blame in this,—
'Tis too much proved—that with devotion's visage
And pious action we do sugar o'er
The devil himself.

KING CLAUDIUS:

[*Aside*] O, 'tis too true!
How smart a lash that speech doth give my conscience!
The harlot's cheek, beautied with plastering art,
Is not more ugly to the thing that helps it
Than is my deed to my most painted word;
O heavy burthen!

LORD POLONIUS:

I hear him coming; let's withdraw, my lord.

[*Exeunt KING CLAUDIUS and POLONIUS*]
[*Enter HAMLET*]

HAMLET:

To be, or not to be; that is the question;
Whether 'tis nobler in the mind to suffer
The slings and arrows of outrageous fortune,
Or to take arms against a sea of troubles,
And by opposing end them? To die, to sleep;

No more; and by a sleep to say we end
The heart-ache and the thousand natural shocks
That flesh is heir to, 'tis a consummation
Devoutly to be wish'd. To die, to sleep;
To sleep; perchance to dream; ay, there's the rub;
For in that sleep of death what dreams may come
When we have shuffled off this mortal coil,
Must give us pause; there's the respect
That makes calamity of so long life;
For who would bear the whips and scorns of time,
The oppressor's wrong, the proud man's contumely,
The pangs of despised love, the law's delay,
The insolence of office and the spurns
That patient merit of the unworthy takes,
When he himself might his quietus make
With a bare bodkin? who would fardels bear,
To grunt and sweat under a weary life,
But that the dread of something after death,
The undiscover'd country from whose bourn
No traveller returns, puzzles the will
And makes us rather bear those ills we have
Than fly to others that we know not of?
Thus conscience does make cowards of us all;

And thus the native hue of resolution
Is sicklied o'er with the pale cast of thought,
And enterprises of great pith and moment
With this regard their currents turn awry,
And lose the name of action. —Soft you now!
The fair Ophelia! Nymph, in thy orisons
Be all my sins remember'd.

OPHELIA:

Good my lord,

How does your honour for this many a day?

HAMLET:

I humbly thank you; well, well, well.

OPHELIA:

My lord, I have remembrances of yours,

That I have longed long to re-deliver;

I pray you, now receive them.

HAMLET:

No, not I;

I never gave you aught.

OPHELIA:

My honour'd lord, you know right well you did;
And, with them, words of so sweet breath composed
As made the things more rich; their perfume lost,

Take these again; for to the noble mind

Rich gifts wax poor when givers prove unkind.

There, my lord.

HAMLET:

Ha, ha! are you honest?

OPHELIA:

My lord?

HAMLET:

Are you fair?

OPHELIA:

What means your lordship?

HAMLET:

That if you be honest and fair, your honesty should admit no discourse to your beauty.

OPHELIA:

Could beauty, my lord, have better commerce than with honesty?

HAMLET:

Ay, truly; for the power of beauty will sooner transform honesty from what it is to a bawd than the force of honesty can translate beauty into his likeness; this was sometime a paradox, but now the time gives it proof. I did love you once.

OPHELIA:

Indeed, my lord, you made me believe so.

HAMLET:

You should not have believed me; for virtue cannot so inoculate our old stock but we shall relish of it; I loved you not.

OPHELIA:

I was the more deceived.

HAMLET:

Get thee to a nunnery; why wouldst thou be a breeder of sinners? I am myself indifferent honest; but yet I could accuse me of such things that it were better my mother had not borne me; I am very proud, revengeful, ambitious, with more offences at my beck than I have thoughts to put them in, imagination to give them shape, or time to act them in. What should such fellows as I do crawling between earth and heaven? We are arrant knaves, all; believe none of us. Go thy ways to a nunnery.

Where's your father?

OPHELIA:

At home, my lord.

HAMLET:

Let the doors be shut upon him, that he may play the fool no where but in's own house. Farewell.

OPHELIA:

O, help him, you sweet heavens!

HAMLET:

If thou dost marry, I'll give thee this plague for thy dowry; be thou as chaste as ice, as pure as snow, thou shalt not escape calumny. Get thee to a nunnery, go; farewell. Or, if thou wilt needs marry, marry a fool; for wise men know well enough what monsters you make of them. To a nunnery, go, and quickly too. Farewell.

OPHELIA:

O heavenly powers, restore him!

HAMLET:

I have heard of your paintings too, well enough; God has given you one face, and you make yourselves another; you jig, you amble, and you lisp, and nick-name God's creatures, and make your wantonness your ignorance. Go to, I'll no more on't; it hath made me mad. I say, we will have no more marriages; those that are married already, all but one, shall live; the rest shall keep as they are. To a nunnery, go.

[*Exit*]

OPHELIA:

O, what a noble mind is here o'erthrown!

The courtier's, soldier's, scholar's, eye, tongue, sword;
The expectancy and rose of the fair state,
The glass of fashion and the mould of form,
The observed of all observers, quite, quite down!
And I, of ladies most deject and wretched,
That suck'd the honey of his music vows,
Now see that noble and most sovereign reason,
Like sweet bells jangled, out of tune and harsh;
That unmatch'd form and feature of blown youth
Blasted with ecstasy; O, woe is me,
To have seen what I have seen, see what I see!
Re-enter KING CLAUDIUS and POLONIUS

KING CLAUDIUS:

Love! his affections do not that way tend;
Nor what he spake, though it lack'd form a little,
Was not like madness. There's something in his soul,
O'er which his melancholy sits on brood;
And I do doubt the hatch and the disclose
Will be some danger; which for to prevent,
I have in quick determination
Thus set it down; he shall with speed to England,
For the demand of our neglected tribute
Haply the seas and countries different

With variable objects shall expel
This something-settled matter in his heart,
Whereon his brains still beating puts him thus
From fashion of himself. What think you on't?

LORD POLONIUS:

It shall do well; but yet do I believe
The origin and commencement of his grief
Sprung from neglected love. How now, Ophelia!
You need not tell us what Lord Hamlet said;
We heard it all. My lord, do as you please;
But, if you hold it fit, after the play
Let his queen mother all alone entreat him
To show his grief; let her be round with him;
And I'll be placed, so please you, in the ear
Of all their conference. If she find him not,
ToEngland send him, or confine him where
Your wisdom best shall think.

KING CLAUDIUS:

It shall be so;
Madness in great ones must not unwatch'd go.

[*Exeunt*]

SCENE II.
A hall in the castle.

[*Enter HAMLET and Players*]

HAMLET:

Speak the speech, I pray you, as I pronounced it to you, trippingly on the tongue; but if you mouth it, as many of your players do, I had as lief the town-crier spoke my lines. Nor do not saw the air too much with your hand, thus, but use all gently; for in the very torrent, tempest, and, as I may say, the whirlwind of passion, you must acquire and beget a temperance that may give it smoothness. O, it offends me to the soul to hear a robustious periwig-pated fellow tear a passion to tatters, to very rags, to split the ears of the groundlings, who for the most part are capable of nothing but inexplicable dumbshows and noise; I would have such a fellow whipped for o'erdoing Termagant; it out-herods Herod; pray you, avoid it.

First Player:

I warrant your honour.

HAMLET:

Be not too tame neither, but let your own discretion be your tutor; suit the action to the word, the word to the action; with this special o'erstep not the modesty of nature; for any thing so overdone is from the purpose of playing, whose end, both at the first and now, was and is, to hold, as 'twere, the mirror up to nature; to show virtue her own feature, scorn her own image, and the very age and body of the time his form and pressure. Now this overdone, or come tardy off, though it make the unskilful laugh, cannot but make the judicious grieve; the censure of the which one must in your allowance o'erweigh a whole theatre of others. O, there be players that I have seen play, and heard others praise, and that highly, not to speak it profanely, that, neither having the accent of Christians nor the gait of Christian, pagan, nor man, have so strutted and bellowed that I have thought some of nature's journeymen had made men and not made them well, they imitated humanity so abominably.

First Player:

I hope we have reformed that indifferently with us, sir.

HAMLET:

O, reform it altogether. And let those that play your clowns speak no more than is set down for them; for there be of them that will themselves laugh, to set on some quantity of barren spectators to laugh too; though, in the mean time, some necessary question of the play be then to be considered; that's villanous, and shows a most pitiful ambition in the fool that uses it. Go, make you ready.

[*Exeunt Players*]

[*Enter POLONIUS, ROSENCRANTZ, and GUILDENSTERN*]

How now, my lord! I will the king hear this piece of work?
LORD POLONIUS:

And the queen too, and that presently.

HAMLET:

Bid the players make haste.

[*Exit POLONIUS*]

Will you two help to hasten them?

ROSENCRANTZ **GUILDENSTERN**:

We will, my lord.

[*Exeunt ROSENCRANTZ and GUILDENSTERN*]

HAMLET:

What ho! Horatio!

Enter HORATIO

HORATIO:

Here, sweet lord, at your service.

HAMLET:

Horatio, thou art e'en as just a man

As e'er my conversation coped withal.

HORATIO:

O, my dear lord,—

HAMLET:

Nay, do not think I flatter;

For what advancement may I hope from thee

That no revenue hast but thy good spirits,

To feed and clothe thee? Why should the poor be flatter'd?

No, let the candied tongue lick absurd pomp,

And crook the pregnant hinges of the knee

Where thrift may follow fawning. Dost thou hear?

Since my dear soul was mistress of her choice

And could of men distinguish, her election

Hath seal'd thee for herself; for thou hast been

As one, in suffering all, that suffers nothing,

A man that fortune's buffets and rewards

Hast ta'en with equal thanks; and blest are those
Whose blood and judgment are so well commingled,
That they are not a pipe for fortune's finger
To sound what stop she please. Give me that man
That is not passion's slave, and I will wear him
In my heart's core, ay, in my heart of heart,
As I do thee. —Something too much of this. —
There is a play to-night before the king;
One scene of it comes near the circumstance
Which I have told thee of my father's death;
I prithee, when thou seest that act afoot,
Even with the very comment of thy soul
Observe mine uncle; if his occulted guilt
Do not itself unkennel in one speech,
It is a damned ghost that we have seen,
And my imaginations are as foul
As Vulcan's stithy. Give him heedful note;
For I mine eyes will rivet to his face,
And after we will both our judgments join
In censure of his seeming.

HORATIO:

Well, my lord;
If he steal aught the whilst this play is playing,

And 'scape detecting, I will pay the theft.

HAMLET:

They are coming to the play; I must be idle;
Get you a place.

[*Danish march. A flourish. Enter KING CLAUDIUS, QUEEN GERTRUDE, POLONIUS, OPHELIA, ROSENCRANTZ, GUILDENSTERN, and others*]

KING CLAUDIUS:

How fares our cousin Hamlet?

HAMLET:

Excellent, i' faith; of the chameleon's dish; I eat
the air, promise-crammed; you cannot feed capons so.

KING CLAUDIUS:

I have nothing with this answer, Hamlet; these words
are not mine.

HAMLET:

No, nor mine now.

[*To POLONIUS*]

My lord, you played once i' the university, you say?

LORD POLONIUS:

That did I, my lord; and was accounted a good actor.

HAMLET:

What did you enact?

LORD POLONIUS:

I did enact Julius Caesar; I was killed i' the
Capitol; Brutus killed me.

HAMLET:

It was a brute part of him to kill so capital a calf there. Be the
players ready?

SENCRANTZ:

Ay, my lord; they stay upon your patience.

QUEEN GERTRUDE:

Come hither, my dear Hamlet, sit by me.

HAMLET:

No, good mother, here's metal more attractive.

LORD POLONIUS:

[*To KING CLAUDIUS*] O, ho! do you mark that?

HAMLET:

Lady, shall I lie in your lap?

Lying down at OPHELIA's feet

OPHELIA:

No, my lord.

HAMLET:

I mean, my head upon your lap?

OPHELIA:

Ay, my lord.

HAMLET:

Do you think I meant country matters?

OPHELIA:

I think nothing, my lord.

HAMLET:

That's a fair thought to lie between maids' legs.

OPHELIA:

What is, my lord?

HAMLET:

Nothing.

OPHELIA:

You are merry, my lord.

HAMLET:

Who, I?

OPHELIA:

Ay, my lord.

HAMLET:

O God, your only jig-maker. What should a man do but be merry? for, look you, how cheerfully my mother looks, and my father died within these two hours.

OPHELIA:

Nay, 'tis twice two months, my lord.

HAMLET:

So long? Nay then, let the devil wear black, for I'll have a suit of sables. O heavens! die two months ago, and not forgotten yet? Then there's hope a great man's memory may outlive his life half a year; but, by'r lady, he must build churches, then; or else shall he suffer not thinking on, with the hobby-horse, whose epitaph is 'For, O, for, O, the hobby-horse is forgot.'

[*Hautboys play. The dumb-show enters*]

[*Enter a King and a Queen very lovingly; the Queen embracing him, and he her. She kneels, and makes show of protestation unto him. He takes her up, and declines his head upon her neck; lays him down upon a bank of flowers; she, seeing him asleep, leaves him. Anon comes in a fellow, takes off his crown, kisses it, and pours poison in the King's ears, and exit. The Queen returns; finds the King dead, and makes passionate action. The Poisoner, with some two or three Mutes, comes in again, seeming to lament with her. The dead body is carried away. The Poisoner wooes the Queen with gifts; she seems loath and unwilling awhile, but in the end accepts his love.*]

[*Exeunt*]

OPHELIA:

What means this, my lord?

HAMLET:

Marry, this is miching mallecho; it means mischief.

OPHELIA:

Belike this show imports the argument of the play.

Enter Prologue

HAMLET:

We shall know by this fellow; the players cannot keep counsel; they'll tell all.

OPHELIA:

Will he tell us what this show meant?

HAMLET:

Ay, or any show that you'll show him; be not you ashamed to show, he'll not shame to tell you what it means.

OPHELIA:

You are naught, you are naught; I'll mark the play.

Prologue

For us, and for our tragedy,

Here stooping to your clemency,

We beg your hearing patiently.

[*Exit*]

HAMLET:

Is this a prologue, or the posy of a ring?

OPHELIA:

'Tis brief, my lord.

HAMLET:

As woman's love.

[*Enter two Players, King and Queen*]

Player King:

Full thirty times hath Phoebus' cart gone round
Neptune's salt wash and Tellus' orbed ground,
And thirty dozen moons with borrow'd sheen
About the world have times twelve thirties been,
Since love our hearts and Hymen did our hands
Unite commutual in most sacred bands.

Player Queen:

So many journeys may the sun and moon
Make us again count o'er ere love be done!
But, woe is me, you are so sick of late,

So far from cheer and from your former state,
That I distrust you. Yet, though I distrust,
Discomfort you, my lord, it nothing must;
For women's fear and love holds quantity;
In neither aught, or in extremity.
Now, what my love is, proof hath made you know;
And as my love is sized, my fear is so;
Where love is great, the littlest doubts are fear;
Where little fears grow great, great love grows there.

Player King:

'Faith, I must leave thee, love, and shortly too;
My operant powers their functions leave to do;
And thou shalt live in this fair world behind,
Honour'd, beloved; and haply one as kind
For husband shalt thou—

Player Queen:

O, confound the rest!
Such love must needs be treason in my breast;
In second husband let me be accurst!
None wed the second but who kill'd the first.

HAMLET:

[*Aside*] Wormwood, wormwood.

Player Queen:

The instances that second marriage move
Are base respects of thrift, but none of love;
A second time I kill my husband dead,
When second husband kisses me in bed.

Player King:
I do believe you think what now you speak;
But what we do determine oft we break.
Purpose is but the slave to memory,
Of violent birth, but poor validity;
Which now, like fruit unripe, sticks on the tree;
But fall, unshaken, when they mellow be.
Most necessary 'tis that we forget
To pay ourselves what to ourselves is debt;
What to ourselves in passion we propose,
The passion ending, doth the purpose lose.
The violence of either grief or joy
Their own enactures with themselves destroy;
Where joy most revels, grief doth most lament;
Grief joys, joy grieves, on slender accident.
This world is not for aye, nor 'tis not strange
That even our loves should with our fortunes change;
For 'tis a question left us yet to prove,
Whether love lead fortune, or else fortune love.

The great man down, you mark his favourite flies;
The poor advanced makes friends of enemies.
And hitherto doth love on fortune tend;
For who not needs shall never lack a friend,
And who in want a hollow friend doth try,
Directly seasons him his enemy.
But, orderly to end where I begun,
Our wills and fates do so contrary run
That our devices still are overthrown;
Our thoughts are ours, their ends none of our own;
So think thou wilt no second husband wed;
But die thy thoughts when thy first lord is dead.

Player Queen:

Nor earth to me give food, nor heaven light!
Sport and repose lock from me day and night!
To desperation turn my trust and hope!
An anchor's cheer in prison be my scope!
Each opposite that blanks the face of joy
Meet what I would have well and it destroy!
Both here and hence pursue me lasting strife,
If, once a widow, ever I be wife!

HAMLET:

If she should break it now!

Player King:

'Tis deeply sworn. Sweet, leave me here awhile;
My spirits grow dull, and fain I would beguile
The tedious day with sleep.

[*Sleeps*]

Player Queen:

Sleep rock thy brain,
And never come mischance between us twain!

[*Exit*]

HAMLET:

Madam, how like you this play?

QUEEN GERTRUDE:

The lady protests too much, methinks.

HAMLET:

O, but she'll keep her word.

KING CLAUDIUS:

Have you heard the argument? Is there no offence in 't?

HAMLET:

No, no, they do but jest, poison in jest; no offence i' the

world.

KING CLAUDIUS:

What do you call the play?

HAMLET:

The Mouse-trap. Marry, how? Tropically. This play is the image of a murder done in Vienna; Gonzago is the duke's name; his wife, Baptista; you shall see anon; 'tis a knavish piece of work; but what o' that? your majesty and we that have free souls, it touches us not; let the galled jade wince, our withers are unwrung.

[*Enter LUCIANUS*]

This is one Lucianus, nephew to the king.

OPHELIA:

You are as good as a chorus, my lord.

HAMLET:

I could interpret between you and your love, if I could see the puppets dallying.

OPHELIA:

You are keen, my lord, you are keen.

HAMLET:

It would cost you a groaning to take off my edge.

OPHELIA:

Still better, and worse.

HAMLET:

So you must take your husbands. Begin, murderer; pox, leave thy damnable faces, and begin. Come; 'the croaking raven doth bellow for revenge.

LUCIANUS:

Thoughts black, hands apt, drugs fit, and time agreeing;
Confederate season, else no creature seeing;
Thou mixture rank, of midnight weeds collected,
With Hecate's ban thrice blasted, thrice infected,
Thy natural magic and dire property,
On wholesome life usurp immediately.

[*Pours the poison into the sleeper's ears*]

HAMLET:

He poisons him i' the garden for's estate. His name's Gonzago; the story is extant, and writ in choice Italian; you shall see anon how the murderer gets the love of Gonzago's wife.

OPHELIA:

The king rises.

HAMLET:

What, frighted with false fire!

QUEEN GERTRUDE:

How fares my lord?

LORD POLONIUS:

Give o'er the play.

KING CLAUDIUS:

Give me some light; away!

All:

Lights, lights, lights!

[*Exeunt all but HAMLET and HORATIO*]

HAMLET:

Why, let the stricken deer go weep,

The hart ungalled play;

For some must watch, while some must sleep;

So runs the world away.

Would not this, sir, and a forest of feathers— if

the rest of my fortunes turn Turk with me—with two

Provincial roses on my razed shoes, get me a

fellowship in a cry of players, sir?

HORATIO:

Half a share.

HAMLET:

A whole one, I.

For thou dost know, O Damon dear,

This realm dismantled was

Of Jove himself; and now reigns here

A very, very—pajock.

HORATIO:

You might have rhymed.

HAMLET:

O good Horatio, I'll take the ghost's word for a thousand pound. Didst perceive?

HORATIO:

Very well, my lord.

HAMLET:

Upon the talk of the poisoning?

HORATIO:

I did very well note him.

HAMLET:

Ah, ha! Come, some music! come, the recorders!

For if the king like not the comedy,

Why then, belike, he likes it not, perdy.

Come, some music!

Re-enter ROSENCRANTZ and GUILDENSTERN

GUILDENSTERN:

Good my lord, vouchsafe me a word with you.

HAMLET:

Sir, a whole history.

GUILDENSTERN:

The king, sir,—

HAMLET:

Ay, sir, what of him?

GUILDENSTERN:

Is in his retirement marvellous distempered.

HAMLET:

With drink, sir?

GUILDENSTERN:

No, my lord, rather with choler.

HAMLET:

Your wisdom should show itself more richer to signify this to his doctor; for, for me to put him to his purgation would perhaps plunge him into far more choler.

GUILDENSTERN:

Good my lord, put your discourse into some frame and start not so wildly from my affair.

HAMLET:

I am tame, sir; pronounce.

GUILDENSTERN:

The queen, your mother, in most great affliction of spirit, hath sent me to you.

HAMLET:

You are welcome.

GUILDENSTERN:

Nay, good my lord, this courtesy is not of the right breed. If it shall please you to make me a wholesome answer, I will do your mother's commandment; if not, your pardon and my return shall be the end of my business.

HAMLET:

Sir, I cannot.

GUILDENSTERN:

What, my lord?

HAMLET:

Make you a wholesome answer; my wit's diseased; but, sir, such answer as I can make, you shall command; or, rather, as you say, my mother; therefore no more, but to the matter; my mother, you say, —

ROSENCRANTZ:

Then thus she says; your behavior hath struck her into amazement and admiration.

HAMLET:

O wonderful son, that can so astonish a mother! But is there no sequel at the heels of this mother's admiration? Impart.

ROSENCRANTZ:

She desires to speak with you in her closet, ere you go to bed.

HAMLET:

We shall obey, were she ten times our mother. Have you any further trade with us?

ROSENCRANTZ:

My lord, you once did love me.

HAMLET:

So I do still, by these pickers and stealers.

ROSENCRANTZ:

Good my lord, what is your cause of distemper? you do, surely, bar the door upon your own liberty, if you deny your griefs to your friend.

HAMLET:

Sir, I lack advancement.

ROSENCRANTZ:

How can that be, when you have the voice of the king himself for your succession in Denmark?

HAMLET:

Ay, but sir, 'While the grass grows,'—the proverb is something musty.

Re-enter Players with recorders

O, the recorders! let me see one. To withdraw with you:—why do you go about to recover the wind of me, as if you would drive me into a toil?

GUILDENSTERN:

O, my lord, if my duty be too bold, my love is too unmannerly.

HAMLET:

I do not well understand that. Will you play upon this pipe?

GUILDENSTERN:

My lord, I cannot.

HAMLET:

I pray you.

GUILDENSTERN:

Believe me, I cannot.

HAMLET:

I do beseech you.

GUILDENSTERN:

I know no touch of it, my lord.

HAMLET:

'Tis as easy as lying; govern these ventages with your lingers and thumb, give it breath with your mouth, and it will discourse most eloquent music.

Look you, these are the stops.

GUILDENSTERN:

But these cannot I command to any utterance of harmony; I have not the skill.

HAMLET:

Why, look you now, how unworthy a thing you make of me! You would play upon me; you would seem to know my stops; you would pluck out the heart of my mystery; you would sound me from my lowest note to the top of my compass; and there is much music, excellent voice, in this little organ; yet cannot you make it speak. 'Sblood, do you think I am easier to be played on than a pipe? Call me what instrument you will, though you can fret me, yet you cannot play upon me.

[*Enter POLONIUS*]

God bless you, sir!

LORD POLONIUS:

My lord, the queen would speak with you, and presently.

HAMLET:

Do you see yonder cloud that's almost in shape of a camel?

LORD POLONIUS:

By the mass, and 'tis like a camel, indeed.

HAMLET:

Methinks it is like a weasel.

LORD POLONIUS:

It is backed like a weasel.

HAMLET:

Or like a whale?

LORD POLONIUS:

Very like a whale.

HAMLET:

Then I will come to my mother by and by. They fool me to the top of my bent. I will come by and by.

LORD POLONIUS:

I will say so.

HAMLET:

By and by is easily said.

[*Exit POLONIUS*]

Leave me, friends.

[*Exeunt all but HAMLET*]

Tis now the very witching time of night,

When churchyards yawn and hell itself breathes out

Contagion to this world; now could I drink hot blood,

And do such bitter business as the day
Would quake to look on. Soft! now to my mother.
O heart, lose not thy nature; let not ever
The soul of Nero enter this firm bosom;
Let me be cruel, not unnatural;
I will speak daggers to her, but use none;
My tongue and soul in this be hypocrites;
How in my words soever she be shent,
To give them seals never, my soul, consent!

[*Exit*]

SCENE III.
A room in the castle.

[*Enter KING CLAUDIUS, ROSENCRANTZ, and GUILDEN-STERN*]

KING CLAUDIUS:
I like him not, nor stands it safe with us
To let his madness range. Therefore prepare you;

I your commission will forthwith dispatch,
And he to England shall along with you;
The terms of our estate may not endure
Hazard so dangerous as doth hourly grow
Out of his lunacies.

GUILDENSTERN:

We will ourselves provide;
Most holy and religious fear it is
To keep those many many bodies safe
That live and feed upon your majesty.

ROSENCRANTZ:

The single and peculiar life is bound,
With all the strength and armour of the mind,
To keep itself from noyance; but much more
That spirit upon whose weal depend and rest
The lives of many. The cease of majesty
Dies not alone; but, like a gulf, doth draw
What's near it with it; it is a massy wheel,
Fix'd on the summit of the highest mount,
To whose huge spokes ten thousand lesser things
Are mortised and adjoin'd; which, when it falls,
Each small annexment, petty consequence,
Attends the boisterous ruin. Never alone

Did the king sigh, but with a general groan.
KING CLAUDIUS:
Arm you, I pray you, to this speedy voyage;
For we will fetters put upon this fear,
Which now goes too free-footed.
ROSENCRANTZ **GUILDENSTERN:**
We will haste us.

[*Exeunt ROSENCRANTZ and GUILDENSTERN*]
[*Enter POLONIUS*]

LORD POLONIUS:
My lord, he's going to his mother's closet;
Behind the arras I'll convey myself,
To hear the process; and warrant she'll tax him home;
And, as you said, and wisely was it said,
'Tis meet that some more audience than a mother,
Since nature makes them partial, should o'erhear
The speech, of vantage. Fare you well, my liege;
I'll call upon you ere you go to bed,
And tell you what I know.
KING CLAUDIUS:
Thanks, dear my lord.

[*Exit POLONIUS*]

O, my offence is rank it smells to heaven;
It hath the primal eldest curse upon't,
A brother's murder. Pray can I not,
Though inclination be as sharp as will;
My stronger guilt defeats my strong intent;
And, like a man to double business bound,
I stand in pause where I shall first begin,
And both neglect. What if this cursed hand
Were thicker than itself with brother's blood,
Is there not rain enough in the sweet heavens
To wash it white as snow? Whereto serves mercy
But to confront the visage of offence?
And what's in prayer but this two-fold force,
To be forestalled ere we come to fall,
Or pardon'd being down? Then I'll look up;
My fault is past. But, O, what form of prayer
Can serve my turn? 'Forgive me my foul murder'?
That cannot be; since I am still possess'd
Of those effects for which I did the murder,
My crown, mine own ambition and my queen.

May one be pardon'd and retain the offence?
In the corrupted currents of this world
Offence's gilded hand may shove by justice,
And oft 'tis seen the wicked prize itself
Buys out the law; but 'tis not so above;
There is no shuffling, there the action lies
In his true nature; and we ourselves compell'd,
Even to the teeth and forehead of our faults,
To give in evidence. What then? what rests?
Try what repentance can; what can it not?
Yet what can it when one can not repent?
O wretched state! O bosom black as death!
O limed soul, that, struggling to be free,
Art more engaged! Help, angels! Make assay!
Bow, stubborn knees; and, heart with strings of steel,
Be soft as sinews of the newborn babe!
All may be well.

[*Retires and kneels*]
[*Enter HAMLET*]

HAMLET:

Now might I do it pat, now he is praying;

And now I'll do't. And so he goes to heaven;
And so am I revenged. That would be scann'd;
A villain kills my father; and for that,
I, his sole son, do this same villain send
To heaven.
O, this is hire and salary, not revenge.
He took my father grossly, full of bread;
With all his crimes broad blown, as flush as May;
And how his audit stands who knows save heaven?
But in our circumstance and course of thought,
'Tis heavy with him; and am I then revenged,
To take him in the purging of his soul,
When he is fit and season'd for his passage?
No!
Up, sword; and know thou a more horrid hent;
When he is drunk asleep, or in his rage,
Or in the incestuous pleasure of his bed;
At gaming, swearing, or about some act
That has no relish of salvation in't;
Then trip him, that his heels may kick at heaven,
And that his soul may be as damn'd and black
As hell, whereto it goes. My mother stays;
This physic but prolongs thy sickly days.

[*Exit*]

KING CLAUDIUS:

[*Rising*] My words fly up, my thoughts remain below;
Words without thoughts never to heaven go.

[*Exit*]

SCENE IV.
The Queen's closet.

[*Enter QUEEN MARGARET and POLONIUS*]

LORD POLONIUS:

He will come straight. Look you lay home to him;
Tell him his pranks have been too broad to bear with,
And that your grace hath screen'd and stood between
Much heat and him. I'll sconce me even here.
Pray you, be round with him.

HAMLET:

[*Within*] Mother, mother, mother!

QUEEN GERTRUDE:

I'll warrant you,

Fear me not; withdraw, I hear him coming.

POLONIUS hides behind the arras

Enter HAMLET

HAMLET:

Now, mother, what's the matter?

QUEEN GERTRUDE:

Hamlet, thou hast thy father much offended.

HAMLET:

Mother, you have my father much offended.

QUEEN GERTRUDE:

Come, come, you answer with an idle tongue.

HAMLET:

Go, go, you question with a wicked tongue.

QUEEN GERTRUDE:

Why, how now, Hamlet!

HAMLET:

What's the matter now?

QUEEN GERTRUDE:

Have you forgot me?

HAMLET:

No, by the rood, not so;

You are the queen, your husband's brother's wife;

And—would it were not so! —you are my mother.

QUEEN GERTRUDE:

Nay, then, I'll set those to you that can speak.

HAMLET:

Come, come, and sit you down; you shall not budge;

You go not till I set you up a glass

Where you may see the inmost part of you.

QUEEN GERTRUDE:

What wilt thou do? thou wilt not murder me?

Help, help, ho!

LORD POLONIUS:

[*Behind*] What, ho! help, help, help!

HAMLET:

[*Drawing*] How now! a rat? Dead, for a ducat, dead!

Makes a pass through the arras

LORD POLONIUS:

[*Behind*] O, I am slain!

Falls and dies

QUEEN GERTRUDE:

O me, what hast thou done?

HAMLET:

Nay, I know not;

Is it the king?

QUEEN GERTRUDE:

O, what a rash and bloody deed is this!

HAMLET:

A bloody deed! almost as bad, good mother,

As kill a king, and marry with his brother.

QUEEN GERTRUDE:

As kill a king!

HAMLET:

Ay, lady, 'twas my word.

Lifts up the array and discovers POLONIUS

Thou wretched, rash, intruding fool, farewell!

I took thee for thy better; take thy fortune;

Thou find'st to be too busy is some danger.

Leave wringing of your hands; peace! sit you down,

And let me wring your heart; for so I shall,

If it be made of penetrable stuff,

If damned custom have not brass'd it so

That it is proof and bulwark against sense.

QUEEN GERTRUDE:

What have I done, that thou darest wag thy tongue In noise so rude against me?

HAMLET:

Such an act

That blurs the grace and blush of modesty,

Calls virtue hypocrite, takes off the rose

From the fair forehead of an innocent love

And sets a blister there, makes marriage-vows

As false as dicers' oaths; O, such a deed

As from the body of contraction plucks

The very soul, and sweet religion makes

A rhapsody of words; heaven's face doth glow;

Yea, this solidity and compound mass,

With tristful visage, as against the doom,

Is thought-sick at the act.

QUEEN GERTRUDE:

Ay me, what act,

That roars so loud, and thunders in the index?

HAMLET:

Look here, upon this picture, and on this,

The counterfeit presentment of two brothers.

See, what a grace was seated on this brow;

Hyperion's curls; the front of Jove himself;

An eye like Mars, to threaten and command;

A station like the herald Mercury

New-lighted on a heaven-kissing hill;
A combination and a form indeed,
Where every god did seem to set his seal,
To give the world assurance of a man;
This was your husband. Look you now, what follows;
Here is your husband; like a mildew'd ear,
Blasting his wholesome brother. Have you eyes?
Could you on this fair mountain leave to feed,
And batten on this moor? Ha! have you eyes?
You cannot call it love; for at your age
The hey-day in the blood is tame, it's humble,
And waits upon the judgment; and what judgment
Would step from this to this? Sense, sure, you have,
Else could you not have motion; but sure, that sense
Is apoplex'd; for madness would not err,
Nor sense to ecstasy was ne'er so thrall'd
But it reserved some quantity of choice,
To serve in such a difference. What devil was't
That thus hath cozen'd you at hoodman-blind?
Eyes without feeling, feeling without sight,
Ears without hands or eyes, smelling sans all,
Or but a sickly part of one true sense
Could not so mope.

O shame! where is thy blush? Rebellious hell,
If thou canst mutine in a matron's bones,
To flaming youth let virtue be as wax,
And melt in her own fire; proclaim no shame
When the compulsive ardour gives the charge,
Since frost itself as actively doth burn
And reason panders will.

QUEEN GERTRUDE:

O Hamlet, speak no more;
Thou turn'st mine eyes into my very soul;
And there I see such black and grained spots
As will not leave their tinct.

HAMLET:

Nay, but to live
In the rank sweat of an enseamed bed,
Stew'd in corruption, honeying and making love
Over the nasty sty,—

QUEEN GERTRUDE:

O, speak to me no more;
These words, like daggers, enter in mine ears;
No more, sweet Hamlet!

HAMLET:

A murderer and a villain;

A slave that is not twentieth part the tithe

Of your precedent lord; a vice of kings;

A cutpurse of the empire and the rule,

That from a shelf the precious diadem stole,

And put it in his pocket!

QUEEN GERTRUDE:

No more!

HAMLET:

A king of shreds and patches,—

Enter Ghost

Save me, and hover o'er me with your wings,

You heavenly guards! What would your gracious figure?

QUEEN GERTRUDE:

Alas, he's mad!

HAMLET:

Do you not come your tardy son to chide,

That, lapsed in time and passion, lets go by

The important acting of your dread command? O, say!

Ghost:

Do not forget; this visitation

Is but to whet thy almost blunted purpose.

But, look, amazement on thy mother sits;

O, step between her and her fighting soul;

Conceit in weakest bodies strongest works;

Speak to her, Hamlet.

HAMLET:

How is it with you, lady?

QUEEN GERTRUDE:

Alas, how is't with you,

That you do bend your eye on vacancy

And with the incorporal air do hold discourse?

Forth at your eyes your spirits wildly peep;

And, as the sleeping soldiers in the alarm,

Your bedded hair, like life in excrements,

Starts up, and stands on end. O gentle son,

Upon the heat and flame of thy distemper

Sprinkle cool patience. Whereon do you look?

HAMLET:

On him, on him! Look you, how pale he glares!

His form and cause conjoin'd, preaching to stones,

Would make them capable. Do not look upon me;

Lest with this piteous action you convert

My stern effects; then what I have to do

Will want true colour; tears perchance for blood.

QUEEN GERTRUDE:

To whom do you speak this?

HAMLET:

Do you see nothing there?

QUEEN GERTRUDE:

Nothing at all; yet all that is I see.

HAMLET:

Nor did you nothing hear?

QUEEN GERTRUDE:

No, nothing but ourselves.

HAMLET:

Why, look you there! look, how it steals away!

My father, in his habit as he lived!

Look, where he goes, even now, out at the portal!

[*Exit Ghost*]

QUEEN GERTRUDE:

This the very coinage of your brain;

This bodiless creation ecstasy

Is very cunning in.

HAMLET:

Ecstasy!

My pulse, as yours, doth temperately keep time,

And makes as healthful music; it is not madness

That I have utter'd; bring me to the test,
And I the matter will re-word; which madness
Would gambol from. Mother, for love of grace,
Lay not that mattering unction to your soul,
That not your trespass, but my madness speaks;
It will but skin and film the ulcerous place,
Whilst rank corruption, mining all within,
Infects unseen. Confess yourself to heaven;
Repent what's past; avoid what is to come;
And do not spread the compost on the weeds,
To make them ranker. Forgive me this my virtue;
For in the fatness of these pursy times
Virtue itself of vice must pardon beg,
Yea, curb and woo for leave to do him good.

QUEEN GERTRUDE:

O Hamlet, thou hast cleft my heart in twain.

HAMLET:

O, throw away the worser part of it,
And live the purer with the other half.
Good night; but go not to mine uncle's bed;
Assume a virtue, if you have it not.
That monster, custom, who all sense doth eat,
Of habits devil, is angel yet in this,

That to the use of actions fair and good
He likewise gives a frock or livery,
That aptly is put on. Refrain to-night,
And that shall lend a kind of easiness
To the next abstinence; the next more easy;
For use almost can change the stamp of nature,
And either master the devil, or throw him out
With wondrous potency. Once more, good night;
And when you are desirous to be bless'd,
I'll blessing beg of you. For this same lord,

[*Pointing to POLONIUS*]

I do repent; but heaven hath pleased it so,
To punish me with this and this with me,
That I must be their scourge and minister.
I will bestow him, and will answer well
The death I gave him. So, again, good night.
I must be cruel, only to be kind;
Thus bad begins and worse remains behind.
One word more, good lady.

QUEEN GERTRUDE:

What shall I do?

HAMLET:

Not this, by no means, that I bid you do;
Let the bloat king tempt you again to bed;
Pinch wanton on your cheek; call you his mouse;
And let him, for a pair of reechy kisses,
Or paddling in your neck with his damn'd fingers,
Make you to ravel all this matter out,
That I essentially am not in madness,
But mad in craft. 'Twere good you let him know;
For who, that's but a queen, fair, sober, wise,
Would from a paddock, from a bat, a gib,
Such dear concernings hide? who would do so?
No, in despite of sense and secrecy,
Unpeg the basket on the house's top.
Let the birds fly, and, like the famous ape,
To try conclusions, in the basket creep,
And break your own neck down.

QUEEN GERTRUDE:

Be thou assured, if words be made of breath,
And breath of life, I have no life to breathe
What thou hast said to me.

HAMLET:

I must to England; you know that?

QUEEN GERTRUDE:

Alack,

I had forgot; 'tis so concluded on.

HAMLET:

There's letters seal'd; and my two schoolfellows,

Whom I will trust as I will adders fang'd,

They bear the mandate; they must sweep my way,

And marshal me to knavery. Let it work;

For 'tis the sport to have the engineer

Hoist with his own petard; and 't shall go hard

But I will delve one yard below their mines,

And blow them at the moon; O, 'tis most sweet,

When in one line two crafts directly meet.

This man shall set me packing;

I'll lug the guts into the neighbour room.

Mother, good night. Indeed this counsellor

Is now most still, most secret and most grave,

Who was in life a foolish prating knave.

Come, sir, to draw toward an end with you.

Good night, mother.

[*Exeunt severally; HAMLET dragging in POLONIUS*]

ACT4

SCENE Ⅰ.
A room in the castle.

[*Enter KING CLAUDIUS, QUEEN GERTRUDE, ROSENCRANTZ, and GUILDENSTERN*]

KING CLAUDIUS:

There's matter in these sighs, these profound heaves;

You must translate; 'tis fit we understand them.

Where is your son?

QUEEN GERTRUDE:

Bestow this place on us a little while.

[*Exeunt ROSENCRANTZ and GUILDENSTERN*]

Ah, my good lord, what have I seen to-night!
KING CLAUDIUS:

What, Gertrude? How does Hamlet?
QUEEN GERTRUDE:

Mad as the sea and wind, when both contend
Which is the mightier; in his lawless fit,
Behind the arras hearing something stir,
Whips out his rapier, cries, 'A rat, a rat! '
And, in this brainish apprehension, kills
The unseen good old man.
KING CLAUDIUS:

O heavy deed!
It had been so with us, had we been there;
His liberty is full of threats to all;
To you yourself, to us, to every one.
Alas, how shall this bloody deed be answer'd?
It will be laid to us, whose providence
Should have kept short, restrain'd and out of haunt,
This mad young man; but so much was our love,
We would not understand what was most fit;
But, like the owner of a foul disease,
To keep it from divulging, let it feed

Even on the pith of Life. Where is he gone?

QUEEN GERTRUDE:

To draw apart the body he hath kill'd;
O'er whom his very madness, like some ore
Among a mineral of metals base,
Shows itself pure; he weeps for what is done.

KING CLAUDIUS:

O Gertrude, come away!
The sun no sooner shall the mountains touch,
But we will ship him hence; and this vile deed
We must, with all our majesty and skill,
Both countenance and excuse. Ho, Guildenstern!
Re-enter ROSENCRANTZ and GUILDENSTERN
Friends both, go join you with some further aid;
Hamlet in madness hath Polonius slain,
And from his mother's closet hath he dragg'd him;
Go seek him out; speak fair, and bring the body
Into the chapel. I pray you, haste in this.
[*Exeunt ROSENCRANTZ and GUILDENSTERN*]
Come, Gertrude, we'll call up our wisest friends;
And let them know, both what we mean to do,
And what's untimely done. O, come away!
My soul is full of discord and dismay.

[*Exeunt*]

SCENE II.
Another room in the castle.

[*Enter HAMLET*]

HAMLET:
 Safely stowed.
ROSENCRANTZ:
 GUILDENSTERN:
 [*Within*] Hamlet! Lord Hamlet!
HAMLET:
 What noise? who calls on Hamlet?
 O, here they come.

[*Enter ROSENCRANTZ and GUILDENSTERN*]

ROSENCRANTZ:
 What have you done, my lord, with the dead body?

HAMLET:

Compounded it with dust, whereto 'tis kin.

ROSENCRANTZ:

Tell us where 'tis, that we may take it thence
And bear it to the chapel.

HAMLET:

Do not believe it.

ROSENCRANTZ:

Believe what?

HAMLET:

That I can keep your counsel and not mine own. Besides, to be demanded of a sponge! what replication should be made by the son of a king?

ROSENCRANTZ:

Take you me for a sponge, my lord?

HAMLET:

Ay, sir, that soaks up the king's countenance, his rewards, his authorities. But such officers do the king best service in the end; he keeps them, like an ape, in the corner of his jaw; first mouthed, to be last swallowed; when he needs what you have gleaned, it is but squeezing you, and, sponge, you shall be dry again.

ROSENCRANTZ:

I understand you not, my lord.

HAMLET:

I am glad of it; a knavish speech sleeps in a foolish ear.

ROSENCRANTZ:

My lord, you must tell us where the body is, and go with us to the king.

HAMLET:

The body is with the king, but the king is not with the body. The king is a thing—

GUILDENSTERN:

A thing, my lord!

HAMLET:

Of nothing; bring me to him. Hide fox, and all after.

[*Exeunt*]

SCENE III.
Another room in the castle.

[*Enter KING CLAUDIUS, attended*]

KING CLAUDIUS:

> I have sent to seek him, and to find the body.
> How dangerous is it that this man goes loose!
> Yet must not we put the strong law on him;
> He's loved of the distracted multitude,
> Who like not in their judgment, but their eyes;
> And where tis so, the offender's scourge is weigh'd,
> But never the offence. To bear all smooth and even,
> This sudden sending him away must seem
> Deliberate pause: diseases desperate grown
> By desperate appliance are relieved,
> Or not at all.
>
> [*Enter ROSENCRANTZ*]
>
> How now! what hath befall'n?

ROSENCRANTZ:

> Where the dead body is bestow'd, my lord,
> We cannot get from him.

KING CLAUDIUS:

> But where is he?

ROSENCRANTZ:

> Without, my lord; guarded, to know your pleasure.

KING CLAUDIUS:

> Bring him before us.

ROSENCRANTZ:

Ho, Guildenstern! bring in my lord.

Enter HAMLET and GUILDENSTERN

KING CLAUDIUS:

Now, Hamlet, where's Polonius?

HAMLET:

At supper.

KING CLAUDIUS:

At supper! where?

HAMLET:

Not where he eats, but where he is eaten; a certain convocation of politic worms are e'en at him. Your worm is your only emperor for diet; we fat all creatures else to fat us, and we fat ourselves for maggots; your fat king and your lean beggar is but variable service, two dishes, but to one table; that's the end.

KING CLAUDIUS:

Alas, alas!

HAMLET:

A man may fish with the worm that hath eat of a king, and cat of the fish that hath fed of that worm.

KING CLAUDIUS:

What dost you mean by this?

HAMLET:

Nothing but to show you how a king may go a progress through the guts of a beggar.

KING CLAUDIUS:

Where is Polonius?

HAMLET:

In heaven; send hither to see; if your messenger find him not there, seek him i' the other place yourself. But indeed, if you find him not within this month, you shall nose him as you go up the stairs into the lobby.

KING CLAUDIUS:

Go seek him there.

[*To some Attendants*]

HAMLET:

He will stay till ye come.

[*Exeunt Attendants*]

KING CLAUDIUS:

Hamlet, this deed, for thine especial safety,—
Which we do tender, as we dearly grieve

For that which thou hast done,—must send thee hence

With fiery quickness; therefore prepare thyself;

The bark is ready, and the wind at help,

The associates tend, and every thing is bent

For England.

HAMLET:

For England!

KING CLAUDIUS:

Ay, Hamlet.

HAMLET:

Good.

KING CLAUDIUS:

So is it, if thou knew'st our purposes.

HAMLET:

I see a cherub that sees them. But, come; for

England! Farewell, dear mother.

KING CLAUDIUS:

Thy loving father, Hamlet.

HAMLET:

My mother; father and mother is man and wife; man and wife is one flesh; and so, my mother. Come, for England!

[*Exit*]

KING CLAUDIUS:

> Follow him at foot; tempt him with speed aboard;
> Delay it not; I'll have him hence to-night.
> Away! for every thing is seal'd and done
> That else leans on the affair; pray you, make haste.

[*Exeunt ROSENCRANTZ and GUILDENSTERN*]

> And, England, if my love thou hold'st at aught—
> As my great power thereof may give thee sense,
> Since yet thy cicatrice looks raw and red
> After the Danish sword, and thy free awe
> Pays homage to us—thou mayst not coldly set
> Our sovereign process; which imports at full,
> By letters congruing to that effect,
> The present death of Hamlet. Do it, England;
> For like the hectic in my blood he rages,
> And thou must cure me; till I know 'tis done,
> Howe'er my haps, my joys were ne'er begun.

[*Exit*]

SCENE IV.
A plain in Denmark.

[*Enter FORTINBRAS, a Captain, and Soldiers, marching*]

PRINCE FORTINBRAS:

　Go, captain, from me greet the Danish king;
　Tell him that, by his licence, Fortinbras
　Craves the conveyance of a promised march
　Over his kingdom. You know the rendezvous.
　If that his majesty would aught with us,
　We shall express our duty in his eye;
　And let him know so.
　Captain
　I will do't, my lord.

PRINCE FORTINBRAS:

　Go softly on.

[*Exeunt FORTINBRAS and Soldiers*]
[*Enter HAMLET, ROSENCRANTZ, GUILDENSTERN, and others*]

HAMLET:

Good sir, whose powers are these?

Captain. They are of Norway, sir.

HAMLET:

How purposed, sir, I pray you?

Captain. Against some part of Poland.

HAMLET:

Who commands them, sir?

Captain. The nephews to old Norway, Fortinbras.

HAMLET:

Goes it against the main of Poland, sir,

Or for some frontier?

Captain. Truly to speak, and with no addition,

We go to gain a little patch of ground

That hath in it no profit but the name.

To pay five ducats, five, I would not farm it;

Nor will it yield to Norway or the Pole

A ranker rate, should it be sold in fee.

HAMLET:

Why, then the Polack never will defend it.

Captain. Yes, it is already garrison'd.

HAMLET:

Two thousand souls and twenty thousand ducats
Will not debate the question of this straw.
This is the imposthume of much wealth and peace,
That inward breaks, and shows no cause without
Why the man dies. I humbly thank you, sir.
Captain. God be wi' you, sir.

[*Exit*]

ROSENCRANTZ:

Wilt please you go, my lord?

HAMLET:

I'll be with you straight go a little before.

[*Exeunt all except HAMLET*]

How all occasions do inform against me,
And spur my dull revenge! What is a man,
If his chief good and market of his time
Be but to sleep and feed? a beast, no more.
Sure, he that made us with such large discourse,
Looking before and after, gave us not
That capability and god-like reason
To fust in us unused. Now, whether it be
Bestial oblivion, or some craven scruple

Of thinking too precisely on the event,
A thought which, quarter'd, hath but one part wisdom
And ever three parts coward, I do not know
Why yet I live to say 'This thing's to do;'
Sith I have cause and will and strength and means
To do't. Examples gross as earth exhort me.
Witness this army of such mass and charge
Led by a delicate and tender prince,
Whose spirit with divine ambition puff'd
Makes mouths at the invisible event,
Exposing what is mortal and unsure
To all that fortune, death and danger dare,
Even for an egg-shell. Rightly to be great
Is not to stir without great argument,
But greatly to find quarrel in a straw
When honour's at the stake. How stand I then,
That have a father kill'd, a mother stain'd,
Excitements of my reason and my blood,
And let all sleep? while, to my shame, I see
The imminent death of twenty thousand men,
That, for a fantasy and trick of fame,
Go to their graves like beds, fight for a plot
Whereon the numbers cannot try the cause,

Which is not tomb enough and continent
To hide the slain? O, from this time forth,
My thoughts be bloody, or be nothing worth!

[*Exit*]

SCENE V.
Elsinore. A room in the castle.

[*Enter QUEEN GERTRUDE, HORATIO, and a Gentleman*]

QUEEN GERTRUDE:
I will not speak with her.
Gentleman. She is importunate, indeed distract.
Her mood will needs be pitied.
QUEEN GERTRUDE:
What would she have?
Gentleman. She speaks much of her father; says she hears
There's tricks i' the world; and hems, and beats her heart;
Spurns enviously at straws; speaks things in doubt,
That carry but half sense; her speech is nothing,

Yet the unshaped use of it doth move

The hearers to collection; they aim at it,

And botch the words up fit to their own thoughts;

Which, as her winks, and nods, and gestures yield them,

Indeed would make one think there might be thought,

Though nothing sure, yet much unhappily.

HORATIO:

'Twere good she were spoken with; for she may strew

Dangerous conjectures in ill-breeding minds.

QUEEN GERTRUDE:

Let her come in.

[*Exit HORATIO*]

To my sick soul, as sin's true nature is,

Each toy seems prologue to some great amiss.

So full of artless jealousy is guilt,

It spills itself in fearing to be spilt.

Re-enter HORATIO, with OPHELIA

OPHELIA:

Where is the beauteous majesty of Denmark?

QUEEN GERTRUDE:

How now, Ophelia!

OPHELIA:

[*Sings*]

How should I your true love know

From another one?

By his cockle hat and staff,

And his sandal shoon.

QUEEN GERTRUDE:

Alas, sweet lady, what imports this song?

OPHELIA:

Say you? nay, pray you, mark.

[*Sings*]

He is dead and gone, lady,

He is dead and gone;

At his head a grass-green turf,

At his heels a stone.

QUEEN GERTRUDE:

Nay, but, Ophelia,—

OPHELIA:

Pray you, mark.

[*Sings*]

White his shroud as the mountain snow,—

Enter KING CLAUDIUS

QUEEN GERTRUDE:

Alas, look here, my lord.

OPHELIA:

[*Sings*]

Larded with sweet flowers

Which bewept to the grave did go

With true-love showers.

KING CLAUDIUS:

How do you, pretty lady?

OPHELIA:

Well, God 'ild you! They say the owl was a baker's daughter.

Lord, we know what we are, but know not what we may be.

God be at your table!

KING CLAUDIUS:

Conceit upon her father.

OPHELIA:

Pray you, let's have no words of this; but when they ask you what it means, say you this:

[*Sings*]

To-morrow is Saint Valentine's day,

All in the morning betime,

And I a maid at your window,

To be your Valentine.

Then up he rose, and donn'd his clothes,

And dupp'd the chamber-door;

Let in the maid, that out a maid

Never departed more.

KING CLAUDIUS:

Pretty Ophelia!

OPHELIA:

Indeed, la, without an oath, I'll make an end on't:

[*Sings*]

By Gis and by Saint Charity,

Alack, and fie for shame!

Young men will do't, if they come to't;

By cock, they are to blame.

Quoth she, before you tumbled me,

You promised me to wed.

So would I ha' done, by yonder sun,

An thou hadst not come to my bed.

KING CLAUDIUS:

How long hath she been thus?

OPHELIA:

I hope all will be well. We must be patient; but I cannot choose but weep, to think they should lay him i' the cold ground. My brother shall know of it; and so I thank you for your good counsel. Come, my coach! Good night, ladies; good night, sweet ladies; good night, good night.

[*Exit*]

KING CLAUDIUS:

Follow her close; give her good watch,

I pray you.

[*Exit HORATIO*]

O, this is the poison of deep grief; it springs

All from her father's death. O Gertrude, Gertrude,

When sorrows come, they come not single spies

But in battalions. First, her father slain.

Next, your son gone; and he most violent author

Of his own just remove; the people muddied,

Thick and unwholesome in their thoughts and whispers,

For good Polonius' death; and we have done but greenly,

In hugger-mugger to inter him; poor Ophelia

Divided from herself and her fair judgment,

Without the which we are pictures, or mere beasts.

Last, and as much containing as all these,

Her brother is in secret come from France;

Feeds on his wonder, keeps himself in clouds,

And wants not buzzers to infect his ear

With pestilent speeches of his father's death;

Wherein necessity, of matter beggar'd,
Will nothing stick our person to arraign
In ear and ear. O my dear Gertrude, this,
Like to a murdering-piece, in many places
Gives me superfluous death.

A noise within

QUEEN GERTRUDE:

Alack, what noise is this?

KING CLAUDIUS:

Where are my Switzers? Let them guard the door.

Enter another Gentleman

What is the matter?

Gentleman. Save yourself, my lord.
The ocean, overpeering of his list,
Eats not the flats with more impetuous haste
Than young Laertes, in a riotous head,
O'erbears your officers. The rabble call him lord;
And, as the world were now but to begin,
Antiquity forgot, custom not known,
The ratifiers and props of every word,
They cry 'Choose we. Laertes shall be king.'
Caps, hands, and tongues, applaud it to the clouds.
'Laertes shall be king, Laertes king!'

QUEEN GERTRUDE:

How cheerfully on the false trail they cry!

O, this is counter, you false Danish dogs!

KING CLAUDIUS:

The doors are broke.

[*Noise within*]

Enter LAERTES, armed; Danes following

LAERTES:

Where is this king? Sirs, stand you all without.

Danes. No, let's come in.

LAERTES:

I pray you, give me leave.

Danes. We will, we will.

They retire without the door

LAERTES:

I thank you; keep the door. O thou vile king,

Give me my father!

QUEEN GERTRUDE:

Calmly, good Laertes.

LAERTES:

That drop of blood that's calm proclaims me bastard,

Cries cuckold to my father, brands the harlot

Even here, between the chaste unsmirched brow

Of my true mother.

KING CLAUDIUS:

What is the cause, Laertes,

That thy rebellion looks so giant-like?

Let him go, Gertrude; do not fear our person.

There's such divinity doth hedge a king,

That treason can but peep to what it would,

Acts little of his will. Tell me, Laertes,

Why thou art thus incensed. Let him go, Gertrude.

Speak, man.

LAERTES:

Where is my father?

KING CLAUDIUS:

Dead.

QUEEN GERTRUDE:

But not by him.

KING CLAUDIUS:

Let him demand his fill.

LAERTES:

How came he dead? I'll not be juggled with.

To hell, allegiance! vows, to the blackest devil!

Conscience and grace, to the profoundest pit!

I dare damnation. To this point I stand,

That both the worlds I give to negligence,

Let come what comes; only I'll be revenged

Most thoroughly for my father.

KING CLAUDIUS:

Who shall stay you?

LAERTES:

My will, not all the world.

And for my means, I'll husband them so well,

They shall go far with little.

KING CLAUDIUS:

Good Laertes,

If you desire to know the certainty

Of your dear father's death, is't writ in your revenge,

That, swoopstake, you will draw both friend and foe,

Winner and loser?

LAERTES:

None but his enemies.

KING CLAUDIUS:

Will you know them then?

LAERTES:

To his good friends thus wide I'll ope my arms;

And like the kind life-rendering pelican,

Repast them with my blood.

KING CLAUDIUS:

Why, now you speak
Like a good child and a true gentleman.
That I am guiltless of your father's death,
And am most sensible in grief for it,
It shall as level to your judgment pierce
As day does to your eye.
Danes. [*Within*] Let her come in.

LAERTES:

How now! what noise is that?
Re-enter OPHELIA
O heat, dry up my brains! tears seven times salt,
Burn out the sense and virtue of mine eye!
By heaven, thy madness shall be paid by weight,
Till our scale turn the beam. O rose of May!
Dear maid, kind sister, sweet Ophelia!
O heavens! is't possible, a young maid's wits
Should be as moral as an old man's life?
Nature is fine in love, and where 'tis fine,
It sends some precious instance of itself
After the thing it loves.

OPHELIA:

[*Sings*]

They bore him barefaced on the bier;

Hey non nonny, nonny, hey nonny;

And in his grave rain'd many a tear:—

Fare you well, my dove!

LAERTES:

Hadst thou thy wits, and didst persuade revenge,

It could not move thus.

OPHELIA:

[*Sings*]

You must sing a-down a-down,

An you call him a-down-a.

O, how the wheel becomes it! It is the false

steward, that stole his master's daughter.

LAERTES:

This nothing's more than matter.

OPHELIA:

There's rosemary, that's for remembrance; pray,

love, remember; and there is pansies. that's for thoughts.

LAERTES:

A document in madness, thoughts and remembrance fitted.

OPHELIA:

There's fennel for you, and columbines; there's rue

for you; and here's some for me; we may call it

herb-grace o' Sundays. O you must wear your rue with
a difference. There's a daisy; I would give you
some violets, but they withered all when my father
died; they say he made a good end,—
[*Sings*]
For bonny sweet Robin is all my joy.

LAERTES:

Thought and affliction, passion, hell itself,
She turns to favour and to prettiness.

OPHELIA:

[*Sings*]
And will he not come again?
And will he not come again?
No, no, he is dead.
Go to thy death-bed.
He never will come again.
His beard was as white as snow,
All flaxen was his poll.
He is gone, he is gone,
And we cast away moan.
God ha' mercy on his soul!
And of all Christian souls, I pray God. God be wi' ye.

[*Exit*]

LAERTES:

Do you see this, O God?

KING CLAUDIUS:

Laertes, I must commune with your grief,
Or you deny me right. Go but apart,
Make choice of whom your wisest friends you will.
And they shall hear and judge 'twixt you and me.
If by direct or by collateral hand
They find us touch'd, we will our kingdom give,
Our crown, our life, and all that we can ours,
To you in satisfaction; but if not,
Be you content to lend your patience to us,
And we shall jointly labour with your soul
To give it due content.

LAERTES:

Let this be so;
His means of death, his obscure funeral—
No trophy, sword, nor hatchment o'er his bones,
No noble rite nor formal ostentation—
Cry to be heard, as 'twere from heaven to earth,
That I must call't in question.

KING CLAUDIUS:

So you shall;

And where the offence is let the great axe fall.

I pray you, go with me.

[*Exeunt*]

SCENE VI.
Another room in the castle.

[*Enter HORATIO and a Servant*] **HORATIO:**

What are they that would speak with me?

Servant. Sailors, sir; they say they have letters for you.

HORATIO:

Let them come in.

[*Exit Servant*]

I do not know from what part of the world

I should be greeted, if not from Lord Hamlet.

Enter Sailors

First Sailor. God bless you, sir.

HORATIO:

Let him bless thee too.

First Sailor. He shall, sir, an't please him. There's a letter for you, sir; it comes from the ambassador that was bound for England; if your name be Horatio, as I am let to know it is.

HORATIO:

[*Reads*] 'Horatio, when thou shalt have overlooked this, give these fellows some means to the king; they have letters for him. Ere we were two days old at sea, a pirate of very warlike appointment gave us chase. Finding ourselves too slow of sail, we put on a compelled valour, and in the grapple I boarded them; on the instant they got clear of our ship; so I alone became their prisoner. They have dealt with me like thieves of mercy; but they knew what they did; I am to do a good turn for them. Let the king have the letters I have sent; and repair thou to me with as much speed as thou wouldst fly death. I have words to speak in thine ear will make thee dumb; yet are they much too light for the bore of the matter. These good fellows will bring thee where I am. Rosencrantz and Guildenstern hold their course for England; of them I have much to tell thee. Farewell.

'He that thou knowest thine, HAMLET.'

Come, I will make you way for these your letters;
And do't the speedier, that you may direct me

To him from whom you brought them.

[*Exeunt*]

SCENE VII.
Another room in the castle.

[*Enter KING CLAUDIUS and LAERTES*]

KING CLAUDIUS:
Now must your conscience my acquaintance seal,
And you must put me in your heart for friend,
Sith you have heard, and with a knowing ear,
That he which hath your noble father slain
Pursued my life.

LAERTES:
It well appears; but tell me
Why you proceeded not against these feats,
So crimeful and so capital in nature,
As by your safety, wisdom, all things else,
You mainly were stirr'd up.

KING CLAUDIUS:

O, for two special reasons;
Which may to you, perhaps, seem much unsinew'd,
But yet to me they are strong. The queen his mother
Lives almost by his looks; and for myself—
My virtue or my plague, be it either which—
She's so conjunctive to my life and soul,
That, as the star moves not but in his sphere,
I could not but by her. The other motive,
Why to a public count I might not go,
Is the great love the general gender bear him;
Who, dipping all his faults in their affection,
Would, like the spring that turneth wood to stone,
Convert his gyves to graces; so that my arrows,
Too slightly timber'd for so loud a wind,
Would have reverted to my bow again,
And not where I had aim'd them.

LAERTES:

And so have I a noble father lost;
A sister driven into desperate terms,
Whose worth, if praises may go back again,
Stood challenger on mount of all the age
For her perfections; but my revenge will come.

KING CLAUDIUS:

Break not your sleeps for that; you must not think
That we are made of stuff so flat and dull
That we can let our beard be shook with danger
And think it pastime. You shortly shall hear more.
I loved your father, and we love ourself;
And that, I hope, will teach you to imagine—
Enter a Messenger
How now! what news?
Messenger. Letters, my lord, from Hamlet.
This to your majesty; this to the queen.

KING CLAUDIUS:

From Hamlet! who brought them?
Messenger. Sailors, my lord, they say; I saw them not.
They were given me by Claudio; he received them
Of him that brought them.

KING CLAUDIUS:

Laertes, you shall hear them. Leave us.
[*Exit Messenger*]
[*Reads*]
'High and mighty, You shall know I am set naked on
your kingdom. To-morrow shall I beg leave to see
your kingly eyes; when I shall, first asking your

pardon thereunto, recount the occasion of my sudden
and more strange return. 'HAMLET.'
What should this mean? Are all the rest come back?
Or is it some abuse, and no such thing?

LAERTES:

Know you the hand?

KING CLAUDIUS:

'Tis Hamlets character. 'Naked!
And in a postscript here, he says 'alone.'
Can you advise me?

LAERTES:

I'm lost in it, my lord. But let him come;
It warms the very sickness in my heart,
That I shall live and tell him to his teeth,
'Thus didest thou.'

KING CLAUDIUS:

If it be so, Laertes—
As how should it be so? how otherwise? —
Will you be ruled by me?

LAERTES:

Ay, my lord;
So you will not o'errule me to a peace.

KING CLAUDIUS:

To thine own peace. If he be now return'd,
As checking at his voyage, and that he means
No more to undertake it, I will work him
To an exploit, now ripe in my device,
Under the which he shall not choose but fall.
And for his death no wind of blame shall breathe,
But even his mother shall uncharge the practise
And call it accident.

LAERTES:

My lord, I will be ruled;
The rather, if you could devise it so
That I might be the organ.

KING CLAUDIUS:

It falls right.
You have been talk'd of since your travel much,
And that in Hamlet's hearing, for a quality
Wherein, they say, you shine; your sum of parts
Did not together pluck such envy from him
As did that one, and that, in my regard,
Of the unworthiest siege.

LAERTES:

What part is that, my lord?

KING CLAUDIUS:

A very riband in the cap of youth,
Yet needful too; for youth no less becomes
The light and careless livery that it wears
Than settled age his sables and his weeds,
Importing health and graveness. Two months since,
Here was a gentleman of Normandy:—
I've seen myself, and served against, the French,
And they can well on horseback; but this gallant
Had witchcraft in't; he grew unto his seat;
And to such wondrous doing brought his horse,
As he had been incorpsed and demi-natured
With the brave beast; so far he topp'd my thought,
That I, in forgery of shapes and tricks,
Come short of what he did.

LAERTES:

A Norman was't?

KING CLAUDIUS:

A Norman.

LAERTES:

Upon my life, Lamond.

KING CLAUDIUS:

The very same.

LAERTES:

I know him well; he is the brooch indeed
And gem of all the nation.

KING CLAUDIUS:

He made confession of you,
And gave you such a masterly report
For art and exercise in your defence
And for your rapier most especially,
That he cried out, 'twould be a sight indeed,
If one could match you; the scrimers of their nation,
He swore, had had neither motion, guard, nor eye,
If you opposed them. Sir, this report of his
Did Hamlet so envenom with his envy
That he could nothing do but wish and beg
Your sudden coming o'er, to play with him.
Now, out of this,—

LAERTES:

What out of this, my lord?

KING CLAUDIUS:

Laertes, was your father dear to you?
Or are you like the painting of a sorrow,
A face without a heart?

LAERTES:

Why ask you this?

KING CLAUDIUS:

> Not that I think you did not love your father;
> But that I know love is begun by time;
> And that I see, in passages of proof,
> Time qualifies the spark and fire of it.
> There lives within the very flame of love
> A kind of wick or snuff that will abate it;
> And nothing is at a like goodness still;
> For goodness, growing to a plurisy,
> Dies in his own too much; that we would do
> We should do when we would; for this 'would' changes
> And hath abatements and delays as many
> As there are tongues, are hands, are accidents;
> And then this 'should' is like a spendthrift sigh,
> That hurts by easing. But, to the quick o' the ulcer:—
> Hamlet comes back; what would you undertake,
> To show yourself your father's son in deed
> More than in words?

LAERTES:

> To cut his throat i' the church.

KING CLAUDIUS:

> No place, indeed, should murder sanctuarize;
> Revenge should have no bounds. But, good Laertes,

Will you do this, keep close within your chamber.
Hamlet return'd shall know you are come home.
We'll put on those shall praise your excellence
And set a double varnish on the fame
The Frenchman gave you, bring you in fine together
And wager on your heads; he, being remiss,
Most generous and free from all contriving,
Will not peruse the foils; so that, with ease,
Or with a little shuffling, you may choose
A sword unbated, and in a pass of practise
Requite him for your father.

LAERTES:

I will do't;
And, for that purpose, I'll anoint my sword.
I bought an unction of a mountebank,
So mortal that, but dip a knife in it,
Where it draws blood no cataplasm so rare,
Collected from all simples that have virtue
Under the moon, can save the thing from death
That is but scratch'd withal; I'll touch my point
With this contagion, that, if I gall him slightly,
It may be death.

KING CLAUDIUS:

Let's further think of this;
Weigh what convenience both of time and means
May fit us to our shape; if this should fail,
And that our drift look through our bad performance,
'Twere better not assay'd; therefore this project
Should have a back or second, that might hold,
If this should blast in proof. Soft! let me see.
We'll make a solemn wager on your cunnings; I ha't.
When in your motion you are hot and dry—
As make your bouts more violent to that end—
And that he calls for drink, I'll have prepared him
A chalice for the nonce, whereon but sipping,
If he by chance escape your venom'd stuck,
Our purpose may hold there.

Enter QUEEN GERTRUDE

How now, sweet queen!

QUEEN GERTRUDE:

One woe doth tread upon another's heel,
So fast they follow; your sister's drown'd, Laertes.

LAERTES:

Drown'd! O, where?

QUEEN GERTRUDE:

There is a willow grows aslant a brook,

That shows his hoar leaves in the glassy stream;
There with fantastic garlands did she come
Of crow-flowers, nettles, daisies, and long purples
That liberal shepherds give a grosser name,
But our cold maids do dead men's fingers call them.
There, on the pendent boughs her coronet weeds
Clambering to hang, an envious sliver broke;
When down her weedy trophies and herself
Fell in the weeping brook. Her clothes spread wide;
And, mermaid-like, awhile they bore her up.
Which time she chanted snatches of old tunes;
As one incapable of her own distress,
Or like a creature native and indued
Unto that element; but long it could not be
Till that her garments, heavy with their drink,
Pull'd the poor wretch from her melodious lay
To muddy death.

LAERTES:

Alas, then, she is drown'd?

QUEEN GERTRUDE:

Drown'd, drown'd.

LAERTES:

Too much of water hast thou, poor Ophelia,

And therefore I forbid my tears; but yet
It is our trick; nature her custom holds,
Let shame say what it will; when these are gone,
The woman will be out. Adieu, my lord.
I have a speech of fire, that fain would blaze,
But that this folly douts it.

[*Exit*]

KING CLAUDIUS:

Let's follow, Gertrude.
How much I had to do to calm his rage!
Now fear I this will give it start again;
Therefore let's follow.

[*Exeunt*]

ACT5

SCENE I.
A churchyard.

[*Enter two Clowns, with spades, & c*]

First Clown:

Is she to be buried in Christian burial that
wilfully seeks her own salvation?

Second Clown:

I tell thee she is; and therefore make her grave
Straight; the crowner hath sat on her, and finds it
Christian burial.

First Clown:

How can that be, unless she drowned herself in her own defence?

Second Clown:

Why, 'tis found so.

First Clown:

It must be 'se offendendo;' it cannot be else. For here lies the point; if I drown myself wittingly, it argues an act; and an act hath three branches; it is, to act, to do, to perform; argal, she drowned herself wittingly.

Second Clown:

Nay, but hear you, goodman delver,—

First Clown:

Give me leave. Here lies the water; good; here stands the man; good; if the man go to this water, and drown himself, it is, will he, nill he, he goes,—mark you that; but if the water come to him and drown him, he drowns not himself; argal, he that is not guilty of his own death shortens not his own life.

Second Clown:

But is this law?

First Clown:

Ay, marry, is't; crowner's quest law.

Second Clown:

Will you ha' the truth on't? If this had not been

a gentlewoman, she should have been buried out o'
Christian burial.

First Clown:

Why, there thou say'st; and the more pity that
great folk should have countenance in this world to
drown or hang themselves, more than their even
Christian. Come, my spade. There is no ancient
gentleman but gardeners, ditchers, and grave-makers;
they hold up Adam's profession.

Second Clown:

Was he a gentleman?

First Clown:

He was the first that ever bore arms.

Second Clown:

Why, he had none.

First Clown:

What, art a heathen? How dost thou understand the
Scripture? The Scripture says 'Adam digged;'
could he dig without arms? I'll put another
question to thee; if thou answerest me not to the
purpose, confess thyself—

Second Clown:

Go to.

First Clown:

What is he that builds stronger than either the mason, the shipwright, or the carpenter?

Second Clown:

The gallows-maker; for that frame outlives a thousand tenants.

First Clown:

I like thy wit well, in good faith; the gallows does well; but how does it well? it does well to those that do in; now thou dost ill to say the gallows is built stronger than the church; argal, the gallows may do well to thee. To't again, come.

Second Clown:

'Who builds stronger than a mason, a shipwright, or a carpenter?'

First Clown:

Ay, tell me that, and unyoke.

Second Clown:

Marry, now I can tell.

First Clown:

To't.

Second Clown:

Mass, I cannot tell.

[*Enter HAMLET and HORATIO, at a distance*]

First Clown:

Cudgel thy brains no more about it, for your dull ass will not mend his pace with beating; and, when you are asked this question next, say 'a grave-maker; 'the houses that he makes last till doomsday. Go, get thee to Yaughan; fetch me a stoup of liquor.

[*Exit Second Clown*]

[*He digs and sings*]

In youth, when I did love, did love,

Methought it was very sweet,

To contract, O, the time, for, ah, my behove,

O, methought, there was nothing meet.

HAMLET:

Has this fellow no feeling of his business, that he sings at grave-making?

HORATIO:

Custom hath made it in him a property of easiness.

HAMLET:

'Tis e'en so; the hand of little employment hath the daintier sense.

First Clown:

[*Sings*]

But age, with his stealing steps,

Hath claw'd me in his clutch,

And hath shipped me intil the land,

As if I had never been such.

[*Throws up a skull*]

HAMLET:

That skull had a tongue in it, and could sing once; how the knave jowls it to the ground, as if it were Cain's jaw-bone, that did the first murder! It might be the pate of a politician, which this ass now o'er-reaches; one that would circumvent God, might it not?

HORATIO:

It might, my lord.

HAMLET:

Or of a courtier; which could say 'Good morrow, sweet lord! How dost thou, good lord?' This might be my lord such-a-one, that praised my lord such-a-one's horse, when he meant to beg it; might it not?

HORATIO:

Ay, my lord.

HAMLET:

Why, e'en so; and now my Lady Worm's; chapless, and knocked about the mazzard with a sexton's spade; here's fine revolution, an we had the trick to see't. Did these bones cost no more the breeding, but to play at loggats with 'em? mine ache to think on't.

First Clown:

[*Sings*]

A pick-axe, and a spade, a spade,
For and a shrouding sheet;
O, a pit of clay for to be made
For such a guest is meet.

[*Throws up another skull*]

HAMLET:

There's another; why may not that be the skull of a lawyer? Where be his quiddities now, his quillets, his cases, his tenures, and his tricks? why does he suffer this rude knave now to knock him about the sconce with a dirty shovel, and will not tell him of his action of battery? Hum! This fellow might be in's time a great buyer of land, with his statutes, his recognizances, his fines, his double vouchers, his recoveries; is this the fine of his fines, and the recovery of his recoveries, to have his fine pate full of fine dirt? will his vouchers vouch him no more of his purchases, and double ones too, than the length and breadth of a pair of indentures? The very conveyances of his lands will hardly lie in this box; and must the inheritor himself have no more, ha?

HORATIO:

Not a jot more, my lord.

HAMLET:

Is not parchment made of sheepskins?

HORATIO:

Ay, my lord, and of calf-skins too.

HAMLET:

They are sheep and calves which seek out assurance in that. I will speak to this fellow. Whose grave's this, sirrah?

First Clown

Mine, sir.

[*Sings*]

O, a pit of clay for to be made

For such a guest is meet.

HAMLET:

I think it be thine, indeed; for thou liest in't.

First Clown:

You lie out on't, sir, and therefore it is not Yours; for my part, I do not lie in't, and yet it is mine.

HAMLET:

'Thou dost lie in't, to be in't and say it is thine; 'tis for the dead, not for the quick; therefore thou liest.

First Clown:

'Tis a quick lie, sir; 'twill away gain, from me to you.

HAMLET:

What man dost thou dig it for?

First Clown:

For no man, sir.

HAMLET:

What woman, then?

First Clown:

For none, neither.

HAMLET:

Who is to be buried in't?

First Clown:

One that was a woman, sir; but, rest her soul, she's dead.

HAMLET:

How absolute the knave is! we must speak by the card, or e-quivocation will undo us. By the Lord,

Horatio, these three years I have taken a note of it; the age is grown so picked that the toe of the peasant comes so near the heel of the courtier, he gaffs his kibe. How long hast thou been a grave-maker?

First Clown:

Of all the days i' the year, I came to't that day that our last king Hamlet overcame Fortinbras.

HAMLET:

How long is that since?

First Clown:

Cannot you tell that? every fool can tell that; it was the very day that young Hamlet was born; he that is mad, and sent into England.

HAMLET:

Ay, marry, why was he sent into England?

First Clown:

Why, because he was mad; he shall recover his wits there; or, if he do not, it's no great matter there.

HAMLET:

Why?

First Clown:

'Twill, a not be seen in him there; there the men are as mad as he.

HAMLET:

How came he mad?

First Clown:

Very strangely, they say.

HAMLET:

How strangely?

First Clown:

Faith, e'en with losing his wits.

HAMLET:

Upon what ground?

First Clown:

Why, here in Denmark. I have been sexton here, man and boy, thirty years.

HAMLET:

How long will a man lie i' the earth ere he rot?

First Clown:

I' faith, if he be not rotten before he die—as we have many pocky corses now-a-days, that will scarce hold the laying in—he will last you some eight year or nine year; a tanner will last you nine year.

HAMLET:

Why he more than another?

First Clown:

Why, sir, his hide is so tanned with his trade, that he will keep out water a great while; and your water is a sore decayer of your whoreson dead body.

Here's a skull now; this skull has lain in the earth three and twenty years.

HAMLET:

Whose was it?

First Clown:

A whoreson mad fellow's it was; whose do you think it was?

HAMLET:

Nay, I know not.

First Clown:

A pestilence on him for a mad rogue! a' poured a flagon of Rhenish on my head once. This same skull, sir, was Yorick's skull, the king's jester.

HAMLET:

This?

First Clown:

E'en that.

HAMLET:

Let me see.

[*Takes the skull*]

Alas, poor Yorick! I knew him, Horatio; a fellow of infinite jest, of most excellent fancy; he hath borne me on his back a thousand times; and now, how abhorred in my imagination it is! my gorge rims at it. Here hung those lips that I have kissed I know not how oft. Where be your gibes now? your gambols? your songs? your flashes of merriment, that were wont to set the table on a roar? Not one now, to mock your own grinning? quite chap-fallen? Now get you to my lady's chamber, and tell her, let her paint an inch thick, to this favour she must come; make her laugh at that. Prithee, Horatio, tell me one thing.

HORATIO:

What's that, my lord?

HAMLET:

Dost thou think Alexander looked o' this fashion i' the earth?

HORATIO:

E'en so.

HAMLET:

And smelt so? pah!

[*Puts down the skull*]

HORATIO:

E'en so, my lord.

HAMLET:

To what base uses we may return, Horatio! Why may not imagination trace the noble dust of Alexander, till he find it stopping a bung-hole?

HORATIO:

'Twere to consider too curiously, to consider so.

HAMLET:

No, faith, not a jot; but to follow him thither with modesty enough, and likelihood to lead it; as thus; Alexander died, Alexander was buried,

Alexander returneth into dust; the dust is earth; of earth we make loam; and why of that loam, whereto he was converted, might they not stop a beer-barrel?

Imperious Caesar, dead and turn'd to clay,

Might stop a hole to keep the wind away;

O, that that earth, which kept the world in awe,

Should patch a wall to expel the winter flaw!

But soft! but soft! aside; here comes the king.

[*Enter Priest, & c. in procession; the Corpse of OPHELIA, LAERTES and Mourners following; KING CLAUDIUS, QUEEN GERTRUDE, their trains, & c*]

The queen, the courtiers; who is this they follow?
And with such maimed rites? This doth betoken
The corse they follow did with desperate hand
Fordo its own life; 'twas of some estate.
Couch we awhile, and mark.

[*Retiring with HORATIO*]

LAERTES:
What ceremony else?
HAMLET:
That is Laertes,
A very noble youth; mark.
LAERTES:
What ceremony else?
First Priest:
Her obsequies have been as far enlarged
As we havewarranties; her death was doubtful;
And, but that great command o'ersways the order,
She should in ground unsanctified have lodged
Till the last trumpet; for charitable prayers,
Shards, flints and pebbles should be thrown on her;
Yet here she is allow'd her virgin crants,

Her maiden strewments and the bringing home

Of bell and burial.

LAERTES:

Must there no more be done?

First Priest:

No more be done.

We should profane the service of the dead

To sing a requiem and such rest to her

As to peace-parted souls.

LAERTES:

Lay her i' the earth.

And from her fair and unpolluted flesh

May violets spring! I tell thee, churlish priest,

A ministering angel shall my sister be,

When thou liest howling.

HAMLET:

What, the fair Ophelia!

QUEEN GERTRUDE:

Sweets to the sweet; farewell!

[*Scattering flowers*]

I hoped thou shouldst have been my Hamlet's wife;

I thought thy bride-bed to have deck'd, sweet maid,

And not have strew'd thy grave.

LAERTES:

O, treble woe

Fall ten times treble on that cursed head,

Whose wicked deed thy most ingenious sense

Deprived thee of! Hold off the earth awhile,

Till I have caught her once more in mine arms.

[*Leaps into the grave*]

Now pile your dust upon the quick and dead,

Till of this flat a mountain you have made,

To o'ertop old Pelion, or the skyish head

Of blue Olympus.

HAMLET:

[*Advancing*] What is he whose grief

Bears such an emphasis? whose phrase of sorrow

Conjures the wandering stars, and makes them stand

Like wonder-wounded hearers? This is I,

Hamlet the Dane.

[*Leaps into the grave*]

LAERTES:

The devil take thy soul!

[*Grappling with him*]

HAMLET:

Thou pray'st not well.

I prithee, take thy fingers from my throat;

For, though I am not splenitive and rash,

Yet have I something in me dangerous,

Which let thy wiseness fear; hold off thy hand.

KING CLAUDIUS:

Pluck them asunder.

QUEEN GERTRUDE:

Hamlet, Hamlet!

All:

Gentlemen,—

HORATIO:

Good my lord, be quiet.

The Attendants part them, and they come out of the grave

HAMLET:

Why I will fight with him upon this theme

Until my eyelids will no longer wag.

QUEEN GERTRUDE:

O my son, what theme?

HAMLET:

I loved Ophelia; forty thousand brothers

Could not, with all their quantity of love,

Make up my sum. What wilt thou do for her?

KING CLAUDIUS:

O, he is mad, Laertes.

QUEEN GERTRUDE:

For love of God, forbear him.

HAMLET:

'Swounds, show me what thou'lt do.

Woo't weep? woo't fight? woo't fast? woo't tear thyself?

Woo't drink up eisel? eat a crocodile?

I'll do't. Dost thou come here to whine?

To outface me with leaping in her grave?

Be buried quick with her, and so will I.

And, if thou prate of mountains, let them throw

Millions of acres on us, till our ground,

Singeing his pate against the burning zone,

Make Ossa like a wart! Nay, an thou'lt mouth,

I'll rant as well as thou.

QUEEN GERTRUDE:

This is mere madness.

And thus awhile the fit will work on him;

Anon, as patient as the female dove,

When that her golden couplets are disclosed,

His silence will sit drooping.

HAMLET:

Hear you, sir;

What is the reason that you use me thus?

I loved you ever; but it is no matter;

Let Hercules himself do what he may,

The cat will mew and dog will have his day.

[*Exit*]

KING CLAUDIUS

I pray you, good Horatio, wait upon him.

[*Exit HORATIO*]

[*To LAERTES*]

Strengthen your patience in our last night's speech;

We'll put the matter to the present push.

Good Gertrude, set some watch over your son.

This grave shall have a living monument.

An hour of quiet shortly shall we see;

Till then, in patience our proceeding be.

[*Exeunt*]

SCENE II.
A hall in the castle.

[*Enter HAMLET and HORATIO*]

HAMLET:

So much for this, sir; now shall you see the other;
You do remember all the circumstance?

HORATIO:

Remember it, my lord?

HAMLET:

Sir, in my heart there was a kind of fighting,
That would not let me sleep; methought I lay
Worse than the mutines in the bilboes. Rashly,
And praised be rashness for it, let us know,
Our indiscretion sometimes serves us well,
When our deep plots do pall; and that should teach us
There's a divinity that shapes our ends,
Rough-hew them how we will,—

HORATIO:

That is most certain.

HAMLET:

Up from my cabin,

My sea-gown scarf'd about me, in the dark

Groped I to find out them; had my desire.

Finger'd their packet, and in fine withdrew

To mine own room again; making so bold,

My fears forgetting manners, to unseal

Their grand commission; where I found, Horatio,—

O royal knavery! —an exact command,

Larded with many several sorts of reasons

Importing Denmark's health and England's too,

With, ho! such bugs and goblins in my life,

That, on the supervise, no leisure bated,

No, not to stay the grinding of the axe,

My head should be struck off.

HORATIO:

Is't possible?

HAMLET:

Here's the commission; read it at more leisure.

But wilt thou hear me how I did proceed?

HORATIO:

I beseech you.

HAMLET:

Being thus be-netted round with villanies,—
Ere I could make a prologue to my brains,
They had begun the play—I sat me down,
Devised a new commission, wrote it fair.
I once did hold it, as our statists do,
A baseness to write fair and labour'd much
How to forget that learning, but, sir, now
It did me yeoman's service; wilt thou know
The effect of what I wrote?

HORATIO:

Ay, good my lord.

HAMLET:

An earnest conjuration from the king,
As England was his faithful tributary,
As love between them like the palm might flourish,
As peace should stiff her wheaten garland wear
And stand a comma 'tween their amities,
And many such-like 'As'es of great charge,
That, on the view and knowing of these contents,
Without debatement further, more or less,
He should the bearers put to sudden death,
Not shriving-time allow'd.

HORATIO:

How was this seal'd?

HAMLET:

Why, even in that was heaven ordinant.
I had my father's signet in my purse,
Which was the model of that Danish seal;
Folded the writ up in form of the other,
Subscribed it, gave't the impression, placed it safely,
The changeling never known. Now, the next day
Was our sea-fight; and what to this was sequent
Thou know'st already.

HORATIO:

So Guildenstern and Rosencrantz go to't.

HAMLET:

Why, man, they did make love to this employment;
They are not near my conscience; their defeat
Does by their own insinuation grow.
'Tis dangerous when the baser nature comes
Between the pass and fell incensed points
Of mighty opposites.

HORATIO:

Why, what a king is this!

HAMLET:

Does it not, think'st thee, stand me now upon—
He that hath kill'd my king and whored my mother,
Popp'd in between the election and my hopes,
Thrown out his angle for my proper life,
And with such cozenage—is't not perfect conscience,
To quit him with this arm? and is't not to be damn'd,
To let this canker of our nature come
In further evil?

HORATIO:

It must be shortly known to him from England
What is the issue of the business there.

HAMLET:

It will be short; the interim is mine;
And a man's life's no more than to say 'One.'
But I am very sorry, good Horatio,
That to Laertes I forgot myself;
For, by the image of my cause, I see
The portraiture of his; I'll court his favours.
But, sure, the bravery of his grief did put me
Into a towering passion.

HORATIO:

Peace! who comes here?

[*Enter OSRIC*]

OSRIC:

Your lordship is right welcome back to Denmark.

HAMLET:

I humbly thank you, sir. Dost know this water-fly?

HORATIO:

No, my good lord.

HAMLET:

Thy state is the more gracious; for 'tis a vice to know him. He hath much land, and fertile; let a beast be lord of beasts, and his crib shall stand at the king's mess; 'tis a chough; but, as I say, spacious in the possession of dirt.

OSRIC:

Sweet lord, if your lordship were at leisure, I should impart a thing to you from his majesty.

HAMLET:

I will receive it, sir, with all diligence of spirit. Put your bonnet to his right use; 'tis for the head.

OSRIC:

I thank your lordship, it is very hot.

HAMLET:

No, believe me, 'tis very cold; the wind is northerly.

OSRIC:

It is indifferent cold, my lord, indeed.

HAMLET:

But yet methinks it is very sultry and hot for my complexion.

OSRIC:

Exceedingly, my lord; it is very sultry,—as 'twere,—I cannot tell how. But, my lord, his majesty bade me signify to you that he has laid a great wager on your head; sir, this is the matter,—

HAMLET:

I beseech you, remember—

[*HAMLET moves him to put on his hat*]

OSRIC:

Nay, good my lord; for mine ease, in good faith.

Sir, here is newly come to court Laertes; believe me, an absolute gentleman, full of most excellent differences, of very soft society and great showing; indeed, to speak feelingly of him, he is the card or calendar of gentry, for you shall find in him the continent of what part a gentleman would see.

HAMLET:

Sir, his definement suffers no perdition in you; though, I

know, to divide him inventorially would dizzy the arithmetic of memory, and yet but yaw neither, in respect of his quick sail. But, in the verity of extolment, I take him to be a soul of great article; and his infusion of such dearth and rareness, as, to make true diction of him, his semblable is his mirror; and who else would trace him, his umbrage, nothing more.

OSRIC:

Your lordship speaks most infallibly of him.

HAMLET:

The concernancy, sir? why do we wrap the gentleman in our more rawer breath?

OSRIC:

Sir?

HORATIO:

Is't not possible to understand in another tongue?
You will do't, sir, really.

HAMLET:

What imports the nomination of this gentleman?

OSRIC:

Of Laertes?

HORATIO:

His purse is empty already; all's golden words are spent.

HAMLET:

Of him, sir.

OSRIC:

I know you are not ignorant—

HAMLET:

I would you did, sir; yet, in faith, if you did, it would not much approve me. Well, sir?

OSRIC:

You are not ignorant of what excellence Laertes is—

HAMLET:

I dare not confess that, lest I should compare with him in excellence; but, to know a man well, were to know himself.

OSRIC:

I mean, sir, for his weapon; but in the imputation laid on him by them, in his meed he's unfellowed.

HAMLET:

What's his weapon?

OSRIC:

Rapier and dagger.

HAMLET:

That's two of his weapons; but, well.

OSRIC:

The king, sir, hath wagered with him six Barbary horses; against the which he has imponed, as I take it, six French rapiers and poniards, with their assigns, as girdle, hangers, and so; three of the carriages, in faith, are very dear to fancy, very responsive to the hilts, most delicate carriages, and of very liberal conceit.

HAMLET:

What call you the carriages?

HORATIO:

I knew you must be edified by the margent ere you had done.

OSRIC:

The carriages, sir, are the hangers.

HAMLET:

The phrase would be more german to the matter, if we could carry cannon by our sides; I would it might be hangers till then. But, on; six Barbary horses against six French swords, their assigns, and three liberal-conceited carriages; that's the French bet against the Danish. Why is this 'imponed,' as you call it?

OSRIC:

The king, sir, hath laid, that in a dozen passes between yourself and him, he shall not exceed you three hits; he hath laid on twelve for nine; and it would come to immediate trial, if your lordship would vouchsafe the answer.

HAMLET:

How if I answer 'no'?
OSRIC:

I mean, my lord, the opposition of your person in trial.
HAMLET:

Sir, I will walk here in the hall; if it please his majesty, 'tis the breathing time of day with me; let the foils be brought, the gentleman willing, and the king hold his purpose, I will win for him an I can; if not, I will gain nothing but my shame and the odd hits.
OSRIC:

Shall I re-deliver you e'en so?
HAMLET:

To this effect, sir; after what flourish your nature will.
OSRIC:

I commend my duty to your lordship.
HAMLET:

Yours, yours.

[*Exit OSRIC*]

He does well to commend it himself; there are no tongues else for's turn.
HORATIO:

This lapwing runs away with the shell on his head.
HAMLET:

He did comply with his dug, before he sucked it.

Thus has he—and many more of the same bevy that I know the dressy age dotes on—only got the tune of the time and outward habit of encounter; a kind of yesty collection, which carries them through and through the most fond and winnowed opinions; and do but blow them to their trial, the bubbles are out.

[*Enter a Lord*]

Lord:

My lord, his majesty commended him to you by young Osric, who brings back to him that you attend him in the hall; he sends to know if your pleasure hold to play with Laertes, or that you will take longer time.

HAMLET:

I am constant to my purpose; they follow the king's pleasure; if his fitness speaks, mine is ready; now or whensoever, provided I be so able as now.

Lord:

The king and queen and all are coming down.

HAMLET:

In happy time.

Lord:

The queen desires you to use some gentle entertainment to Laertes before you fall to play.

HAMLET:

She well instructs me.

[*Exit Lord*]

HORATIO:

You will lose this wager, my lord.

HAMLET:

I do not think so; since he went into France, I have been in continualpractice; I shall win at the
odds. But thou wouldst not think how ill all's here about my heart; but it is no matter.

HORATIO:

Nay, good my lord,—

HAMLET:

It is but foolery; but it is such a kind of gain-giving, as would perhaps trouble a woman.

HORATIO:

If your mind dislike any thing, obey it; I will forestall their repair hither, and say you are not fit.

HAMLET:

Not a whit, we defy augury; there's a special providence in the fall of a sparrow. If it be now, 'tis not to come; if it be not to come, it will be now; if it be not now, yet it will come; the readiness is all; since no man has aught of what he leaves, what is't to leave betimes?

[*Enter KING CLAUDIUS, QUEEN GERTRUDE, LAERTES, Lords, OSRIC, and Attendants with foils, & c*]

KING CLAUDIUS:

Come, Hamlet, come, and take this hand from me.

[*KING CLAUDIUS puts LAERTES' hand into HAMLET's*]

HAMLET:

Give me your pardon, sir; I've done you wrong;
But pardon't, as you are a gentleman.
This presence knows,
And you must needs have heard, how I am punish'd
With sore distraction. What I have done,
That might your nature, honour and exception
Roughly awake, I here proclaim was madness.

Was't Hamlet wrong'd Laertes? Never Hamlet;
If Hamlet from himself be ta'en away,
And when he's not himself does wrong Laertes,
Then Hamlet does it not, Hamlet denies it.
Who does it, then? His madness; if't be so,
Hamlet is of the faction that is wrong'd;
His madness is poor Hamlet's enemy.
Sir, in this audience,
Let my disclaiming from a purposed evil
Free me so far in your most generous thoughts,
That I have shot mine arrow o'er the house,
And hurt my brother.

LAERTES:

I am satisfied in nature,
Whose motive, in this case, should stir me most
To my revenge; but in my terms of honour
I stand aloof; and will no reconcilement,
Till by some elder masters, of known honour,
I have a voice and precedent of peace,
To keep my name ungored. But till that time,
I do receive your offer'd love like love,
And will not wrong it.

HAMLET:

I embrace it freely;

And will this brother's wager frankly play.

Give us the foils. Come on.

LAERTES:

Come, one for me.

HAMLET:

I'll be your foil, Laertes; in mine ignorance

Your skill shall, like a star i' the darkest night,

Stick fiery off indeed.

LAERTES:

You mock me, sir.

HAMLET:

No, by this hand.

KING CLAUDIUS:

Give them the foils, young Osric. Cousin Hamlet,

You know the wager?

HAMLET:

Very well, my lord

Your grace hath laid the odds o' the weaker side.

KING CLAUDIUS:

I do not fear it; I have seen you both.

But since he is better'd, we have therefore odds.

LAERTES:

This is too heavy, let me see another.

HAMLET:

This likes me well. These foils have all a length?

[*They prepare to play*]

OSRIC:

Ay, my good lord.

KING CLAUDIUS:

Set me the stoops of wine upon that table.

If Hamlet give the first or second hit,

Or quit in answer of the third exchange,

Let all the battlements their ordnance fire.

The king shall drink to Hamlet's better breath;

And in the cup an union shall he throw,

Richer than that which four successive kings

In Denmark's crown have worn. Give me the cups;

And let the kettle to the trumpet speak,

The trumpet to the cannoneer without,

The cannons to the heavens, the heavens to earth,

'Now the king dunks to Hamlet.' Come, begin.

And you, the judges, bear a wary eye.

HAMLET:

Come on, sir.
LAERTES:
Come, my lord.

[*They play*]

HAMLET:
One.
LAERTES:
No.
HAMLET:
Judgment.
OSRIC:
A hit, a very palpable hit.
LAERTES:
Well; again.
KING CLAUDIUS:
Stay; give me drink. Hamlet, this pearl is thine;
Here's to thy health.
[*Trumpets sound, and cannon shot off within*]
Give him the cup.
HAMLET:
I'll play this bout first; set it by awhile. Come.

[*They play*]

Another hit; what say you?

LAERTES:

A touch, a touch, I do confess.

KING CLAUDIUS:

Our son shall win.

QUEEN GERTRUDE:

He's fat, and scant of breath.

Here, Hamlet, take my napkin, rub thy brows;

The queen carouses to thy fortune, Hamlet.

HAMLET:

Good madam!

KING CLAUDIUS:

Gertrude, do not drink.

QUEEN GERTRUDE:

I will, my lord; I pray you, pardon me.

KING CLAUDIUS:

[*Aside*] It is the poison'd cup; it is too late.

HAMLET:

I dare not drink yet, madam; by and by.

QUEEN GERTRUDE:

Come, let me wipe thy face.

LAERTES:

My lord, I'll hit him now.

KING CLAUDIUS:

I do not think't.

LAERTES:

[*Aside*] And yet 'tis almost 'gainst my conscience.

HAMLET:

Come, for the third, Laertes; you but dally;

I pray you, pass with your best violence;

I am afeard you make a wanton of me.

LAERTES:

Say you so? come on.

[*They play*]

OSRIC:

Nothing, neither way.

LAERTES:

Have at you now!

[*LAERTES wounds HAMLET; then in scuffling, they change rapiers, and HAMLET wounds LAERTES*]

KING CLAUDIUS:

Part them; they are incensed.

HAMLET:

Nay, come, again.

[*QUEEN GERTRUDE falls*]

OSRIC:

Look to the queen there, ho!

HORATIO:

They bleed on both sides. How is it, my lord?

OSRIC:

How is't, Laertes?

LAERTES:

Why, as a woodcock to mine own springe, Osric;

I am justly kill'd with mine own treachery.

HAMLET:

How does the queen?

KING CLAUDIUS:

She swounds to see them bleed.

QUEEN GERTRUDE:

No, no, the drink, the drink,—O my dear Hamlet,—

The drink, the drink! I am poison'd.

[*Dies*]

HAMLET:

O villany! Ho! let the door be lock'd.
Treachery! Seek it out.

LAERTES:

It is here, Hamlet; Hamlet, thou art slain;
No medicine in the world can do thee good;
In thee there is not half an hour of life;
The treacherous instrument is in thy hand,
Unbated and envenom'd; the foul practise
Hath turn'd itself on me lo, here I lie,
Never to rise again; thy mother's poison'd.
I can no more; the king, the king's to blame.

HAMLET:

The point! —envenom'd too!
Then, venom, to thy work.

[*Stabs KING CLAUDIUS*]

All:

Treason! treason!

KING CLAUDIUS:

O, yet defend me, friends; I am but hurt.

HAMLET:

Here, thou incestuous, murderous, damned Dane,
Drink off this potion. Is thy union here?
Follow my mother.

[*KING CLAUDIUS dies*]

LAERTES:

He is justly served;
It is a poison temper'd by himself.
Exchange forgiveness with me, noble Hamlet.
Mine and my father's death come not upon thee,
Nor thine on me.

[*Dies*]

HAMLET:

Heaven make thee free of it! I follow thee.
I am dead, **HORATIO:**
Wretched queen, adieu!

You that look pale and tremble at this chance,

That are but mutes or audience to this act,

Had I but time—as this fell sergeant, death,

Is strict in his arrest—O, I could tell you—

But let it be. Horatio, I am dead;

Thou livest; report me and my cause aright

To the unsatisfied.

HORATIO:

Never believe it.

I am more an antique Roman than a Dane.

Here's yet some liquor left.

HAMLET:

As thou'rt a man,

Give me the cup; let go; by heaven, I'll have't.

O good Horatio, what a wounded name,

Things standing thus unknown, shall live behind me!

If thou didst ever hold me in thy heart

Absent thee from felicity awhile,

And in this harsh world draw thy breath in pain,

To tell my story.

[*March afar off, and shot within*]

What warlike noise is this?

OSRIC:

Young Fortinbras, with conquest come from Poland,
To the ambassadors of England gives
This warlike volley.

HAMLET:

O, I die, Horatio;
The potent poison quite o'er-crows my spirit.
I cannot live to hear the news from England;
But I do prophesy the election lights
On Fortinbras; he has my dying voice;
So tell him, with the occurrents, more and less,
Which have solicited. The rest is silence.

[*Dies*]

HORATIO:

Now cracks a noble heart. Good night sweet prince.
And flights of angels sing thee to thy rest!
Why does the drum come hither?

[*March within*]
[*Enter FORTINBRAS, the English Ambassadors, and others*]

PRINCE FORTINBRAS:

Where is this sight?

HORATIO:

What is it ye would see?

If aught of woe or wonder, cease your search.

PRINCE FORTINBRAS:

This quarry cries on havoc. O proud death,

What feast is toward in thine eternal cell,

That thou so many princes at a shot

So bloodily hast struck?

First Ambassador. The sight is dismal;

And our affairs from England come too late.

The ears are senseless that should give us hearing,

To tell him his commandment is fulfill'd,

That Rosencrantz and Guildenstern are dead.

Where should we have our thanks?

HORATIO:

Not from his mouth,

Had it the ability of life to thank you.

He never gave commandment for their death.

But since, so jump upon this bloody question,

You from the Polack wars, and you from England,

Are here arrived give order that these bodies

High on a stage be placed to the view;

And let me speak to the yet unknowing world
How these things came about; so shall you hear
Of carnal, bloody, and unnatural acts,
Of accidental judgments, casual slaughters,
Of deaths put on by cunning and forced cause,
And, in this upshot, purposes mistook
Fall'n on the inventors' reads; all this can I
Truly deliver.

PRINCE FORTINBRAS:

Let us haste to hear it,
And call the noblest to the audience.
For me, with sorrow I embrace my fortune.
I have some rights of memory in this kingdom,
Which now to claim my vantage doth invite me.

HORATIO:

Of that I shall have also cause to speak,
And from his mouth whose voice will draw on more;
But let this same be presently perform'd,
Even while men's minds are wild; lest more mischance
On plots and errors, happen.

PRINCE FORTINBRAS:

Let four captains
Bear Hamlet, like a soldier, to the stage;

For he was likely, had he been put on,
To have proved most royally; and, for his passage,
The soldiers' music and the rites of war
Speak loudly for him.
Take up the bodies; such a sight as this
Becomes the field, but here shows much amiss.
Go, bid the soldiers shoot.

[*A dead march. Exeunt, bearing off the dead bodies; after which a peal of ordnance is shot off.*]